*Two delightfully dark Hun*

# BENEATH A WANING MOON

In A VERY PROPER MONSTER, Josephine Shaw spends long nights filling the pages of her Gothic stories with the fantastic and the macabre, unaware that the suitor her father has arranged is one of the dark creatures she's always dreamed. For Tom Dargin, courting an ailing spinster was only one duty in a long life of service to his sire. But after he meets the curious Miss Shaw, will Tom become the seducer or the seduced? Can a love fated to end in tragedy survive a looming grave?

In GASLIGHT HADES, Nathaniel Gordon walks two worlds—that of the living and the dead. Barely human, he's earned the reputation of a Bonekeeper, the scourge of grave robbers. He believes his old life over, until one dreary burial he meets the woman he once loved and almost married. Lenore Kenward stands at her father's grave, begging the protection of the mysterious guardian, not knowing he is her lost love. Resolved to keep his distance, Nathaniel is forced to abandon his plan and accompany Lenore on a journey into the mouth of Hell where sea meets sky, and the abominations that exist beyond its barrier wait to destroy them.

*Praise for* Gaslight Hades...
"It's so gracefully steampunk. Effortless."
—Ilona Andrews, NYT Bestselling author

*Praise for* A Very Proper Monster...
"Heart wrenchingly emotional. Perfectly Gothic."
—Nocturnal Book Reviews

"Once again the combined work of this talented duo is well worth the small expense."
—Rabid Reads

# Beneath a Waning Moon

a duo of Gothic Romances

(( ✤ ))

## Grace Draven & Elizabeth Hunter

☦

But oh! that deep romantic chasm which slanted
Down the green hill athwart a cedarn cover!
A savage place! as holy and enchanted
As e'er beneath a waning moon was haunted
By woman wailing for her demon-lover!

Samuel Taylor Coleridge
*Kubla Khan*

BENEATH A WANING MOON
Copyright © 2015
ISBN: 9781518694233

A Very Proper Monster
Copyright © 2015
Elizabeth Hunter

Gaslight Hades
Copyright © 2011
Grace Draven

All rights reserved. No part of this book may be used or reproduced by any means, graphic, electronic, or mechanical, including photocopying, recording, taping, or by any information storage retrieval system without the written permission of the publisher except in the case of brief quotations embodied in critical articles and reviews.

This is a work of fiction. Names, characters, places, and incidents are the products of the author's imagination or are used fictitiously. Any resemblance to actual persons, living or dead, business establishments, events, or locales is entirely coincidental.

Editors: Mel Sterling, Lora Gasway, Anne Victory
Formatted: Elizabeth Hunter
Cover art: Grace Draven/Elizabeth Hunter

This e-book is licensed for your personal enjoyment only. This e-book may not be resold or given away to other people. If you would like to share this book with another person, please purchase an additional copy for each recipient. If you're reading this book and did not purchase it, or it was not purchased for your use only, then please delete it and purchase your own copy from an authorized retailer. Thank you for respecting the hard work of this author.

# A Very Proper Monster

An Elemental World novella

(( ✦ ))

# Elizabeth Hunter

✝

*For my writing friends*

*You know who you are*

Girls are caterpillars when they live in the world, to be finally butterflies when the summer comes;
but in the meantime there are grubs and larvae…
each with their peculiar propensities,

necessities

and structures.

—*Carmilla*
Joseph Sheridan Le Fanu

## Prologue

*Dublin, 1886*

My dearest Miss Tetley,

Enclosed you will find the final draft of Viviana Dioli's "The Countess's Dark Lover," a story within which you will no doubt find numerous additional faults. Signorina Dioli turns an indifferent profile to you, her harsh editor. I'm afraid she simply cannot find it in her cold heart to remove the balcony scene and subsequent mortal fall. Gothic romance, my dear Miss Tetley, so rarely comes to a happy end. And after all, what would be your actions when pursued by the grim monster which Warwick was revealed to be?

As for your other inquiries, rest assured I am no better or worse than when last I wrote. If I am completely honest, Lenore, I seem to be in some terrible stasis. The physicians know I am not so foolish as to hope for a cure, nor am I morbid enough to welcome my inevitable end peacefully. Part of me wishes that the sanatoriums they continue to suggest were possible, but I cannot bear the thought of leaving Father alone, even if I am ill.

So I trudge on, writing my stories, traveling to take the sea air when possible, and worrying about Father. No doubt you've heard of his own failing health. I know he wrote to your dear parents only last week, and I do hope he was frank. He is not well.

I have no worries about his businesses, for he has spent the past few years affixing the most competent men in positions of authority. But my own failing health, combined with his inevitable retirement, means that he does worry about the continuance of his legacy. Shaw mills have employed hundreds, but the boat works are poised to be entirely more impressive than the mills. And you know, for your father has the same honorable bent, how much the well-being of those many men and women weighs on his mind.

Would that I were a healthy son!

But alas, then I would have been forced to turn my head to business instead of literature of questionable moral value, and the world would have been robbed of Miss Dioli's and Mister Doyle's brilliance. (You know, of course, that I speak in false pride, for my own wit does amuse me too much.)

While I wish my cousin were of a mind to manage the businesses in good temper, I fear he is not. Neville eyes my every discreet cough with a kind of manic glee. Or is it my own morbid fascination that finds his expression so? I confess I am not impartial, having never liked the boy. I like even less the man he has become.

I do believe Father will seek to sell if his health shows no sign of improving. There are more than a few eager speculators, but he will sell only to someone who sees the boat works as he does. Not only industry, but the realization of a dream. If he could find an honorable benefactor to carry on his legacy, I believe he would happily sell.

For now, my dear Lenore, think of me and the dark depths of madness I must plumb to write this next horrible tale. I do say living in Miss Dioli's fanciful (if morbid) mind makes your friend a far pleasanter companion for poor Mrs. Porter. While Mr. Doyle's terrible imagination provides more pennies per word, he does take a terrible toll on the household staff. There will be no living with me, I am afraid, until this next monster has been exorcized on the page.

Wish me happy ink stains, Miss Tetley. No doubt you will see the beginnings of horror, though not the ghastly results, within the next fortnight.

    Yours always,
    Josephine Shaw

## Chapter One

"THE MILLS AND THE BOAT works are both profitable," Tom Dargin said. "The business is well run, and his workers even like the man. Foremen have naught to say against him."

Tom waited as Murphy read the report Declan had drafted. Tom didn't want to rely on the numbers alone, but the report, combined with his own discreet inquiries about how Shaw ran his businesses, had led him to believe his sire was making the right move pursuing Shaw's boat works.

"I like all of this," Murphy said, raising his head. "The mills and the boat works *are* both profitable. So why are there rumors he's looking to sell?"

"Health," Tom said. "That's what some are speculating. He's gettin' on and his health isn't what it was. That's the rumor, anyway."

Murphy frowned. "And no children?"

"A daughter," Declan said. "Josephine Shaw. But she's consumptive. Rarely seen out in society, not for the past five years. There's a nephew, but they're not close."

"And a sick daughter means a son-in-law is hardly likely," Murphy mused, rubbing his chin. "Has he said anything publicly?"

"No," Tom said. "Though it seems pretty common knowledge among his foremen."

"Beecham's sniffing," Declan said. "As are a few human investors."

William Beecham, the vampire lord of Dublin, would be happy to pounce on the struggling company. They'd have to tread carefully.

"Has Shaw a manager?" Murphy asked.

"He did, but the man was hired away." Tom tried not to let the smile touch his lips. "I believe by one of Hamilton's works in Belfast."

"That bloody woman," Murphy said. "Why am I not surprised? At least it wasn't Beecham. Buying with a manager installed would be a hell of a lot easier."

"It would," Tom said, "but I can see two or more of the men I talked to rising to the position if given the proper incentive. Shaw hired lads for brains, not just strong backs."

"Smart," Declan said. "What do you think, boss?"

Murphy tapped his pen for a moment, fiddling with the new watch fob his mate, Anne, had given him. Tom wished the woman were there that evening, but she was visiting a friend in Wicklow that week. Murphy always made up his mind more quickly when Anne was around.

"He won't be going for money," Murphy said. "Or at least not only money. He has no son. He won't have any grandchildren. These businesses are his legacy."

"Agreed," Tom said. His sire could have acquired Shaw's assets through mental manipulation like many of their kind did. It was a point of honor for Murphy that he didn't and one of the reasons Tom had been so keen to join his former student in immortality.

It wasn't as if Patrick Murphy needed the old pugilist at his side for fighting advice anymore. But Murphy could be a little too trusting in Tom's opinion. He needed a bruiser at his back, and Tom had been happy to volunteer, even if it did mean having to feed on blood when the need arose.

He'd been a vampire for over thirty years, and all in all, it wasn't that bad. He missed the sun, but if he was honest, he'd been living the last years of his human life at night, hustling through Dublin and even over to London with Murphy, trying to scrounge enough money with boxing matches to make it worth the blood.

Now the blood came from donors, and Murphy was the one in charge. At least, that's what it looked like to outsiders. Murphy, Tom, and Declan presented themselves as brothers to mortal society. No one questioned their connection. In time they'd have to adjust, but for now it worked. Tom just had to remember to answer to "Mr. Murphy" on occasion.

"If Shaw is truly looking to sell, he will want someone who'll invest more than money," Tom said. "Someone who cares about the workers. That's my take, anyway."

"Agreed," Declan said.

"No harm in calling on the man," Murphy said. "We've already been introduced. Perhaps I come to him asking about improvements for my own millworks..."

Tom nodded. "Show him you're the kind who cares. A boss willing to invest for the long term."

Declan said, "Plus he might have something to help with the dust problem in Whitechurch."

"True." Murphy set his pen down. "Declan, write up a letter, will you? Ask Shaw for a meeting next week if he's amenable. Let's see if John Shaw is a man willing to work with creatures of the night."

THE meeting had been six months coming, at least, and Tom had watched Shaw deteriorate in that time. The once-robust man had grown wan and pale as Tom and Murphy's respect for the human grew stronger.

"You know," Shaw said, "I spotted your intentions in our second meeting, Mr. Murphy."

Murphy smiled. "And yet you kept meeting me."

"It's the same kind of tactic I would have used when I was young," Shaw said with a drawn smile. "Of course I kept meeting with you."

Shaw was a hell of a businessman, but Tom approved of the core of honor in the man. When he'd been human, he would have felt privileged to work for a man like John Robert Shaw.

"And so," Murphy said more quietly, "we come to the sticking point. I want to buy the works, John. The mills and the boat works. You know that. What I need you to know is that it's not just about the money to me. I respect what you've done. I'm no Englishman to see only the profit in them. I see what the boat works have the potential to do for Dublin. For the whole of Ireland. That's important to me."

"I know." Shaw took a sip of his whiskey, and Tom noticed his hand trembling just a little. "I've made a study of you, young man. And while there are some... curious things rumored about you, I know a gentleman of good character when I see one. I like your wife. I like your brothers. You're a man who understands family."

Tom cocked his head. Shaw talked more than a little about family, which made the relative secrecy around his own something of a mystery. It was well-known he had a daughter, but Tom had never seen her. Neither had Murphy or Declan. She was a mystery. One that Tom Dargin couldn't help but wonder about.

"You're right. Family is very important to me," Murphy said.

"And me." Shaw dabbed at his brow. "I had this all planned, and now I find myself nervous to speak of it. Perhaps I'm absorbing some of Jo's fancy after all."

"Jo?" Tom asked from the settee.

Shaw had asked both Tom and Declan to join Murphy and him that night for a drink. Tom felt as he always did in company, like the prized ox accidentally let into someone's parlor. He was an unfashionably big man, and the scars on his face often led those in polite society to avoid his gaze. He was more at home with the factory workers than the bosses.

"My daughter, Josephine." Shaw took a deep breath. "As I imagine you have heard, she is not well. She has been unwell for years, despite the efforts of numerous physicians."

Tuberculosis, they called it now. Consumption, his mam had said. If the disease had progressed as far as rumors claimed, there would be no cure for Josephine Shaw, and Tom could see the knowledge in her father's eyes.

"Your own health...," Murphy said cautiously. "You fear you are deteriorating."

"I *am* deteriorating. And faster than my daughter. She will be alone."

Tom knew Shaw was worried about his daughter's protection after he died. Those with consumption could linger for years. And while she might not hurt for money, a woman without a family to protect her was still at risk of being taken advantage of.

Murphy said, "Her family—"

"She has little to none. She has friends—good friends—but mostly in England where she went to school. Her cousin should be the one to care for her, but Neville has little interest in anyone but himself, and he will be furious when he learns I am looking to sell the businesses. He expects to inherit."

Tom's ears perked, and he made a mental note to keep an eye on this Neville. A disappointed would-be heir was nothing to trifle with. The quicker Shaw sold the whole works to Murphy, the better it would be for everyone. Let Neville become accustomed to disappointment while his uncle was alive to manage him.

"Mr. Shaw," Murphy said, "if you are concerned about your daughter, you needn't be. You have met my wife. Mrs. Murphy is a generous woman, both of heart and attention. And I'm sure Miss Shaw has inherited her father's good sense. My family would be happy to count your daughter a friend, as I have come to think of you as a fr—"

"She doesn't need a friend, she needs a husband," Shaw said abruptly.

The whole room fell silent.

Murphy stammered. "John... I say, I'm already married."

"And you've two brothers who aren't."

Tom glanced at Declan, whose eyes were the size of saucers. Declan knew Tom's taciturn demeanor and age hardly made him husband material, especially for a young woman not yet thirty. That left Declan the obvious choice, and he didn't look like he was jumping at the opportunity, even if the woman was an heiress.

Tom glued his lips shut. Let Murphy talk them out of taking on some consumptive spinster. He was the one with the silver tongue.

"John, wouldn't it be wiser to—"

"She doesn't think she needs a husband," Shaw said. "Has always resisted any attempts at matchmaking. Says she'd only be a burden. Foolish girl." Shaw's whole face softened. "She has been the delight of my heart. She deserves any happiness I can give her."

Murphy tread carefully. "If the young woman doesn't wish to be married," he said, "wouldn't it be more prudent to find a reliable companion for her as she declines? Anne's and my offer of friendship remains. We are more than willing—"

"If one of your brothers marries Josephine, it settles the whole business, don't you see?" Shaw said. "You will be *family*. There will be no one to contest your purchase. There will be no one to wrest Josephine's fortune from her if she takes a turn. An employee cannot protect her from unscrupulous relations, Mr. Murphy. You know that." Shaw's face grew even paler. "The moment I pass from this world, the vultures will circle, particularly my nephew."

"How sick is she?" Tom asked quietly. "I don't mean to be indelicate, sir, but you may be seeing too dire a circumstance. Your daughter could very well—"

"Her last doctor said she could expect two years. At the most." Shaw looked at Murphy, then at Declan sitting quietly beside him. "Two years, young man. Surely any honorable gentleman understands my concern as her father. It would be nothing to give her two years. She is educated. Independent. And when she passes—"

"Mr. Shaw," Declan interrupted. "While I am sure your daughter is a most agreeable young woman, I do not know her, nor does she know me. Surely she would not consent to this."

9

"She would if you charmed her," Shaw said. "As if all of Dublin doesn't know of the Murphy brothers' charm! Surely, Mr. Murphy, you could persuade her. I would not try to hide my machinations, of course. But she's a practical girl, my Jo." Shaw grimaced. "When she wants to be."

Tom's mind was racing. Courts could be unpredictable, especially when it came to issues of inheritance. Wills could be contested. And Beecham was always sniffing around Murphy, watching the younger vampire with jealous eyes. He would use any excuse—manipulate any connection—to thwart Murphy, though he couldn't do it openly.

Shaw was right. If Declan married the Shaw heiress, it would solve everything. Murphy would buy Shaw's businesses without argument. Shaw would be seen as handing over the reins to his daughter's new family. Not even Beecham would be able to manipulate Murphy's claim to the boat works.

And when the girl died... it wasn't as if she didn't have a fortune of her own. In a way, marriage to the Shaw spinster would mean they were getting Shaw's businesses for little less than the cost of a wedding and care for a consumptive.

But Declan looked as if he were steps away from execution.

Ninny.

Murphy also saw the terrified look on his brother's face and leaned forward. "John, as much as I want to buy your factories, I cannot force my brother—"

"I'll do it," Tom said quietly. "If Miss Shaw would consent to marry me, I will wed her."

Wide eyes turned toward Tom.

"But only if she consents," he said again. "I won't force the girl or put up with having her coerced. From what you've said, Miss Shaw has little enough time left without her being miserable in a marriage she doesn't want."

Murphy's mouth was gaping open. Declan finally took a breath. And John Shaw was smiling.

"Good man," Shaw said.

Tom nodded, uncomfortable being the center of their attention. "Don't be too certain she'll accept me. She's the one who'll have to look at this ugly mug every night."

"Tom," Murphy said. "You don't have to do this. Shaw, I promise we will ensure your daughter—"

"It's little enough, Murphy." Tom glanced at Shaw, interrupting his sire before he could offend their host. "Little enough to ensure the protection of a young woman. I'm no prize. But if she'll have me, I'll have her."

Murphy looked at Tom a long time until Tom looked his sire in the eye and nodded. Murphy's shoulders relaxed and he turned to Shaw. "John, why don't you talk to your daughter first. We can wait to have my solicitor draw up the paperwork. Perhaps you could arrange a dinner sometime this week so my brother and your daughter could meet? I think we'd all like to meet Miss Shaw."

"CHRIST, Tom. Did you have to go and offer for the spinster?" Declan stormed into the room while Murphy and Tom were throwing back a pint of ale. Declan had stayed behind, talking to Shaw's family solicitor.

"Did you have to act like marrying the woman was such a torture?" Tom asked. "You'd have thrown the whole deal off with your clumsy excuses, Dec."

His brother pointed at him. "You've no business marrying the girl. Sure, we can fool Shaw and avoid the daylight when we do business with him, but have you thought about the consequences of trying to fool a wife? She'll have a staff. Servants. What the hell do you think you're going to do?"

"Be very careful," Murphy said. "This is Tom, Declan. Who's more careful than Tom?"

Tom didn't feel very careful, and for the first time in thirty years, he wished he could fall into the sweet oblivion liquor had once brought him and not just taste it. For the first ten years of immortality, it had haunted him. He still had all the same reasons to drink with none of the relief alcohol had once afforded.

When he'd finally turned his mind to controlling the baser urges that had driven him as a human, he'd found some peace. Now he was voluntarily taking on the care of a wife. A sick wife. He had no business taking care of anyone, much less a sick spinster.

Murphy looked at him with an expression that said he could hear all Tom's doubts rising to the surface. "It'll be fine, Tom," his sire said. "If you need to, you can touch her mind. Or have Anne do it. She has the most control."

"Jayzuz," Declan groaned. "What's Anne going to say? She'll have your head for this, Murphy."

"She'll not," Tom said. "I'm the one that put us all in this by offering. I'll tell Anne."

None of them wanted to anger Murphy's mate. She was the glue that held their small family together. But Tom knew she'd be keen to protect a vulnerable human woman, even if it meant inconvenience for the rest of them for a couple of years. Anne had a soft heart.

"I'm going out," Tom said, placing his glass carefully on the bar in Murphy's office.

"I saw some of Beecham's crew on the way here," Declan said. "Be careful. They're sniffing."

Murphy had taken the space near the docks because Beecham never dirtied his fine leather shoes by the waterfront. Their crew could operate with some amount of discretion there away from the finer eyes of Dublin immortal society and the corruption of its lord.

And Tom's upcoming marriage might blow that all to hell.

"Don't think of it," Murphy said, reading Tom's mind. "We always knew we'd attract attention with a move to take over Shaw's boat works. There was no avoiding this. Marriage to the Shaw girl won't make that any better or worse."

Declan shrugged. "At least she's not popular in society. She won't have to explain your lack of social graces. I inquired discreetly after you both left. The woman is practically an invalid.

Twenty-eight years old, but her health started failing soon after she came out in society. Most of her education was in England. She maintains correspondence but hardly leaves the grounds unless she's going to their house by the sea for her lungs. Very few callers. No one mentioned her looks, which means she's plain. Probably dim too. Otherwise she'd have an offer of marriage, even if she was on the edge of death, solely for her fortune." Declan laughed. "Probably more than one."

"She went to school," Tom said, already feeling protective of the lady. "I highly doubt any daughter of Shaw's is a dullard. Besides that, how do you know she hasn't had an offer? Shaw said she never wanted a husband. Said she was 'independent.'"

He found himself admiring her for it, even though *independent* might be polite society code for foolish and stubborn. As long as the girl had her wits, Tom wouldn't be miserable. He could respect a stubborn woman. He was no pushover himself.

"Why don't we all withhold judgment until we've met the woman?" Murphy said. "If she's anything like her father, I expect she and Tom will get along well. The details can be worked out in time. Tom, take your walk if you've a mind, but keep an eye out for Beecham's lads."

"Will do, boss."

Tom left the warehouse, slipping down the back alleys along the river and heading south toward the Shaws' fine house on Merrion Square. He had a mind to watch it. Why? He didn't exactly know.

He wasn't in any kind of rush, so he stretched the walk out for an hour or so, plenty of time for most of the city to fall asleep. Tom liked the silence. He was a quiet man and always had been, even in human life. It was hard enough to avoid gathering notice when you were over six feet tall and built like a brick wall, as his mam had told him. He was only ever going to be a brute with size like that.

It was pure luck he'd fallen into boxing as a human. More luck that when his own body had started to give out, he'd run into a brash young Traveller who needed coaching and a companion to watch his back. Tom Dargin had thrown in with Murphy within weeks of meeting the young man, seeing in him the kind of luck Tom had always admired but never captured.

And now he'd be marrying a proper society woman if that woman would have him.

Wasn't life unexpected?

He lurked across the way from the Shaw house, surprised by the number of lights still on inside. Comfortable in the shadows, he crossed the main thoroughfare on the north side of the square and walked down a side street, curious to see if the Shaws' garden was accessible. He wanted to know who was awake. Who would be using gas lamps so late at night? Surely not one of the servants. Was it old Mr. Shaw himself, worried about his company and his failing health? Or perhaps it was Miss Shaw, unable to sleep or discomforted by her illness.

Either way, Tom was curious. And a curious Tom was a stubborn thing.

He walked across the muddy road behind the house where delivery carts had left deep grooves in the mud. A light mist was falling, and he drank it in, replete with the surge of power it lent his amnis. Unlike Murphy, who preferred fresh water, Tom felt most at home near the sea. But any water would do. He'd never been a particular man.

Following the lights led him past numerous walled gardens until he finally arrived at the back side of the stately redbrick Georgian home belonging to John Robert Shaw. It was handsome but not ostentatious. Respectable but not ancient. He'd watched Shaw exit the front of the house on more than one night, but he'd never investigated the gardens. Declan might have looked through the Shaw books, but it was Tom who gathered information on the ground.

That night, Tom Dargin scaled the garden wall and dropped into another world.

Far from the well-tended, orderly garden he'd imagined from Shaw's tidy appearance, this garden was a wild tangle of trees and flowers. Statuary hid among rocks tumbled artfully around the bases of trees, giving the dark garden a fantastical appearance. A miniature glass house lit up the center of the lawn, sparkling from the inside with candlelight. Tom felt as if he'd slipped into one of the fairy stories his grandmother had been fond of telling.

For standing in the center of a lush lawn, dressed in a white dressing gown, was a tall woman, as willowy as the trees that lined the garden. She stood, swaying a little, her pale skin touched by the moon's silver light as she held a book in her hand and turned in place. Her feet were bare, her dark hair fell past her waist, and her long gown was drenched in the evening dew.

It must be Miss Shaw. No servant would take a book out into the garden in the middle of the night. Certainly not in their dressing gown.

"'But dreams come through stone walls...'" She held up the book to the moon's light and spoke quietly, though his immortal hearing could pick up the words easily. "'...light up dark rooms, or darken light ones, and their persons make their exits and their entrances as they please, and laugh at locksmiths.'"

She twirled on the lawn, lifting the book over her head and humming a tune as her hair lifted while she spun.

"Dreams come through stone walls...," she whispered into the night as Tom watched from the dark shelter of a drooping willow.

"Oh, feck me," he muttered under his breath, letting out a sigh. "She's mad as a March hare."

## Chapter Two

JOSEPHINE ROBERTA DOYLE SHAW was a practical woman. Despite her rather eccentric writings, she ran her father's household with quiet efficiency, though she was wise enough to bow to the expert opinion of Mrs. Morse, the housekeeper her mother had hired before her untimely—and, Josephine preferred to think, tragic—death. As her mother had died in childbirth, Josephine had never felt her loss, though she liked to imagine she and her mother would have been the closest of confidantes and the dearest of friends.

As it was, Eloisa Shaw had left her daughter with an excellent and loving nanny, an efficient housekeeper, and an extensive and not-at-all proper library with books in Italian, French, and Spanish, as well as all the more conventional writings. This had motivated Josephine to excel early in languages, and by the time she was thirteen, she could explore the forbidden tomes her mother had left behind.

Josephine had not been disappointed.

As well as firing her imagination in very improper ways, her mother's own notes in the margins of the most scandalous books gave Josephine a peek into the mind of the woman she must have been.

Which was why when she embarrassed her father—as she inevitably did—Josephine reminded him that he had been the one to marry Eloisa Francesca Dioli Doyle in the first place.

Therefore, if any scandal resulted from her reading Italian romances and French philosophy, it was entirely his own fault.

She was sitting in her library when her father presented his latest idea to ensure her future.

"You want me to *what*?" she said, laughing lightly so as not to provoke her lungs. "Marry him? One of your business partner's brothers?"

He leaned toward her, her gentle father who had always indulged her every whim. If she were a petulant child, he would have ruined her. Luckily, Josephine was eminently good-natured and had been blessed with a very strict nanny.

"Jo, you know you must."

"No, I don't know I must. Father, in addition to the rather large fortune you have worked very hard for, I also have my own income, modest though it may be. I will never be destitute. You are fretting for nothing."

"And when I die? When your cousin tries to take the house?"

She shrugged. "He could try. But if you should pass before me—though I think you are not quite as ill as you imagine—I will sell the house to some eager buyer with Mr. Macon's help, then I shall take Mrs. Porter and Mrs. Morse with me to the house in Bray. You know I don't like society." She let a sad smile touch her lips. "And you know it will not be for long. I am happy as I am."

"But if you were married..." He sighed. "Jo, I would worry so much less."

"I know."

The soft pang in her chest was not only from the tuberculosis that plagued her. For though Josephine Shaw was a practical woman, she also had the fiery heart of a romantic. It wasn't that she'd never longed for love. She had. When she was younger, she'd longed most desperately! But she'd known by the age of twenty-three that her health was becoming more and more fragile. And by twenty-five that the doctors' treatments would not save her life. It seemed cruel to hope for any happiness besides her own small fancies.

She wrote her stories, and they were read and enjoyed—or so Lenore claimed—by many. Josephine enjoyed quiet society and music and books and gardening. She loved her father to distraction.

It was with that love in mind that she took his hand. "Father, I promise I will be fine."

She tried to ignore the tears in the corners of his eyes when he squeezed her hand tightly.

"You deserve much more than 'fine,' my dear girl. You deserve a love like your mother and I had. I only had her for four years, but it has been enough to sustain me for twenty-nine."

"And do you think I will find love in an arranged marriage?" She had to smile. "You cannot make a young man love me because you do. I do not think that is the way love works."

"If he only meets you, he will have to love you."

"Oh, Papa!" Josephine laughed harder, and she couldn't stop the cough that followed. She muffled it in the handkerchief Lenore had embroidered for her. No blood—thank God—yet. "I think you are biased in my favor, but I will take the compliment. Surely Mr. Murphy will love me on sight. But shall I love him? This young man who would agree to a marriage to seal a business deal for his brother? No doubt he sees in our marriage a way to make his own fortune. Not that I begrudge ambition, but it doesn't lend itself to romance, does it?"

Shaw looked thoughtful. "If it was Declan Murphy, I might say you have the right of it, my dear. But it is not. Mr. Thomas Murphy, the oldest of the brothers, has offered for you."

"The oldest, is it?" Josephine quipped. "Well then, I might have a chance to outlive him after all."

Her father was abashed. "Not as old as that. But he is... a mature man. Perhaps in his forties. Not overly talkative. Not a pretty fellow at all, I suppose. Though I've noticed the serving girls all take note of him."

Josephine nodded solemnly. "I do bow to the measured opinion of observant serving girls when I consider suitors."

Shaw let go of her hand and leaned back, crossing his legs and brushing a hand over his trouser leg. "You're teasing your father."

She smiled. "It's just so silly. Why do I have need of a husband?"

"To protect you."

"I can protect myself. Or set the dogs on the marauders if they ignore my shrill and desperate cries."

His lips twitched with a smile. "To make you happy."

"You have no guarantee this Thomas Murphy is capable of that."

"Fine." He took her hand again. "To give your poor papa a measure of peace that I will leave you secure. I don't have long, Jo. I know that. If the Tetleys lived in Dublin, I would have no worry in your situation, for I know Margaret and Daniel love you as their own. But they do not live here, and you are not well enough to travel so far. All I am asking is that you give this man a chance to win your regard."

Josephine paused, persuaded by her father's worried pleas. "Very well, I will meet him."

"That is all I am asking."

"But if he thinks this union is somehow assured—"

"Mr. Murphy specifically said he would have you *only* if you would have him. He was quite clear that any kind of coercion on my part was unacceptable."

"Oh." That was... rather thoughtful. "I appreciate his regard in that matter."

"Meet him, Jo. You never know. Thomas Murphy may not be one of your romance heroes, but you might find him far more to your liking than you expect."

My dearest Miss Tetley,

You will be most astonished to find not only the pages of Mr. Doyle's latest horror enclosed, but also news of an even more alarming nature.

Father has found a gentleman to marry me!

I know you will be as dismayed as I am, dear Lenore. For herein lies the ruin of our plans in joint spinsterhood. I doubt my domineering (for surely he must be very domineering) future husband will consent to our scandalous plans to run away to the seaside and live out our lives wearing pantaloons.

Alas, no doubt the rogue will lock me in a tower or an attic until I wither away from disappointed love. With my fortune, he will have ample funds to find an appropriate tower or attic within easy distance of town as he is also a man of business and must surely not neglect his familial responsibilities.

I jest, of course. I have only allowed that I will meet Mr. Thomas Murphy, and Father has made every concession to my consent in the matter. I have no cause to presume lack of character in the gentleman, though the housemaids have rumored a rather hopeful and frightening scar on one side of his face. Further portent of illicit intent? Or perhaps a mere carriage accident in childhood? You know which one I would prefer, of course.

Father's health continues to fail. He is wracked with worry, which is the only reason I have consented to meet Mr. Murphy. I very much doubt a sick spinster of eight and twenty will tempt him, but as he has given his word to offer, it seems the engagement is mine to refuse. I will determine the truth in the man's face and decide my course. If he is a kind sort of man whose company I could endure, perhaps the engagement will give Father some comfort and me some amusement.

I long, my friend, though I dare not hope. You know that for which I have always wished. Perhaps fate is just cruel enough to see me madly in love before I die.

For I will die. You and Mrs. Porter will accuse me of consorting with the fairies, but I know it. I feel it in the night. I can feel Death's footsteps stalking me at the edges of the wild, and more and more, I find I do not want to run. I hope I will welcome him when he comes. Perhaps, in that pale lover, I will find the satisfaction that has so long eluded me in life.

Of course, I could also fling myself from the tower window in the midst of a violent thunderstorm. That would have more dramatic impact.

Your faithful (and sadly doomed) friend,
Josephine Shaw


SHE couldn't sleep, but then, did she ever sleep? Except for some lazy afternoons, Josephine had always been a restless creature, especially at night. By her calculations, if she slept only half as long as the average person, her life would not be cut in half. Merely... a third at the most.

She took an oil lamp to the garden and hid in the small glass house their gardener, Mr. Connelly, had built for her when she had returned from school. It was supposed to be for delicate plants, but it had become, much to no one's surprise, her own private study. Josephine didn't store her manuscripts in the glass house because she worried about the damp. But she often wrote there late into the night, the reflection of the lamp on the glass casting eerie shadows around her writing desk.

Josephine had never needed sleep to dream.

That night, she was neglecting her pen in favor of rereading one of the most-favored books in her library. It was a small volume that had appeared mysteriously when she was only fifteen. Josephine still had no idea who had gifted her the lovely horror of *Carmilla*, but she owed her nameless benefactor an enormous debt. Her personal guess was a briefly employed footman who had seen her reading her mother's well-worn copy of *The Mysteries of Udolpho* and confessed his own forbidden love of Poe.

The slim volume of Le Fanu's Gothic horror stories had been hidden well into adulthood. As it wasn't her father's habit to investigate her reading choices, concealment might have been more for dramatic effect than real fear of discovery.

Josephine read by lamplight, curled into an old chaise and basking in the sweet isolation of darkness as she mouthed well-loved passages from her favorite vampire tale.

> *"For some nights I slept profoundly; but still every morning I felt the same lassitude, and a languor weighed upon me all day. I felt myself a changed girl. A strange melancholy was stealing over me, a melancholy that I would not have interrupted. Dim thoughts of death began to open, and an idea that I was slowly sinking took gentle, and, somehow, not unwelcome possession of me."*

She slammed the book shut.

How had she turned so morbid?

For while Josephine had long known she would not live to old age, she thought she had resigned herself to it. She made a point of fighting the melancholy that threatened her. If she had any regret, it was that she would not live long enough to write all the stories she wanted. Sometimes she felt a longing to shout them into the night, offering them up to any wandering soul that they might be heard so they could live.

So many voices beating in her chest. So many tales to write and whisper and shout. Her eyes fell to the book she'd slammed shut.

> *"'You are afraid to die?'*
> *"Yes, everyone is."*

Josephine stood and pushed her way out of the glass house, into the garden where the mist enveloped her. She lifted her face to the moon and felt the tears cold on her cheeks.

"'Girls are caterpillars,'" she whispered, "'when they live in the world, to be finally butterflies when the summer comes; but in the meantime there are grubs and larvae, don't you see?'"

But the summer would never come for Josephine. She beat back the despair that threatened to envelop her.

*You are afraid to die?*

*Yes, everyone is.*

She lifted her face and opened her eyes to the starry night, speaking her secret longing into the night. "'But to die as lovers may—to die together, so that they may live together.'"

How she longed for love! For passion. How she ached to be seen. To be cherished. To be *known*.

She could pour her soul onto the page and still find loneliness in the dark. She strangled her heart to keep it alive, knowing it was only a matter of time until the palest lover took her to his bosom. Already, she could feel the tightness in her chest.

Tomorrow would not be a good day.

Nevertheless, she lifted her arms like an offering to a pagan god. "'Thus fortified I might take my rest in peace,'" she said, lifting her voice in defiance of the darkness. "'But dreams come through stone walls, light up dark rooms, or darken light ones, and their persons make their exits and their entrances as they please...'" She smiled. "'And laugh at locksmiths...' because they are clever dreams."

The sound of quiet laughter drifted through the garden.

She spun and glared into the darkness. "Who is there?" Josephine gathered her dressing gown, wrapping it closer around her body. "Who are you?"

Surely only a neighbor's servant, gawking at her foolishness. She should have been embarrassed, but she wasn't. She knew the neighbors considered her eccentric. It was the privilege of the dying.

"If you're going to spy on me"—Josephine stepped toward the bushes—"you will only see folly."

"I saw no folly tonight," a quiet voice replied. "Only perhaps a bit of fancy."

The voice was low and rough, coming from the edge of the garden. A man's voice, not a boy's. Coming from the other side of the wall? She couldn't tell for certain. But whoever was watching her, she didn't sense him moving away.

"Are you planning to kidnap me?" She cocked her head, stepping closer to the edge of darkness. "I'll warn you, I'm consumptive. I'll probably make you sick if you try."

"My kind don't fall ill easily."

She froze. "Your kind?"

"Who were you talking to? The moon? God? Perhaps the fairies?"

"None of them, I think. Death, maybe."

He sounded amused when he said, "'Tis a foolish woman who courts Death. He is the most jealous lover."

Josephine stopped at the edge of the grass, not wanting to discover his secret. Whoever he was—servant or tramp, beggar or gentleman—she didn't feel fear. He had *heard* her, and she was grateful.

Josephine offered a sad smile into the shadows. "As I don't have any other lover, I suppose Death can have me."

She thought he came closer, though she had no idea why.

"Are you afraid to die?" her shadowed friend asked.

"No."

He waited.

"Yes," she whispered into his silence. "Everyone is."

A silent pause, then a murmur so close she felt his breath on her neck.

"Goodnight, Josephine."

But when she spun around, he was gone.

## Chapter Three

*GIRLS ARE CATERPILLARS when they live in the world...*

Tom tried not to fidget in the carriage on the way to Shaw's town house. Girls might be caterpillars according to Miss Shaw, but Tom felt like he was the one wrapped in a cocoon. The amount of clothing he'd been forced to don was verging on torture.

Normally he'd be able to get by with a more casual suit, even when socializing among Murphy's cronies. Tom Dargin hardly spoke. He was known as the stern older brother with dubious connections and a noted air of violence. Gentlemen respected him, greeted him properly if they met at clubs, but kept their distance.

Unfortunately, his sire's mate and valet had gotten ahold of him and forced Tom into his most formal attire.

He was miserable.

"You look very handsome," Anne said, leaning forward. "Please stop fidgeting."

"I'm a league off of handsome, Annie. And I'm not fidgeting."

"You've nearly torn the hem of that waistcoat. And if you cross your arms again, you're liable to tear the seams of that coat across the shoulders. Relax."

Relax? Tom had faced monsters in the boxing ring that unnerved him less than the thought of meeting a proper lady like

Josephine Shaw. Especially when he already knew what the woman looked like in her dressing gown.

Did it bother him that his possible betrothed might be slightly insane? He hadn't quite decided yet. He thought probably not. Some of the most interesting people he'd known were a bit gone in the head, and he'd hardly be bored with her should she decide on him.

What he didn't like was that the decision was entirely in Josephine Shaw's hands. He'd promised to offer for the woman *if she wanted him*. Oddly enough, the thought that she might not was what made him worry his waistcoat. Because—and this had kept him pacing for three nights—Miss Shaw had surprised him by being entirely more desirable than anticipated.

"We're here."

Murphy's words pulled him from his mental dithering. The carriage jerked to a halt and the door opened. Tom had to stop himself from exiting first and looking around for threats. This wasn't a meeting with Beecham where vampires might be waiting with swords. This was a civilized dinner party with Murphy's mate, his new business partner, and a woman who ran around in her garden in the middle of the night quoting morbid poetry.

"Feck me," Tom muttered as he disembarked from the carriage. Murphy and Anne were waiting at the foot of the stairs. Declan—the sorry little ninny—had begged off.

Anne scowled. "You absolutely must not use language like that in front of Miss Shaw."

"She might like it," Tom said. "You'd be surprised at the ladies who do."

Murphy covered a smile with cough and put his arm out for Anne. "Come now, Anne. Tom knows how to speak with a lady."

"No, I don't."

"And he'll even use a knife and fork when it's necessary," Murphy said.

"I promise not to stab anyone unless they try to steal my food," Tom added.

Anne shook her head. "I don't know why I put up with you scoundrels."

Murphy leaned closer to his mate and whispered something that would have made Tom blush if he could.

"Oh," Anne said in a slightly higher voice. "Yes, that's why. Well, God help Miss Shaw anyway if she likes you, Tom. I know you're as bad as this one, if not worse."

"Not our Tom," Murphy said. "He's the boring, responsible brother."

"I'd punch you, boss, but I might bust my seams," Tom said. "Come on now. Let's stop stalling." He could already see the butler waiting at the door.

They walked up the ruthlessly neat steps to the redbrick town house with tall glowing windows. Thank heaven the sun was setting earlier this time of year, otherwise they'd have to make excuses about the dinner hour.

The butler took Tom's hat and overcoat at the door before he led him, Murphy, and Anne back to the drawing room and announced them.

A rush of voices surrounded them, but Tom's eyes found his target immediately. She was standing awkwardly near the bookcases, next to an older woman who looked like a companion. He could see a hastily set-aside book on the small table next to the lamp. Josephine Shaw was brushing at her skirts and slouching slightly, as if trying to conceal her height.

"And Mr. Murphy"—Tom blinked when he realized Shaw was speaking to him—"allow me to introduce you to my only daughter, Miss Josephine Shaw."

Tom stepped toward her.

*Girls are caterpillars...*

No girl here, but Tom thought he saw the caterpillar. Miss Shaw was... not pretty, though he thought she might be what some would call handsome. What had suited the darkness and moonlight appeared awkward in the artificial light of the drawing room. Her skin was pale, not luminous. Her hair was mouse-brown and tied back in a complicated, heavy knot. Her height and dramatic features were not flattered by the fashions she'd been buttoned into. But her eyes...

Too big for her face. Too dark. Too wide. Too... much.

Far too much for a very proper drawing room.

Tom thought her eyes might trap him if he wasn't careful.

"Miss Shaw." He bowed respectfully. "A pleasure to meet you."

*Wake up, caterpillar.*

She smiled politely and inclined her head, her shoulders still bent. Tom watched her ink-stained hand as he straightened, imagining what the skin would feel like in his rough palm. He stretched his shoulders back. Those large, dark eyes that had been hovering somewhere around his cravat rose and kept rising to meet his own gaze.

"I find," he said quietly, "that it's quite useless to apologize for how tall the good Lord made me."

She blinked. "Pardon me, sir?"

He liked her voice even more when it wasn't whispered in a garden. And Anne would probably thrash him for it, but he'd say it anyway. "No need to slouch, Miss Shaw. In my opinion, there's nothing grander than a tall woman."

Miss Shaw blinked again. Then her face lit with a smile, she threw back her shoulders and let out a laugh as improper as dancing in the garden at midnight.

The laugh transformed her.

The older woman behind Miss Shaw met his eyes with an approving look, and Shaw clapped him on the shoulder as Miss Shaw continued to laugh.

"You young people," Shaw said. "Mr. Murphy, I have a good whiskey I've opened for the evening. May I get you a glass?"

"Please," Tom said. "And what are you drinking tonight, Miss Shaw?"

An attractive flush lent a little color to her face. "I rarely drink spirits, sir. I only take a bit of wine as my doctor recommends."

He liked that she made no pretense of hiding her disease.

Tom led Miss Shaw away from the bookcases and toward the fireplace where he found a seat for her near the cheerful hearth. She introduced Mrs. Porter, her companion, and asked him all the proper questions a young lady asks a young man of trade.

Tom answered, even though he was far from a young man of trade.

It was very, very awkward.

"Tell me, Mr. Murphy, do you enjoy working with your brothers?"

He'd been watching the fire and thinking about how long it would be before dinner, so the answer slipped out before he thought. "Better than a team of asses, but not by much."

He heard Miss Shaw stifle a snort and barely contain a spit of wine that would have sprayed over her lovely green frock. Mrs. Porter's mouth hung open a little, though her eyes were alight in amusement.

"Bollocks," Tom muttered before he pressed a knuckle to his lips and tried not to growl. *Language, man. Watch your language.* "My sincerest apologies, Miss Shaw. I am too accustomed to the company of men. Please forgive my vulgarity."

Her voice was low and conspiratorial as she leaned toward him slightly. "I accept your apology. I hate dinner parties. Would you like to know why?"

"Yes."

"Because it takes five times as long to say something in polite language as it does by being forward. And all the really good jokes are forbidden."

"Don't you believe in manners, Miss Shaw?" He let the corner of his mouth turn up. "Are you trying to shock me?"

"I have a strong inclination that it would take quite a lot to shock you, Mr. Murphy."

"You might be correct."

If their self-appointed matchmakers were watching, Tom thought they would probably be cackling with glee. Miss Shaw leaned toward him and he toward her. He couldn't help it. Something about her nature spoke to him. She was, despite her proper upbringing, an outsider by nature and circumstance. A caterpillar in a world that was not ready to see the butterfly she might become.

Tom wanted to see it.

He could smell the scent of gardenia in her hair and india ink on her fingers. And layered beneath that, he realized with an unexpected pang of sorrow, was the smell of her sickness. Of tonics and herbs she probably took to let her breathe easier.

"Miss Shaw, may I call on you tomorrow evening?"

She smiled, a sweet, cheerful expression with no artifice at all. "I would like that. I think... you and I might get on very well, Mr. Murphy."


THEY toasted him later, Murphy and Anne and Declan, who had miraculously appeared once Tom hadn't bollixed the whole affair.

"To Tom!" Murphy crowed. "Who knew a charming gentleman lurked beneath that ugly exterior?"

"Fuck off." Tom took a hearty drink of his ale and managed not to toss his sire into the wall.

Anne's eyes were sparkling. "I liked her. Very much. She's delightful, Tom. Pleasant, mature, and sensible."

Tom would have listed "sensible" fairly far down on the list of Miss Shaw's attributes. Anne's recitation of her virtues made Josephine Shaw sound dull. And the woman was anything but dull. But then, Tom had seen Miss Shaw running around the garden in her nightclothes and Anne hadn't. That probably influenced his impression of her.

Anne continued to rave. "She's very intelligent. She seems a voracious reader, and she speaks six languages. Can you imagine? Six! English, Irish, French, Latin, Greek, and Italian. Her great-grandmother was Italian. I think her mother's family were all quite artistic. What fun company she will be!"

Italian, eh? That might explain her fairy eyes. But good Lord, how could Tom possibly keep the interest of a woman who spoke six languages? He barely spoke one.

"You know," Declan said, "if you wore that fancy getup out more, I think the ladies would be a bit keener on you, old man. Something about a rough-looking bloke in a suit."

"Tom doesn't need to worry about all the ladies," Anne said. "Only one for right now. And Miss Shaw could barely keep her eyes off him."

"Oh really now?" Tom tried not to squirm. "Well, she seems a nice enough girl."

"She's *not* a girl," Murphy said thoughtfully. "She's a smart, intelligent woman. I think she's appeasing her father with this whole business, because I felt no sense of the desperate spinster about her."

Tom nodded. "Agreed. She is very independent."

"She may like Tom," Anne said. "But do you think she'd marry him? And if she doesn't, will Shaw still follow through on the contract?"

"I think he'll follow through, but it would leave room for his relations to challenge in the courts if we don't have any family connection," Declan said. "The nephew, Neville Burke, could be problematic."

Murphy shrugged. "Does he have any influence? Any political allies we're unaware of?"

"He has Beecham," Declan muttered.

Tom sat up straight. "He has who?"

"Beecham." Declan raised his hand when Murphy started to speak. "I know. I discovered they've developed an acquaintance only tonight."

"Damn," Anne said quietly. "So much for Beecham not noticing this deal."

"There was never any real question of that," Murphy said as he sat next to his mate. He took her hand, kissing it absently. "We knew he'd not be able to ignore me once I made my move with Shaw. Once I buy Shaw's boat works, I'll control more jobs on the waterfront than he does. A good third, even counting the humans. There was no way that crazy old bastard wouldn't notice."

Tom asked, "Dec, did he have any acquaintance with Neville Burke before now? Any history of business with the man?"

"Not that I could find. According to Burke's driver, they've only been socializing for the past month or so."

"But often?"

Declan nodded and Tom scowled. Suddenly, romancing Josephine Shaw had taken on an entirely new urgency. If Beecham was cultivating a friendship with the human, it could only be because he saw some vulnerability in Murphy and Shaw's alliance.

An even more alarming thought struck him. "Murphy, do we have guards around the Shaws' home?"

"No." Murphy shook his head. "I didn't think it was necessary."

"It is." Tom stood up and walked toward the door. "I'll take care of it. Right now."

All Tom could picture was Josephine dancing in the garden under the moonlight. She was as vulnerable as a babe. Anything could happen to her. Violence. Vampire influence. Hell, she'd been chatting with him in the shadows as if she hadn't a care in the world only three nights before.

Well, Tom decided, proper lady or not, Josephine Shaw would be getting a few more guards, and they'd be the most vicious lads he could find. No one, save him, was touching her.

TOM spotted her assigned guards the next night when he called on Miss Shaw. The two humans nodded at him, then went back to chatting behind newspapers as they waited in the square. He knew two more guards would be concealed in the garden behind the house, including a young vampire from Cornwall who'd come under Murphy's aegis only two years before.

She was a merciless little bit of an earth vampire whose lover was originally from Dublin. Kerra looked like a waif. If any of the humans spotted her, they'd likely try to feed her and give her a hand-me-down coat, not knowing she could tear their throat out before they'd have time to scream. She was the perfect guard for his woman.

He knocked on the door, a slim book he hoped Miss Shaw would like clasped in his hand, and the solemn butler ushered him into the gaslit entryway. He could hear voices coming from down the hall before he took off his hat.

"...know his supposed interest is only about your money, cousin."

"And I'm sure your interest is purely familial."

"I'm your cousin. I care about you."

A wry laugh. "It's almost as if you think I've forgotten all your slights over the years."

"Josephine—"

"Don't insult my intelligence, Neville. We both know you're angry that you won't inherit my money if I marry. Let me enlighten you: you wouldn't have inherited anyway. My will is something I saw to years ago. So whatever happens between me and Mr. Thomas Murphy, you can be assured my fortune—and father's—is well out of your reach."

Tom put a hand on the butler's arm, holding him back from announcing his presence. The butler, who was obviously not a fool, nodded silently. Tom waited outside the library, curious what Neville Burke's response would be.

"You're a foolish girl, Jo. And wills, especially those made by sick old spinsters, are always subject to interpretation. I have friends who can be very influential."

*Jo.* It was a darling nickname, but Tom didn't like the cousin using it. Neville Burke should only call her Josephine, if he had to speak to her at all.

"I am not a girl. Nor am I foolish. But you *are* foolish if you think you've hired better attorneys than mine. Good-bye, Neville. I'm expecting company, and I don't want you around. Is that plain enough language for you? And don't bother my father again. Make no mistake: I run this household, and you are not welcome in it unless you have an invitation."

Tom nodded at the butler, who knocked a second before he pushed the door open.

"Mr. Thomas Murphy, Miss Shaw. Here to see you."

"Ah." Josephine stood, and Tom would have missed the slight tremble in her hand if he hadn't been looking for signs of her temper. "Thank you, Mr. Carver. Would you see Mr. Burke out, please? He was just leaving."

"Of course."

Neville glared, but he didn't argue. He nodded toward his cousin. "Josephine, I wish you well."

"Of course you do."

Tom suppressed the smile at her sarcasm and held out a hand to the pale gentleman. "Mr. Neville Burke, I take it?"

The young Mr. Burke could hardly refuse his hand without it seeming awkward. He took it and Tom squeezed it firmly. Neville Burke looked like a man who'd spent his whole life in clubs and at dinner parties. His clothes were fashionable, his face soft. His pale blond excuse for a mustache hung limp beneath his narrow nose, as if it too had given up on any proper attempt at manliness.

Tom squeezed his hand a little harder to amuse himself.

"Mr. Thomas Murphy," Neville said through clenched teeth. "Your reputation, sir, proceeds you."

"I'm glad." He let go of the human's hand, resisting the urge to plant some mental manipulation that would banish him from Josephine's house forever. No, as offensive as Burke was, they needed to use him to understand what Beecham was up to.

"I understand," Tom said, "we have a mutual acquaintance. Mr. William Beecham."

Neville's face grew pale. "Ah. I mean yes, I am acquainted with the gentleman. You know Mr. Beecham?"

"Oh yes," Tom said. "I know all about Mr. Beecham. My brothers and I have known him for years."

"Is that so? How... remarkable."

Tom heard the waver in Neville's voice and noticed Josephine's eyes darting between the two men. This was taking too long. And Josephine was too bright not to pick up on the innuendo. He liked her intelligence, but he had to admit it was inconvenient at the moment.

"Good evening to you." He nodded to dismiss Neville Burke and turned his attention to Josephine. "Miss Shaw, I am honored to see your library." He bent and kissed her knuckles as the butler saw her cousin to the door. "My sister-in-law led me to believe it was extensive, and it does not disappoint."

"Thank you, Mr. Murphy!"

"It also gives me hope you will enjoy this gift."

He held out the slim volume to her and watched as she unwrapped it, meanwhile nodding politely at Mrs. Porter, who was knitting in the corner, and listening intently to make sure Neville Burke left the house.

Tom forgot the cousin entirely when Josephine's face lit. "*Ivanhoe*!"

"It is only the first volume, I'm afraid. I found it years ago at a bookshop in London. But the binding is good, and there's an intriguing inscription in the front I thought you might enjoy."

She held the book to her breast. "You brought me a book."

"You seemed more the book sort than the flower sort. Though I'd be happy to get you those as well."

"A book." Her face was glowing. "You are quite adept at courting."

"No, I'm afraid I'm rather inexperienced in it. That's why I'm trying everything in the hope I'll hit on something that strikes your fancy."

She laughed then, and the butterflies took flight in her eyes. She opened the book and looked at the first page. "'To my own Rebecca,'" she read on the frontispiece. "'Yours always, T.'" She looked up. "Your given name is Thomas."

"Aye, but I'm afraid I did not write the verse. Only acquired it with the book."

"Rebecca, not Rowena," she murmured. Her fingers traced over the script.

"Well," Tom said, "Rebecca was the more interesting of the two, wasn't she?"

"Yet Ivanhoe married Rowena at the end," Josephine said. "There's a story in this inscription, I think."

Tom shrugged. "Isn't there always?"

She held the book as if she'd found a treasure. "You're a *reader*, Mr. Murphy!"

If he could spend every night making her smile like that, proper manners and fancy dress might just be worth the trouble. "I am, Miss Shaw."

She motioned to two chairs by the fire, and Tom moved his seat a fraction closer to hers as they sat down.

"I would not have guessed," Josephine said. "Most of the gentlemen I've met since leaving school are not much for reading unless it is the newspapers."

"I can't claim to read philosophy or any kind of scholarly books. But I work nights mostly, so a good adventure story is always welcome to pass the time. *Ivanhoe* is one of my favorites."

"You work mostly at night? That's unusual, I think."

"I oversee most of our warehouses on the waterfront. Ships come in all hours of the day. Deliveries happen very early in the morning." *And the sun will burn me to a crisp.* "So yes, most of my hours are at night." He paused because the question was important. "Would that bother you? Should we...?"

She shook her head. "Not at all. I've always been a night bird. I sleep most afternoons and blame it on feeling ill." She glanced at Mrs. Porter, who only chuckled a little in the corner. "Mostly I just prefer the night. Sunlight can be quite harsh, don't you think?"

"I quite agree."

She started talking about books, a subject she was clearly passionate about. They talked about art and museums. About London and her favorite places and why she'd moved back to Dublin after school. Conversation didn't stop for two hours straight, even when Mrs. Porter started snoring in the corner.

Tom couldn't keep his eyes off her. She was delightful, as Anne had said. She was also intriguing, smart, and becoming more attractive every moment he spent in her presence. He was no longer merely resigned to marrying the woman; he was shocked to discover he truly desired it. And her.

"I wish you'd call me Tom," he said quietly, hoping not to wake her chaperone. "I know that's not very proper, is it?"

"Tom?" she asked, staring at him with wide eyes. "Only Tom? Not Thomas?"

"Just Tom."

She looked down for a moment before she looked up and met his eyes. "If I do, will you call me Josephine?"

"I don't think so." His heart kicked in his chest. "But I might call you Josie."

Her cheeks pinked. "Josie? No one calls me Josie."

"I do."

"Very well," she whispered, "Tom."

He took her hand in both of his. "Do you think... you might like to marry me, Josie?"

Josephine's smile lit up the room. "I believe I might."

*Hello, butterfly.*

## Chapter Four

My dearest Lenore,

You'll think me caught up in one of my stories, but indeed, I am not. I am engaged to be married. His name is Mister Thomas Murphy of Dublin. He has two brothers, and he is old! But not too old. He is not handsome, but he is very tall. And, I daresay, his shoulders are dramatically broad. He does, as the housemaids have mentioned, cut a very striking figure.

We suit each other, Lenore. Far more than I ever expected a man to suit me.

I don't think we will have a large wedding. I don't want one, and I don't think Father will insist on it. Tom and I are both too old for foolishness.

I am happy and maybe a little frightened by it. It seems too easy. At some point a monster is sure to intrude, don't you think? We're going to the theater tonight. Tom (he insists I call him Tom) said we must celebrate because I did not cough once yesterday.

I like that he does not avoid my illness. He is thoughtful but not overly solicitous.

I haven't told him about Miss Dioli or Mr. Doyle yet. It might be foolish, but I find I want to ensnare the poor man in matrimony before I announce my alter egos.

(This will surely be my tragic downfall, don't you think? I can see the shadows lurking at the edge of this letter.)

He is no flattering suitor, which I like. He is, however, very excellent company and has a dry wit I value highly. He also gave me a copy of *Ivanhoe* with a very sentimental inscription. Do not reveal this to anyone (unless you're taken by villains and tortured for it, of course), but my intended might be a romantic.

Wish me luck, dearest Lenore. I have absolutely no idea what to do with him.

Your faithful friend,
Josephine Shaw

P.S. Tom calls me Josie. Isn't that grand?

JOSEPHINE held the handkerchief to her mouth, wishing she could shrink back into the seat. Wishing for the first time since she'd met him two months before that Tom Murphy would disappear.

"It was likely all that close air in the theater," Tom said, flipping open his watch and closing it. "I nearly passed out myself from Mrs. Lark's perfume. Horrid stuff."

Fidgeting. He was fidgeting. Tom didn't fidget.

"It's not too late to change your mind," she rasped out, then put the muslin to her mouth again to catch the cough. After the spell had passed, she continued. "It's not going to get better, Tom." Josephine looked up and almost reeled back at the anger on his face.

"Get your mind off that," he said. "What kind of man do you think I am?"

"A single man until next week. A healthy man. Not one who needs to be saddled with a—"

"Do not finish that sentence, Josephine Shaw, or you'll be insulting both of us."

She fell silent and watched the dark streets of Dublin pass, the steady trickling rain pattering on the roof of the carriage. Tom, never shy about ignoring propriety, shifted across the carriage to sit next to her. He closed his hand around hers, and she struggled not to pull it away.

"I want to marry you, Josie."

"Why?"

He was silent for a moment. "Well...," he finally drawled. "I'm quite eager to bed you, and you seem the kind who'll want matrimony for that."

Josie's eyes popped open and her jaw dropped. She swung her shocked gaze to his laughing one and tried pulling her hand away, but he only pulled it closer. "Tom!"

His eyes were all innocence, but the devil was lurking around his mouth. "What?"

"You did not just say that to me."

"I did. It's the truth."

Cough forgotten, her face felt as if it were on fire. "Mr. Murphy!"

"Is that what you're gonna call me when we f—"

She slapped a hand over his mouth. "Don't you dare."

He nipped at her fingers and pulled them away. He'd captured both her hands, and Josephine sat helpless, not sure whether she was more shocked or aroused.

Tom took a deep breath and smiled wickedly. "You knew I was lacking in manners when you agreed to marry me, Miss Shaw."

"What if Mrs. Porter were here?"

"Mrs. Porter isn't here. And I'd hardly talk about the pleasures of the marriage bed with my future wife while her companion was in attendance, now would I?"

Her heart raced. "Pleasures of the marriage bed?"

"Don't tell me you haven't thought of it. I know what kind of books you read."

"Tom—"

"Why are you embarrassed?"

Tom hadn't let go of her hands. He'd crossed them over his chest as if embracing her. Her fingertips flexed against the crisp cotton of his shirt, and she wondered at the thick muscle on his chest. He was solid as a wall. She couldn't even feel his heart beat, though her own was racing. His eyes were intent and his smile was still wicked.

"Come now, Josie. Why are you embarrassed? You're no blushing miss. Are you frightened?"

"I don't want to say." Her voice sounded tiny to her ears. She cleared her throat and tried to take a deep breath, but it rasped out of her.

Tom immediately let one of her hands go and put a cool palm on the side of her neck. "Shhh," he murmured. "Easy now. I'm sorry. I was just teasing you. Try to relax."

"Hard to do with you so close."

He leaned away, but she grabbed his sleeve and pulled.

"Josie, I'm trying to—"

"I *am* afraid."

They both fell silent, and the only sound was the rain on the roof. She felt her face flush with embarrassment again. She closed her eyes and pressed her lips together when Tom's thumb stroked her neck.

"Why are you afraid?" he asked, his voice as hoarse as hers. "Is it me? I know I'm not—"

"*No.* Just... the unknown, I suppose. Reading isn't doing, is it?"

"No, it's not."

"And I can assume you have...?"

"Yes."

"Probably a good thing one of us knows what goes where then."

His chest rumbled with laughter, but his voice was gentle. "Josephine, open your eyes."

"Is my face still very, very red?"

"Yes, but it's lovely."

"Oooh," she groaned and let her head fall forward, only to feel his shoulder catch it. She pressed her face into his coat. "I'm very glad Mrs. Porter is not here."

"So am I." His lips touched her forehead. "Josie?"

"I'm going to hide here until we reach my home. As my intended, it is your duty to let me use your shoulder this way."

The aforementioned shoulder shook with more laughter. "What are you frightened by?"

"Are you truly forcing me to speak of this?"

"Yes."

"Fine." She sat up but kept her eyes closed. "I have been informed by several well-meaning but terror-inducing friends and household staff that things do... hurt quite a bit."

"Hmm."

"That's the only thing you're going to say? 'Hmm?'"

"Nothing much to say about men who don't know their way about pleasing a woman."

Josephine had no vocabulary to respond to that.

"I can assume you know the mechanics of the act?" he asked.

"I'm an educated woman. Obviously, yes. Also... I have read more than one book that mentioned it."

"You're going to keep your eyes closed the entire way home, aren't you?"

"Yes, I am."

Tom laughed. "Fine. But even though you're hiding, you have to tell me..." He leaned close enough that she could feel his breath on her neck. "Your books? Do they... excite you?"

His voice moved along her skin like a physical caress.

"Josephine?"

"You know they do."

"Aye, I can tell they do by that gorgeous color on your face. Your lips are flushed and swollen. Your breathing is faster. But do you know what, Josie?"

"You have no manners at all, Tom Murphy."

"I know. Don't change the subject." His finger trailed along the curve of her ear. "Do you know what?"

She was going to burst out of her skin. "What?"

His lips were at her ear. "I'm better than your books."

And when the gasp left her lips, he captured them with his own. Tom's kiss burned through her. One hand cupped her jaw while the other hand stroked her neck. His mouth wasn't still or chaste. His hands lifted her face to his until the angle suited him. Then, he devoured her.

His tongue licked out at hers, darting to taste her as if she was a delicacy he wanted to sample. He captured her lower lip with his front teeth and bit softly. Then his lips seized hers again. She heard him groan.

The hand holding her jaw slid back, and his fingers dug into her hair. They caressed the nape of her neck, tugging at her hair as his mouth—wondrous mouth—continued to kiss her senseless. Josephine felt the dampness between her thighs. Felt her small breasts swell as they pressed against his chest. His lips left her mouth and traveled across her cheek, nibbled her earlobe, slipped down to her neck.

"Tom..." Her eyes still closed, she held him close. One hand gripped the lapel of his coat while the other pressed to the nape of his neck. She could feel the shorn hair at his collar, the rough texture of his skin. She must have been feverish, because his skin felt *so* cool. She sighed when she felt the bite of his teeth at her flesh. A tingling against her skin. Sharp and teasing.

Tom's hand was still tugging at her hair.

"What are you doing?" she asked as he licked and kissed her neck. She finally opened her eyes, only to have them roll back in pleasure.

"Want your hair down."

She blinked. "What?"

"Hair. Want it—"

"No!" She pulled away. "Tom, we're in a carriage."

Did he actually just growl?

"Do you know how long it takes to pin my hair up? If you take it down, everyone in Merrion Square will know what you've been doing."

He pulled back, his lips pressed together. His chest heaved as he attempted to control himself, and Josephine saw him not-at-all discreetly adjust his trousers. Her eyes widened before she swung her gaze to the window again.

"You're marrying me next week, and then I'll have it down," he muttered.

"I usually braid it when I sleep."

"Not when I'm sleeping with you."

Could her heart beat any faster? "Oh."

"You still frightened?"

"Possibly more than I was before."

For some reason this amused him, and he laughed. "No, you're not." He reached out and took her hand, sliding his fingers between hers in a suggestive way.

Josephine shivered.

"You're marrying me next week," he said again, his voice bordering on smug. "I'll bed you then, and Josie? You'll like it."

"MISS Shaw? Mrs. Murphy, that is. Josephine?"

Was that Tom? Something cold touched her chest. Her back. Cool pillows at her neck as someone pulled the damp ones away and replaced them.

"Her temperature is no longer rising, but it is still very high. I would recommend a cool bath for most fevers, but because of her lungs—"

"Just tell us what to do."

Not Tom. The doctor. Tom had that lovely, deep voice that made her belly tremble for mysterious and exciting reasons. His voice had sounded so lovely in the church. It had resonated through the stone chapel as he said his vows. He was always so serious...

She heard someone sigh. "She needs fresh air. Relaxation." It was the doctor again. "Get her out of the city if you can. The air right now is noxious. It's the worst place for her."

Josephine struggled to open her eyes. "Tom?" she whispered.

He grabbed her hand. She'd know those calluses anywhere. "Josie?"

"Not... Not the wedding night we planned," she said before her chest was racked by another cough.

"Hush, Miss Jo." Mrs. Porter was there. She propped her up and untied her shift at the neck.

"Louisa." She tried to protest, but the cough surged up and stopped her voice.

"Now, child, you're married. I'll send the others away. None but your own husband here. Nothing to be embarrassed about."

Nothing to be embarrassed about? Her wedding night had ended in a fever, wracking coughs, and a house call from the doctor. Thank God Mrs. Porter had come with her to her new home. Poor Tom would have had no idea what to do otherwise.

Josephine finally felt strong enough to open her eyes. The room was lit by lamplight and full of more people than she was accustomed to. She could see her wedding dress draped over the chair in the corner of the room. Her new brother-in-law and sister-in-law were speaking with the doctor, and Tom and Mrs. Porter knelt by her bed.

He held a cool cloth to her head as Mrs. Porter eased her back.

"Wait here," she said. "I'll clear the room and bring the onions."

Her fevered eyes shifted to Tom. "And thus begins the romance of marriage," she wheezed. "It all begins with onions." She reached out and tried to smooth away the groove between his eyebrows. "Careful now. You'll look an old man too soon, husband."

"The doctor said it was likely the stress of the wedding and all," Tom said. "We should a' just run away, Josie."

"It's not your fault I fainted walking out of the church."

"No, but it'll give the papers something to write about." He pressed her hand to his freshly shaved cheek. "The poor Shaw heiress overcome by the idea of her wedding night with the scandalous Murphy brother."

Her rasping laughs turned into coughs. She closed her eyes again and focused on relaxing her chest. In. Out.

"Have you ever felt," she wheezed out, "as if you were trying to breathe through water?"

"Jaysus," he swore. "Don't do this to me, sweet girl. Give me a little longer, eh?"

She blinked her eyes open and lifted a hand to the corner of his eyes where the skin was creased with age and worry. "Your eyes are all red, Tom."

He blinked and looked away. "Must be all the smoke. And worrying about you."

"I told you..." She traced a fingertip around his stern mouth. "I'm not going to get better."

"And I told you I was marrying you. And I did, wife."

She smiled. "That's right. We're married."

"We are."

"I like you so much, Tom. Far... more than I could have imagined. So unfair—"

Another coughing fit took her, and Tom helped her sit up, rubbing her back and placing the cool cloth at the nape of her neck.

"Tell me what to do," he whispered. "Anything."

"There's nothing... The onions will help," she rasped when the cough had passed.

Mrs. Porter bustled in, a smelly poultice in her hands and a stern look on her face.

"Mr. Murphy, sir, I must insist you clear your brother and sister-in-law from the room. The less company the better for Miss Shaw. I'm in no danger of infection, you see. I had it as a child and recovered. But the rest of you could be at risk."

"I'll clear them out," he growled. "But then I'm coming back to sit with *Mrs. Murphy*, so don't you bar the door."

She pursed her lips. "As you like."

The door closed a few moments later, and Mrs. Porter opened up Josephine's gown, carefully placing the steaming poultice on her chest. It was so hot she felt as if her skin would peel off.

"Oh, the smell," she groaned. "What horrid thing did you add this time, Louisa?"

"Smells like clear breathing is what it smells like. And the Murphys' cook had garlic. She said it might help."

"Well, it certainly"—Josephine coughed some more—"smells vile enough to be medicinal."

Mrs. Porter sat silently for a few more moments while Josephine breathed in the onion fumes.

"I think I heard them mention the house in Bray."

"Bray would be nice," she wheezed. "Take... you and Tom."

"And his valet, of course. Young man by the name of Henry. Seems a nice boy, and Mr. Murphy said he was good driver too."

The house at Bray was hers. Father had put it in her name years before. Josephine found she liked the idea of sharing the simple house with Tom. They'd planned to travel to Wicklow for their honeymoon, but Bray would be far more relaxing.

She felt herself slipping to sleep as her breathing eased. "Tell Tom..."

"What, dear?"

"See him in my dreams."

Mrs. Porter brushed Josephine's hair back from her damp forehead. "Course you will, lovey. Rest now."

But when she dreamed, Josephine was steeped in nightmares. Tom was there, but his eyes were bloodred and his skin ice-cold. He took her in his arms and kissed her, but when she pulled away, her mouth was bleeding and a childish voice whispered:

*Are you afraid to die?*


THE next time she woke, Tom was carrying her. She took a breath and realized the horrid onions had done their job and her breathing had eased. She pressed her cheek into Tom's shoulder, amazed by his strength.

"You're not even breathing heavily," she murmured.

"Are you awake then?"

"Hmmm." She burrowed into his shoulder. "Are we in Bray already?"

"We've just arrived."

"How long did I sleep?"

"Your fever broke around noon today, Mrs. Porter said. We both slept until late afternoon, then I decided we'd better get started. You woke a little in the carriage, but not for long. No coughing."

"Oh good." She took another easy breath. Ah, the wondrous onions. Vile, but effective. "I feel like a damsel in a novel with you carrying me like this."

A laugh rumbled in his chest. "Just to the house."

"No, no," she murmured. "You must carry me up to the top of a tower and ravish me. Or perhaps carry me over a hill as we run from bandits."

"I'm afraid there will be no ravishing until your strength is back." His voice wore a smile. He almost sounded as if he was laughing. "What an imagination you have, Josie."

"You have no idea."

"Are you a good one for stories? I love a good story."

"You might say that."

She felt him jostle her feet a bit as he maneuvered her through the small entry hall. The sea air nipped her too-long nose, and she could still feel the edge of the fever, but she didn't care. She felt as romantic as a heroine in one of her Gothic tales.

Which, being Gothic, didn't bode well for her long-term health.

She started to laugh out loud.

"What's so funny?" Tom asked. "Am I too clumsy for you?"

"Not at all. It strikes me that I am the sick maiden who is going to an isolated country house with the mysterious man who swept her off her feet and threatened to ravage her. This would make an excellent novel."

"Do you think so?" Tom leaned down and played with her, snapping his teeth at the tip of her nose. "Never fear, Josie, my girl. If I'm a monster, I'm a proper sort of one."

"Oh dear," she sighed. "A proper sort of monster? How very disappointing."

## Chapter Five

TOM WOKE FOR THE NIGHT, his face already turned toward the door where Henry was chattering on to himself about some letters that had arrived from Dublin. The lad must have heard him move because he turned and gave Tom a silent nod that everything was well as he continued the one-sided conversation designed to give the illusion that Tom had been awake for hours.

"No sir, Mr. Murphy. I got them off to the post today, but there was nothing yet to bring to you." The lad paused. "Yes, sir. I'll check in the morning. Would you like to prepare for dinner, sir?"

Tom cleared his throat and said, "Yes, Henry. Please ask Mrs. Murphy to join me for a drink if she's feeling up to it tonight."

"Yes, sir."

Stepping closer to the side of the bed where Henry had already laid out a set of evening clothes, the lad leaned down and said, "Nothing unusual today, sir."

"Has my wife slept at all?"

"Yes, sir. Believe she woke for breakfast, then was locked in her room awhile with something or other. Slept this afternoon."

"No coughing?"

"Not that I heard, sir."

"Thank you, Henry."

"Did you need help getting dressed, Mr. Murphy?"

Tom waved him away, and Henry slipped out of the room.

It was one thing to plan to marry a human and conceal his immortal nature; it was quite another thing to accomplish it. Especially while traveling. The house he'd intended to rent in Wicklow was owned by immortals and had a staff who was fully aware of their secrets. But when Josie's doctor had suggested the seaside, he and Anne had quickly cobbled together a plan for Bray.

For the hundredth time since they'd arrived, Tom thanked the gods for Henry Flynn. The boy had been born to a couple who'd worked for Tom almost as long as he'd been a vampire. The lad had known about immortals since he was a child. Had never been terrified and had always known what it was to keep secrets.

Tom supposed every vampire had families like the Flynns. Or they did if they were lucky.

He kept his own chamber in Bray, which fortunately had very heavy drapes. And while he normally lay solitary in his secure day-chamber in his Dublin house, in the Bray house, Henry needed access to his rooms to maintain the illusion of humanity. The boy was trustworthy. That didn't mean Tom didn't help his loyalty along with a touch of amnis at times.

He'd planted subtle suggestions not to question his odd sleeping patterns in all the household staff and, unfortunately, his new wife. He hated doing anything to touch her mind, but it was necessary. Josie was simply too intelligent to fool by human means.

And gods, she was so very human.

Tom thought he'd planned for everything. But he could never have prepared himself for the feeling of helplessness that struck him when Josie was having one of her coughing fits. Or the raw guilt when he was forced to leave her at daybreak instead of staying at her bedside.

Tom wasn't used to feeling helpless. His relief at hearing she'd had another day with no breathing problems struck him as more profound than it should have been for a man who'd only met his wife two months before.

That made six days with no coughing since they'd come to the seaside. He'd promised himself to stay away from her for at least a week after her collapse following their wedding ceremony. Seven full days without coughing before he attempted more than a chaste kiss.

Oh, he'd have her, but Tom had to admit he'd been an insensitive fool. He'd not taken many lovers as an immortal. He found controlling his urges to be hard enough without adding in lust.

But Josie...

For once in his life, Tom had found a woman he enjoyed looking after. Maybe it was because she was so independent. Looking after her was a challenge. Her barely contained sensuality, a bonus. He still thought about their kiss in the carriage, though it did nothing to help his self-control.

His unexpected eagerness for matrimony and the anticipation of bedding his new wife had been all he'd been thinking of in the days leading up to the small church ceremony. She'd looked lovely in the church. In the back of Tom's mind, he'd imagined Josie dressed in a medieval costume with a flowing train and her hair falling past her waist rather than the fashionable dress and pinned hair she wore. That's what her dressing gown had reminded him of that first night in the garden. *No matter,* he'd thought. He'd have her hair down that very night and finally indulge his imagination.

But then came the horror of her collapse. The unexpected terror of her wracking coughs that simply *would not stop*. Tom had torn open her dress and corset in the carriage, which had helped, but it wasn't enough. Then her fever spiked. Then more coughing. Her father had tears in his eyes, terrified he was losing his daughter, though the sensible Mrs. Porter simply barked instructions at his staff as soon as she arrived, accustomed to her mistress's spells.

Tom finished tying his cravat, eager to see her again.

Six days. Tomorrow, perhaps.

Apparently his body still thought he was a boy of twenty, because even the thought of seeing Josie's hair fall down her back caused a very ungentlemanlike reaction. He straightened his waistcoat in the mirror and left his room, nodding to the maid as she passed him in the hall, noting her downcast eyes and ghost of a curtsy.

He truly hated acting the gentleman.

Following the sweet sound of Josie's voice, he headed toward the library where they usually enjoyed a drink before dinner. His wife was sitting by the fire, a book on her lap, interrogating poor Henry about his education.

"But you never went to school? Not even for a few years?"

"Not... exactly, Mrs. Murphy. See, Mr. Patrick Murphy always kept... Well, see, there was—"

"Tutors," Tom said, rescuing Henry from the relentless curiosity of his wife. "My brother kept a tutor employed for all the servants' children. There were enough to justify it, and that way the girls could take the same lessons as the boys, which Anne insists on." He leaned down and pressed a kiss to Josephine's cool cheek, happy to smell less sickness and more of the gardenia-scented soap she preferred. "Good evening, wife."

"Good evening." Josie turned her head slightly, avoiding his gaze and the kiss he usually pressed to the corner of her mouth. "That's very generous of him. It's not many gentlemen who would keep tutors for their household staff."

Tom straightened, feeling the slight turn as if she'd given him a physical push. "Henry, if you would excuse us."

"Yes, sir."

The lad fled the room, and Tom stood next to her. "Tell me what's wrong."

A flush in her cheeks. "Nothing, Tom. You'll be happy to know I'm feeling well tonight. No coughing at all today. Did you accomplish everything you needed to for work?"

"Did I anger you? I did tell you I'd need to see to—"

"It's fine." Her pulse was rushing, and her flush grew. "I had... matters to attend to this morning as well. Cook found some lovely fish at the market today. I hope you'll enjoy—"

"Don't ignore me, Josephine. Tell me what I've done that made you turn away from me just now."

Her face reddened more, the flush spreading down her throat and across the high-necked dress...

One of her old dresses. Not one of the more fashionable evening dresses she'd ordered for their honeymoon like she'd worn the night before.

They'd played chess and he'd beaten her. Badly. Josie claimed she had no head for the game, but mostly she'd been making Tom laugh too hard with her stories as she narrated a melodramatic—and ultimately doomed—romance between the black queen and the white knight. It had him laughing so hard he could barely think to make a move.

They'd been laughing. Then he'd lost patience with her silly commentary and swung her onto his lap, kissing her soundly before...

He'd given her a chaste kiss and sent her to her bed because his own body was raging.

And tonight she was wearing one of her old dresses, and all the teasing light had gone out of her eyes because she'd mistaken his self-control for disinterest.

"Blast it, Josie!" He fell to his knees beside her. "No, no, no. It isn't you. I'm only worried—"

"It's fine." She turned her face to the fire. "I'm being silly. And... dramatic. It's a failing of mine. I know my spell after the wedding put everything in perspective. We're friends, Tom. I don't want to damage that. I value your company too much—"

"Friends?" He leaned forward, caging her on the blue chair though she still wouldn't turn her eyes to him. "You think I no longer want you as my wife?"

"Of course not. I know you'll make an excellent husband—"

"I'm not such an excellent husband if I've been ignoring what you need, am I?"

She shook her head, still staring at the fire. "I won't... I don't want to be a duty or an obligation. I have my pride. I'd rather have friendship than pity."

"Bloody hell." He grabbed her chin and forced her face to him. "You think my kisses are pity, do you? You think I don't want you? That I don't have to think of cold baths and the like when I leave you at night? I thought you were *dying* ten days ago, Josephine."

Her mouth trembled, and he saw the tears in her great dark eyes, though she blinked them back.

"I *am* dying, Tom." She put a hand on his jaw when he clenched it. "And I understand—"

He cut her off with an angry kiss. How dare she! Tom grabbed the back of her neck and pressed her mouth to his, swallowing the quick cry she let out before her hands came to rest on his chest and her slim fingers dug into the muscle there. She kissed him back, opening her mouth to his, and he tasted the sherry she'd been drinking. A hint of pear and a bite of something salty on her tongue.

"You understand nothing." Tom hissed before he kissed her again. He wasn't careful or chaste. She thought he didn't want her, or wanted her only for pity.

How dare she? How dare she make him laugh so? Make him hunger for her as he did? How dare she be so clever and generous?

So terribly mortal.

He pulled away from her mouth and bent to her ear, biting the lobe before he soothed the sting with his tongue. He pressed his forehead to her warm temple and fought to control the drop of his fangs when he heard the swift beat of her heart.

"I *want* you," he whispered. "I want to see you naked in the firelight. I want to see your hair loose when you're wearing nothing but your skin. Want to see it brush the top of your arse. I want to see it tickle the tips of your pretty tits, Josie. I want my mouth on every inch of you. Want to feel you around me. Hot and—"

Josie slammed a hand over his mouth. "I don't want supper," she gasped. "Take me to my room."

Had he shocked her? Offended her? Tom swore. "Jo—"

"Take me to my room, Tom, and if you leave me without doing everything you just said, I'll... do something horrible to you. I don't know what. I can't think right now. But I have a good imagination."

He picked her up without another word and carried her out of the library, almost running over Henry on the way toward the stairs.

"Henry, tell Cook we don't need supper."

The lad's cheeks turned red, and he muttered, "Perhaps a tray later, sir."

"See that we're not disturbed."

"Yes, sir, Mr. Murphy." He nodded. "Mrs. Murphy."

Josie, seemingly oblivious to the interchange, had her lips against his neck. Her skin was burning, but it was the healthy flush of arousal, not sickness. He carried her to her bedchamber on the second floor. The evening maid was bending over the newly lit fire and jumped when he practically kicked in the door.

"Out."

"Yes, sir!"

She slammed the door on the way out, and Tom locked it behind her.

"We're shocking the servants," Josie whispered against his neck.

"If they're not scandalized by the time this night is over, then I'll consider it a personal failure."

He laid her on the bed and immediately set to undoing the buttons at her neck.

"I hate this dress," he muttered as he stripped it off. "Don't ever wear it again. Wear your new clothes. All the pretty things you bought. You should have pretty things."

"You can rip it if you'd like."

Leave it to the woman to make him laugh when his cock felt like it was going to revolt in his trousers if it wasn't released soon.

"Ripping corsets," he said as he unhooked her at the back, "is seldom as comfortable or as quick as novels make it out to be."

"Do you speak from personal experience?"

Her proper accent undid him. "You do ask the most inconvenient questions."

"I consider it part of my charm. Good God, you're right. Why are there so many layers?"

He finally removed everything but the thin cotton of her camisole. Her breasts pressed against it and he bent down, putting his mouth on them as she arched under his hands.

"Oh Tom!" she gasped. "That feels... I'm finding it very hard to describe at the moment."

Teasing his tongue over the thin cotton, Tom lifted her and tried to remove all the skirts hindering him. "Much prefer the dressing gown," he muttered.

"What?"

"Nothing. Take everything off if you don't want it ripped." He started removing his own clothes, more than ready to join her.

"I thought you didn't believe in ripping clothes."

"I'm losing patience with ladies' fashions."

He stripped off the blasted waistcoat and shirt, ridding himself of the excess clothing before he turned back to the bed.

"Oh, I..." Her face was burning as she surveyed his bare chest. "Oh, my."

Josie lifted the edge of her camisole but didn't pull it off. Clad only in the light cotton of her undergarments, she was as bare as Tom had ever seen her. He decided to wait to take off his trousers. Best not to scare the woman.

She was nervous, which he supposed was natural. He climbed into bed next to her and pressed soothing kisses to her shoulder.

"We'll slow down," he said. "I'm losing my head like a randy lad, aren't I?"

She laughed nervously. "I lost my nerve when your shirt came off. You have a startling number of muscles."

And scars. And burns. His human life hadn't been an easy one. "I'm not so easy on the eyes as you, sweet girl."

"You?" Her eyes widened. "You're magnificent. Like one of those statues the Italians sculpt. And I'm so very thin."

He continued kissing her shoulder, teasing the edges of the lace camisole with his callused fingers. "You're good for my ego. I know I'm not a handsome gentleman. And you're not thin. You're..." His fingers drifted between her breasts. "Slender. Gorgeous. Like one of the willow trees in your garden."

Her heart raced under his fingertips, but she said nothing. Tom's fangs throbbed in his mouth, but he beat back his instinct to bite. Tonight was about taking care of Josie. Bloodlust had no place here.

"Can I see you?" He reached up to tug at the pins he could see in her hair. "Here now, sit up."

She did, and he scooted her forward so he was sitting behind her. He leaned against the headboard, pleased at her shiver when he drew her back against his bare chest. "I've been dreaming about feeling all that hair against my skin. Let me take it down."

"If you thought the buttons were frustrating..."

He laughed and her small breasts shook with the movement. He grew impossibly harder, and he knew she felt it because her shoulders tensed.

"That does seem... rather impossible from my perspective. You realize that, don't you?"

"It's as natural as breathing. Just takes a bit of getting used to, like anything else."

"Are you abnormally large? Or are things always... proportional?"

Tom bit his lip to keep from laughing. "I think you're assuming a level of knowledge on a subject I haven't taken time to study."

"Oh?"

"And you're talking too much."

Her head fell to the side when he put his mouth there and tasted her. His left hand continued extracting the pins in her hair while his right cupped her breast over her camisole. Slowly, he worked his hand under the fabric and finally, finally he felt her skin.

He groaned. "You're so soft."

"And you're not soft at all."

Her hair tumbled down, and Tom luxuriated in the chestnut silk that smelled of gardenias and lilac. Dark scents from her garden. Heady scents that wrapped around him as she arched back into his chest. He drew her hair around her as he eased the camisole off. Silk and warm skin and Josie. He banished the sickness from his memory and set his mind to her pleasure. He slowly turned his wife until her breasts were against his chest, and his hands trailed down her back, over the curve of her hips and the swell of her bottom.

"Let me," he said against her neck. He fought back the instinct to bite. "Let me—"

"Yes. Anything." Her voice was high and needy. "Everything, Tom."

Her trust undid him. He lay back, Josie draped across his chest, her hair falling around them like a curtain. His hands slid down, caressing the slick heat between her legs. He slowly worked her body until her eyes glazed over with longing and she fell to the side, begging for release. Then, with a gentle kiss, he pushed her over and she arched her back, shuddering with pleasure.

He carefully removed the rest of their clothes, scattering kisses over her skin and murmuring soft words to soothe her.

"So lovely, my wife." He lay at her side, his hands and lips arousing her again. "So perfect. So soft." He wasn't a small man, and he didn't want to hurt her, but some pain would be inevitable.

"Please," she whispered. "Don't make me wait."

Tom drew back. There were tears in her eyes and a tremulous smile on her lips.

"Josie?"

"I've waited so long," she said, her voice soft and urgent. "For you. For this. Don't make me wait, Tom."

He kissed her, pressing their lips together as he rose and parted her legs. He shifted up and felt the tight squeeze of her body. Slow. So slow. When her muscles tensed, he whispered and kissed her neck, pausing until her body melted for him again. He worked himself slowly to the hilt and then stopped.

"Josie?"

She nodded. "I'm... it hurts a little, but not as bad as I'd imagined."

"Well, you do have an awful imagination," he said with a smile, his body locked still so she could grow accustomed to him.

"You're not moving."

She squirmed beneath him, and he groaned.

"Wait for it. God, you feel good. Just want to give you a moment."

Josie reached up, stroking his cheek with her hand. "Oh, my Tom. You take such care with me."

She filled his heart and broke it all at once.

Tom couldn't hold back longer. He started to move. Josie's eyes fluttered closed, but her lips were flushed and red. Her heart raced, and he could feel the swell of her body around his, tight and slick. Her neck arched back, and he bent to kiss her again.

"I will never forget this," he whispered against her lips. "Not a moment. If I live a thousand years, I will never forget this. Do you understand? I will *never* forget you."

She cried out and threw her arms around his shoulders, wrapping herself around him as he let himself go. Tom lost himself in her body, in the smell and taste and feel of her. Hunger for her blood forgotten, he fisted a hand around her wild tangle of hair and tugged, holding her in place as she writhed beneath him.

Josie. Josie. Josie.

She had captured him. Enchanted him. He'd never stood a chance.

He fell.

## Chapter Six

JOSIE'S CHEEKS ACHED from laughing as she walked into the library, Anne on her heels. The two had taken in a concert that had been advertised heavily for the previous month but had proved to be less than promised in person. They'd left early, and Josie had agreed to a drink with Anne before she slipped away to write.

"But the tenor—" Anne was laughing. "I think he might have been a she. I've never heard a man sing that high."

"It was extraordinary. Pity he was the only talented one among— Oh! Hello, Tom. What are you doing home?"

Tom was sitting near the fireplace... glowering.

Yes, she did believe that was the appropriate verb. To glower. Her normally composed husband was glowering.

Unsurprisingly, this did not make him any less attractive to her. Josie had become quite his sycophant, though she'd never tell him. In the three months they'd been married, her feelings had deepened to far more than mere affection for her rough-mannered, taciturn husband. She was, quite simply, besotted. And glowering did nothing to quash that.

"What are you doing back from the warehouse?" she asked, frowning.

Anne asked, "Is everything all right? I know there was supposed to be a meeting with Beecham tonight."

"And I forgot one of my reports. Realized I'd left it in Josie's sitting room last night, so I went looking for it." He held up an envelope. "What is this?"

"As I'm rather far away at the moment, I cannot tell you." Josie stepped forward with her hand out. "Give it here, Tom."

He flipped it away from her fingers.

"Tom!" She heard Anne slip from the room. "What on earth—"

"Who is Joseph Doyle?"

Her mouth dropped open. Her heart sped. "It isn't... I mean—"

"I can hear your heart racing from here. Tell me."

Josie frowned. "That's impossible. There's no way for you to hear—"

"Who is he, Josephine? Why is someone sending letters to a Joseph Doyle care of you at your father's house? Who is he? Is that why you've been spending your days over there?"

"You're mad." She'd raced past embarrassed and straight into furious. "I'm at my father's house every day because my father is *dying* and you're locked in your rooms working all the time! So don't question my—"

"Who is he?"

"He's me!" Angry tears pricked her eyes. She didn't know how to fight with Tom. He'd always been too kind. He was gentle with her, sometimes to frustration. A model of quiet humor and utter patience, even when she was at her most distracted. He'd never once raised his voice.

Glowering had turned to confusion. "What do you mean, he's you?" He frowned at the letter again. "Did someone mistake your—"

"Joseph Doyle is... a writer of... of Gothic stories and mysteries. He... That is, he writes for several of the more... popular papers in... in London. And he is... me." Her face was burning. She stared at the red and blue whorls of the rug at her feet. "Joseph Doyle is one of my noms de plume." She finally tipped her chin up. "I am sorry I concealed this from you, but I am not sorry I write such stories, nor do I have any plans to stop."

He was frowning at the letter, flipping it over in his hands. He stared at it, then cocked his head. Then looked up, a grin slashed across his scarred face. "Are you saying you write penny dreadfuls?"

She put her hands on her hips. "There are many fine writers in the Gothic genre who write for papers that—"

He cut her off with a clap of his hand on his thigh. "That's why you write so many letters. They're not letters; they're stories." He stood and started pacing. "Joseph Doyle sounds—" He snapped his fingers. "Did you write the one about the doctor who was murdering the old women?"

Josie stood frozen, blinking her eyes rapidly as Tom walked to her. "Did I write the... The one with the scalpel or the one who used poison?"

"Scalpel."

"No, I wrote the poisoner. Only it wasn't the doctor in the end. He was framed. It was—"

"The kitchen maid!"

Josie slapped a hand over her mouth.

Tom burst into laughter. "There's a lad on the docks who brings them from London every month. You have the most horrid imagination! The way you described those murders had my stomach churning, Josie. The jerking and frothing at the mouth—"

"And you *read* it?"

He was still laughing. He pulled her hand away from her flushed face and put the letter in it. "One of your noms de plume? Do you have more names I don't know about?"

"Viviana Dioli," she murmured. Surely she would wake up any moment to find that Tom disapproved of his wife pursuing such... unladylike hobbies. Not that she would stop, but she'd been braced for disapproval. Had her arguments planned in advance. But he—

"Viviana Dioli?" he asked. "Something tells me she doesn't write horror stories."

"Gothic tales of a more romantic nature."

His grin turned wicked. "I bet those stories have been getting a bit more detailed over the past few months, eh?"

Her face burned. Well, obviously.

"Any others I need to know about, Josie?"

"No, just... Are you telling me you don't mind that I write scandalous stories for London newspapers?"

He leaned closer. "Is it more fun if I disapprove?" He reached back and pinched the back of her thigh. "I knew that naughty imagination couldn't be just from reading books."

"No, it's been years of wicked mental cultivation." She batted his hand away. "Are you laughing at me?"

"No." He smacked a kiss on her lips. "I'm relieved."

A spark of anger flared to life. "Did you really think I was having some kind of affair?"

"No!" He paused. "Perhaps. There's no way to answer that question correctly. To be fair, you were hiding things from me."

"I was hiding my hobby! Not a lover. And are you implying you don't have any secrets? *You*?"

He grew instantly silent. "Josie—"

"No." She turned toward the fire. "I'm still angry. Glad, yes, that you're not bothered by my writing, but also angry you assumed I'd do something so horrible. I would never be unfaithful to you, Tom."

She could feel him at her back. He carefully put his arms around her and rested his chin on top of her head.

"Forgive me, sweet girl? Jealousy isn't something I'm used to."

"I was a spinster for twenty-eight years. I hardly think—"

"You're clever and funny," he said, cutting her off. "You're generous and kind and beautiful."

"You're the only one who's ever thought so."

His arms tightened around her, and she ignored the tickle in her chest. Pushed back the threat of a cough.

"'Girls are caterpillars,'" he whispered, "'when they live in the world, to be finally butterflies when the summer comes.'"

She tried to turn, but he had her locked in place. "Where did you—"

"I see the butterfly you've become. And so do others. I don't like having to share you with the world."

Had he read *Carmilla* too? Or...

*I saw no folly tonight. Only perhaps a bit of fancy.*

That low voice in the garden months ago was utterly familiar now that she'd heard it in the bedroom.

"It was you," she said. "In the garden that night. You were the one I talked to."

"You were beautiful in the moonlight. Are you angry with me?"

"You saw me in my dressing gown."

The arms around her shoulders tightened, and she felt the laughter in his chest.

"I suppose... I'm not angry," she said. "Not about that. I wasn't angry when I thought it was one of our neighbor's servants, so why should I be angry it was you? Why did you—?"

"I was curious about you. I certainly never expected you'd be out in the garden in the middle of the night. I just wanted to see your home. And then I saw you, and I thought you looked like a fairy queen. In your white gown with your hair falling down your back. You had no fear."

"Oh no," Josie said. She managed to turn in his arms and lay her head on his chest. "I was wrapped in fear. I still am some nights."

Tom kissed the top of her head. "I don't ever want you to fear again. And don't hide anything from me. I want all of you."

"Then you can have it." *For as long as we have.*

---

AFTER they returned from Bray, Josie and Tom never spoke of her illness. While Tom had never shied from it before their marriage, something about them had shifted after those quiet, gentle nights of lovemaking by the seaside. Perhaps they were both living in a state of denial. Her breathing had been marginally better since their return to town, and she avoided any situation or event that could trigger an episode. She spent most nights writing or making love to Tom, who seemed to have an endless, fervent hunger for her.

He was her favorite form of madness.

They explored everything. After her initial nerves had been conquered, she found in her new husband an eager teacher. No question was unanswered. Often, demonstrations were required. They laughed when they loved, and Josie knew she'd fallen in love with Tom quite thoroughly, though she hesitated to say it.

There was a restlessness in her husband, and she knew, however he might accuse her of keeping secrets from him, his own secrets were a weight between them. There was a darkness in him. Too often, a sense of foreboding enveloped her. And her thoughts were... muddled. There was something she knew she wasn't seeing. She sensed he was a breath away from confessing something too many times to count. But the confession never came, and she didn't want to press him.

She didn't want to know.

She wanted to love. To revel in him. To gorge herself on life for as long as she had.

The heaviness in her lungs told her she didn't have long.


TOM and Murphy had announced the dinner party three nights before, and Josie had found herself curious to meet some of Tom's business associates. The name of William Beecham was certainly one she'd heard in passing between Tom, Murphy, and their younger brother, Declan, but not with any great humor. She was surprised to find him invited to dinner. Even more surprised her cousin, Neville, would also be present.

"Has Neville tried to call on your father again?" Tom asked, straightening his suit in the mirror in his room before they descended to the drawing room. Because he worked mostly at night, he insisted on keeping separate bedrooms. If she were healthier, Josie would have objected, for she hated waking in the mornings without him. But for their situation, it made sense.

"Not that anyone has said. The servants would have told me."

"Any change today?"

She shook her head.

Tom feathered a caress across her cheek before he bent to kiss it. "He had a good life, sweet girl. And he's not in any pain."

"I know." She blinked back tears. "It doesn't make it any easier."

"No, it doesn't."

He turned to her with his cravat in hand and waited for her to tie it for him. It was a task she enjoyed and one he loathed.

"You know," she said as she tied the simple knot he preferred, "I never thought I'd do this."

"Tie a cravat? I agree. Wouldn't suit you."

"You know what I mean." Josie smoothed a hand down the front of his crisp white shirt. "I enjoy these wifely things. They're like… little gifts I never expected."

Tom caught her hand and held it silently. He opened his mouth, then closed it. He pressed a kiss to her knuckles and held her hand there.

"Tom?"

"I don't suppose those fantastic creatures you write of are real, are they?"

Josie laughed. "Vampires and demons and monsters in the night? Thank God, no. We'd all be doomed, wouldn't we?"

"Aye, but it wouldn't be such a bad thing to live forever," he said, almost silently, "if you could hold on to the people you loved. It wouldn't be so bad then, would it?"

It was as close as he'd come to speaking of her failing health since they'd been married.

"Was I unfair to you?" she asked. "Should I have refused this?"

"Never." He tipped her face up to his, and she could see the odd redness in his eyes again. Or perhaps it was only the light. "I'd not trade a moment of our time together, Josephine Shaw."

"Even when I'm acting like a madwoman when a story strikes me?"

"Especially then."

She choked back the lump in her throat and patted his chest. "You are the most patient of husbands, Thomas Murphy. We should go down before our guests arrive."

"Hang our guests. Murphy's the one who invited them."

"But I should not neglect my cousin. Even if I do find him somewhat loathsome."

Tom grunted and held the door for her. "Why did we agree to host this?"

"Because Neville technically belongs to me. And our cook is better than your brother's."

"Don't say that. I might fire her if her food invites company." He kissed her neck. "Shall we?"

Though they were separate houses, Tom and Murphy's town houses near Mountjoy Square were adjoining and even connected through the lower floors. It was, in essence, one very large household, which suited Josie to the ground and allowed her and Anne to share much of the domestic burden.

Josie had been tickled to learn her night-loving tendencies were entirely indulged in Tom's household. Indeed, as her sister-in-law was usually busy during the days, Josie spent most of her time writing, which left the evenings free for family.

As they descended to the drawing room, she heard Anne's tinkling laughter rising above her cousin's nasal voice. As Neville had never been particularly amusing, Josie had to guess Anne was humoring him. Tom ushered her in, and she immediately caught the slightly pained look on her sister-in-law's face.

"You're finally here," Anne said. "Did Tom 'accidentally' lose his dinner jacket again?"

"Have no idea what you're talking about," her husband grumbled, kissing his sister-in-law on the cheek.

"Neville," Josie said. "How good of you to come."

Her cousin looked irritated that he'd been distracted from the lovely Anne Murphy.

"Hello, cousin. And belated felicitations on your union."

"Thank you."

Murphy came over accompanied by a pale gentleman with a rather unexpected halo of blond curls and a narrow nose.

"My dear Josephine," her brother-in-law said, "may I introduce Mr. William Beecham?"

"Of course," Josie said, inclining her head. "Mr. Beecham, welcome to our home. And thank you for joining us for dinner."

Cunning green eyes glinted at her before he bowed. His skin was frightfully pale, and Josie wondered at the temperature outside. They'd been having a mild winter, but Dublin weather could be unpredictable.

"I thank you for your hospitality, madam," Beecham said. "And my felicitations on your union as well. Seems Tom fooled you after all."

There was a meanness in his voice that made Josie want to curl into her husband. Perversely, that fear compelled her to be as clever as possible.

"I assure you," Josie said, tucking her hand in the crook of Tom's elbow, "any subterfuge was on my part. I hid all my most irritating qualities and hurried him to the altar. Poor Mr. Murphy never stood a chance."

The company laughed, but Mr. Beecham's gaze never left hers. They rested on her with a kind of furtive glee. As if he knew a secret she would soon discover and hate.

"Mr. Beecham, you must be a villain," she quipped.

Neville laughed, unaware the rest of the room had gone silent. "Why must he be a villain, cousin?" He nudged Beecham's shoulder. "Josephine tells the most amusing stories, William. She has since she was a child."

"Has she?" The handsome man's eyes hadn't left her. "Pray tell, Mrs. Murphy, why must I be a villain?"

"Your face is too handsome, sir, and your hair too angelic." She smiled innocently. "I daresay it is your fate to be a villain or a saint. And isn't a villain the more interesting role?"

Beecham threw his head back and laughed. "Tom, your wife amuses me. I quite approve."

She felt her husband tense when Beecham said he "approved," but he only said, "Thank you, Mr. Beecham."

It was the oddest dinner party Josie had ever attended.

Mr. Beecham clearly occupied some role of authority among the gentlemen, though he was vague about his occupation. Neville seemed to worship the man. Murphy and Tom offered him grudging respect, and Anne ignored him as much as possible. It was so unlike her husband to condescend to a man of Beecham's character that Josie thought she must have frowned at Tom through dessert.

She and Anne were the only ladies in attendance, so when the gentlemen called for the port and cigars, they both retired for the night. Anne, she could tell, had something troubling her. And though she was growing closer to her new sister-in-law, she did not yet consider herself a confidante.

She went to her sitting room, which doubled as her study, and started to work on the next chapter of the new story she'd been sending to Lenore. It was a departure for her, inspired by some of the fantastical tales of Jules Verne she'd been recently engrossed in. Her new husband was a fan of the scientific adventures, and she'd taken a liking to them as well. She was so engrossed in the tale of airships, resurrectionists, and questionably honorable demons that she missed Tom's entrance entirely. She looked up when the coals shifted in the fireplace, and he was sitting across from her, watching her work.

"Tom! I didn't see you there. Is it very late?" Josie struggled to focus. She was still lost in the story and wanted to finish the scene.

"Not so late," he said quietly. "Why don't I go change out of this jacket? I was smoking."

And smoke bothered her lungs, so he would change. Because he was Tom.

"Thank you, darling. Just give me a few more minutes. The heroine..." She drifted off, still thick in the middle of describing a haunting scene in a foggy graveyard. She was considering a new villain for the story. One with a high forehead, a halo of curls, and unnatural, glowing green eyes. After all, it was the most beautiful faces that hid the most horrible demons.

The fire was dying by the time she put her pen down. Tom was watching her again, stripped down to his trousers and shirtsleeves, lounging on the couch across from her desk.

"I love watching you work," he said quietly. "You frown and scowl. Then smile and cry. Sometimes I see your mouth moving when you say their words. Every emotion is on your face as you write. Is it whatever the character is feeling?"

She tried not to be embarrassed. "I don't know. Probably. Do you want to read this chapter?"

Josie had found Tom to be quite the excellent editor. Talking over story ideas with him had become one of her favorite pastimes, though he often laughed at the outlandish plot devices the newspaper audiences seemed to love.

"Course I want to read it. Has she discovered the hero isn't what he seems?"

"Yes, but I'm thinking about adding a new villain. One with blond curls and green eyes."

Tom smiled, but only for a moment. "Not too obvious, all right?"

"Would he even know?"

"William Beecham is... resourceful. Dangerous. If you ever meet him in town, avoid him. If you can't avoid him, speak as little to him as possible. And don't be clever or interesting. You don't want Beecham interested in you. He's interested enough as it is."

Josie blinked. "Tom, I was joking, but you act as if he *is* a villain."

"He's powerful. And not to be crossed lightly."

"Is Neville safe?" A chill crept over her, despite the warm room. "Why was he in our house?"

"He wanted to meet my new wife. Murphy thought it would be a good idea."

"Why?"

"We must do business with the man. We... condescend when we must. For now."

"He said he 'approved' of us." She couldn't stop the shiver. Mrs. Porter would say someone had walked over her grave. "What an odd thing to say. Who is he to approve of us?"

"He's..." Tom's eyes burned. "It doesn't matter. He didn't approve enough."

"What—"

"Forget William Beecham." He leaned forward, elbows on his knees. "Josie, if there were a way to... cure you. If there were a way to get better—even if you had to leave Dublin—would you want it?"

She could feel the color drain from her face. "What?"

"If there were a treatment—"

"Stop." Her voice grew hoarse. "There's nothing, Tom."

"But if there were—"

"Don't you think Father looked? Do you know how many years I spent being poked and prodded? I've inhaled the most horrendous concoctions you could imagine. We tried sanatoriums and hospitals. I went to Switzerland, for God's sake. Don't be cruel."

"I never want to hurt you." His eyes were red again. "But if there was a way—"

"Stop!" She stood, knocking over her inkwell in her haste. She must have stood too fast, because it seemed Tom was there before she could blink, righting the bottle and blotting the ink so it didn't spill over her manuscript.

"Careful," he murmured. "I'm only asking. Didn't mean to upset you."

"Of course I'd want it," she said. "Don't you think I'd do anything to stay with you? I... I love you, Tom. So much. But there's nothing." She cleared her throat and felt the beginning press of tightness in her chest. "So please don't give me some kind of false hope. It's not fair."

He said nothing more. Tom straightened her desk, laid aside her work for the evening, then took her to bed. He spent hours making silent love to her. He didn't return her words, because he didn't have to. Josie knew her husband wasn't a talkative man. His touch. His kiss. Every caress was its own declaration.

*But to die as lovers may—to die together, so that they may live together.*

What foolish words she'd once found romantic. Her lover could not die! Tom had to live so he could remember. Because if he remembered she had lived and loved him, then Josie could find the courage to say good-bye.

## Chapter Seven

TOM TAPPED A PEN on the table as Declan finished up the monthly financial report for Murphy.

"I'd say the boat works will be profitable within two years with this expansion. While merging our existing works with Shaw's will cost in the short term, it'll be worth the investment."

"And Beecham?" Murphy asked.

"We'll be bigger, not just in holdings but in name. He won't like it."

Tom gritted his teeth. Murphy's refusal to confront William Beecham had become a bone of contention between them. Once Beecham had flat out stated the Shaw heiress was not to be turned—even before Tom had brought it up with his sire—any interest in concession had flown out the window. He wanted Beecham gone. Wanted Murphy to take over. And he wasn't quite rational about it.

Murphy tapped a long finger on the papers in front of him. "Beecham is... problematic."

"Beecham's a monster," Tom muttered. "And you'd have the support of more than half the immortals in Dublin. You don't hear what I do among the workers."

"And you don't hear what Anne and I do among the gentry," Murphy said. "It's not a simple thing, Tom. If I'm to avoid bloodshed, we must tread carefully."

"There'll be no avoiding bloodshed," Tom said. "That's not how these things work."

"I have no interest in ruling a city where half the immortal population has been slaughtered and the other half only follows me out of fear."

"Why not?" Tom asked. "It works. Vampires respect power."

"They also respect intelligence. A bloody coup is not what Dublin needs right now. Not with all the unrest in human politics and not when the city is finally beginning to prosper. It's simply not wise. Neither is turning humans who are notable in society."

It was the closest they'd ever come to speaking of it, though Tom knew his anger at his wife's failing health had not gone unnoticed by his sire.

Declan was completely silent, and Tom felt an irrational spike of anger toward his brother. If Declan had been the one to marry Josephine Shaw, Tom would barely have known her. He'd not feel this tearing pain at the thought of her loss. He'd not have tasted the joy of her devotion only to have human disease snatch it away.

"Tom," Murphy said softly, "you knew it would end this way. It was why I forbade you from revealing yourself. It has nothing to do with my trust, respect, or affection for Josephine."

Tom slammed his hand down and stood. He tried to keep his voice level, but he knew he failed.

"If it were Anne—"

"But it's not Anne. There is a reason I've never allowed myself to become emotionally attached to humans. Added to that, Beecham has flatly denied—"

"Fuck Beecham!" he yelled. "We dance politely around the monster as he runs this city into the ground. He doesn't care about the people, vampire or human. He'll drain it like a docklands whore, and don't think he hasn't been doing more of that too. Is that the kind of men we are? To give allegiance to a monster like him? He isn't as smart as you, isn't as cunning as you, and he doesn't have the loyalty you've built. So why aren't you challenging him, boss? Why?"

Murphy stood and Tom tried not to shrink from the censure on his sire's face. It was instinctual, this need to please him. But other loyalties now tore at him, and Tom didn't shrink away.

"Your wife is human, and she is ill. There are reasons we do not turn the sick, Tom Dargin. And prematurely confronting a rival can lead to disaster. I'll not upend my plans for sentiment."

Declan slammed into Tom's chest and pushed him back before he could reach Murphy with bared fangs.

"Tom, stop!" his brother yelled. "Dammit, man. Leave it!"

He punched Declan in the face, tossing the man halfway across the room before Murphy was on him. He gripped Tom by the neck and shoved him into the wall.

"What do you think you're doing, Dargin?" Murphy said, his fangs bloody from piercing his own lips. "Stop acting the fool."

"You'll kill 'er," he choked out.

"She was dead before you met her."

Tom shook his head and shoved Murphy away. He had to leave. If he stayed, he'd do something unforgivable.

He couldn't change her himself. He knew that much. Any love they had would be twisted by the bond between sire and child. Stories of lovers who'd been changed inevitably led to nothing but tragedy and usually the death of one or both vampires.

But Murphy could change her. Anne could. Even Declan. Vampires he thought of as family. And yet they watched her every night as she withered away. She was failing along with her father. Her breathing was shallower, the smell of sickness around her more pronounced. More, her spirit—the playful, passionate spirit he'd fallen in love with—was withering. The haunted love in her eyes was enough to drive him to madness.

The water in the air drew to his skin as he walked, attracted by the rush of his anger and pain.

She couldn't die. If his sire refused to change her, then they would leave Dublin. Once her father was gone, he could convince her. He could go to Mary Hamilton in the north. He knew Anne wasn't unsympathetic. She loved Josie too. Tom thought

Hamilton might turn her if Tom pledged himself to her service. She'd love to steal one of Murphy's top men.

Loyalty between his sire and the woman he loved tore him in two, but he could finally admit the truth.

Tom no longer wanted to live an eternity without Josie at his side.

"MR. MURPHY?"

Tom tried not to cringe at the name. Much of his household didn't know his real name. His own wife didn't even know it. And the way he was feeling toward his sire at the moment, the last thing he needed was a reminder his life was not his own.

He turned and met Josie's companion in the hall. "Yes, Mrs. Porter?"

"She's not been feeling well today. Are you home for the evening, sir?"

"I am."

"She might enjoy the company. She can't seem to focus on her writing. I think she may be running a slight fever."

"I'll find a book to read to her then. Is she in bed?"

Mrs. Porter shook her head. "She didn't want the bed. I've settled her on the chaise in her room. Make sure she stays propped up. It's easing her breathing."

"Any news on Mr. Shaw?"

Mrs. Porter smiled sadly. "Mr. Carver did send word this morning that he thought it would be a matter of days, if that. Mrs. Murphy was planning on spending the night there, but I held her off until tomorrow. I thought she could use another night of rest."

"I'll try to get her to sleep."

"Thank you, sir. She's had a poultice tonight, so her breathing is easier."

"Thank you, Mrs. Porter."

Mrs. Porter started down the hallway, then paused. Turning to him, she said, "No, sir, thank you. She's had more joy and life in the past six months than the whole of the past six years, I think. I know your family is... different, sir. I wouldn't say anything more. But thank you. Thank you for caring for her as you do."

She swept down the hall before he could respond. And Tom turned to his wife's bedroom with a heavier heart and a renewed sense of purpose.

Six months of living was not enough. Not for Josie. Not for him.

He stopped by the library to grab a copy of Verne's *Around the World in Eighty Days*, which they'd been reading on nights she couldn't seem to focus on her writing. Not even the new adventure story she'd started seemed to be able to hold her attention for long. And if she was feverish, her mind would wander.

"Josie?" he said, peeking into the room to see if she'd fallen asleep.

Her eyes blinked open. "Hello, darling. How are Patrick and Declan tonight? Everything all right with work? You're home early. Anne was by earlier. Did you know she has a sister in Belfast? Isn't that interesting?"

Tom wondered if Anne's thoughts were running parallel to his. "I did. She and Murphy don't get along well."

"So I heard. What a drama." Josie smiled wanly. "Perhaps I should write it into a story."

Tom saw the unhealthy flush on her cheeks. "I brought a book to read. I thought we'd get back to old Phileas, if you like."

She held up her old copy of *In a Glass Darkly*. "I've been getting lost in this old favorite again. Read for me?"

"Vampires again?"

Did she know on some level? She'd never questioned his odd schedule, though Tom continued to use a nudge of amnis sometimes when she started to question why they spent every night together and yet he was always gone in the daylight. He hated it. Hated the deception. But if she discovered it on her own...

"I keep coming back to it," she murmured. "Something... I don't know. Familiar stories are like old friends, aren't they?

They're comforting." She held out the book. "Please? We'll come back to Phileas another night."

And so Tom sat at the foot of the chaise lounge and put Josie's slender legs on his lap, stroking her ankles as he read from the tale of the mysterious vampire girl and the proper young lady she seduced.

> *"Dearest, your little heart is wounded; think me not cruel because I obey the irresistible law of my strength and weakness; if your dear heart is wounded, my wild heart bleeds with yours. In the rapture of my enormous humiliation I live in your warm life, and you shall die—die, sweetly die—into mine. I cannot help it; as I draw near to you, you, in your turn, will draw near to others, and learn the rapture of that cruelty, which yet is love; so, for a while, seek to know no more of me and mine, but trust me with all your loving spirit."*

He watched her as she dozed and he read the familiar words. Abruptly, she sat up.

"Josie?"

"I'd love for it to be real," she rasped. "Wouldn't it be grand, Tom? Do you think it could be real?"

"What's real, love?"

"The vampires, of course. Carmilla and Laura."

He choked on his desire to reveal himself to her, and she continued, the fever now burning in her eyes.

"There is so much more to this life than we know, isn't there? It could be real. It could be. Fairies and shape-shifters. Airships and demon lovers. Why couldn't they be real, Tom? Why would we dream of them if they weren't real?"

She'd started to cry, and he put the book away, pulling her to his lap so that he could hold her. He put his cheek against her burning forehead.

"'You will think me cruel, very selfish, but love is always selfish...' Oh, Tom! She was right. I'm sorry. It's horrible, isn't it? This love. To love someone and know they cannot be yours. We only borrow each other for a time, don't we? I'm too cruel to you, darling. Please don't hate me. I couldn't bear it if you hated me."

He rocked her back and forth. "Josie, please—"

"He was Irish. Did you know he was Irish? Joseph Sheridan Le Fanu. What a wonderful name. Not like Josephine. Who wants to read a story from a Josephine?"

"I do. I love reading stories by Josephine." Her skin was burning.

"Why aren't there more vampire stories? I wish there were. I wish I could have known him. My mother met him. They were... friends. Perhaps it wasn't the footman after all. He only liked Poe. But who doesn't like Poe, after all?"

She was rambling, her fever overtaking her reason. Tom stood and walked to the bed, stripping her out of her robe and ringing for the maid to bring some ice. Murphy kept a basement of it for blood stores, and Tom was tempted to take her down and hold her in the frigid walls of the cool room. He knew it wouldn't help.

"Josie," he said again. "Please, love. Take a deep breath. Try to calm down."

The breath she took rattled in her chest and made Tom want to rip the sheets and punch his fist through the wall. He put more pillows behind her and stripped the heavy, feather-filled blanket that only seemed to make her cough worse. The maid came, along with Mrs. Porter, and they began to see to his wife.

His wife. The love of his life. Tom could smell it in the breath she coughed out.

His Josie was dying.

Tom turned away before the women could see the bloody tears that filled his eyes.

TOM received word the next evening that John Shaw had passed away in his sleep, but Josie wouldn't hear it. Her eyes were half-open, and her breathing labored. She hadn't woken since her rambles the night before. Tom had been forced to his day rest, raging in fear that his wife would slip away while he was dead to the world.

Her breathing seemed a little better when he woke, but her fever had not lessened. Mrs. Porter and Josie's day maid had banished the doctor after it was clear there was nothing he could do.

Tom sat in despair, knowing she would never be well enough to travel to Belfast. He would lose her. But then he could end things. After all, he'd lived over seventy-five years, mortal and immortal life combined. That was a good run, he thought.

And Murphy?

Murphy could go to hell.

Tom lay next to Josie in bed, dabbing at her mouth with blood-stained cloths when she coughed. He paid no attention when he heard the door open or when Mrs. Porter announced Murphy and Anne's presence. He refused to look at his sire. These hours were not for him. He would hold his woman as long as he could. And when the end came, he would follow. Loyalty to his sire be damned. After all his years of service, what had Murphy done but let the woman Tom loved die a painful death?

"Tom," Anne called him. "Tom Dargin, look at me."

He didn't.

"Go away." Tom didn't want to leave her side, even to throw them both out. "Her father's dead. She's dying. Leave me alone. You won't have to bother with me much longer."

Murphy's voice was stiff. "Tom, stop this madness."

"Go fuck yourself." He brushed her cheek. "Sorry, sweet girl. I know you don't like rough language."

Anne was there, clutching his shoulder. "Tom, please."

"Won't be the same. Nothing was the same from the night I met her. My butterfly girl. Only woman as ever saw the whole of me. Loved me, she did. It'll be fine, Annie. No need to ask your sister for that favor. I'll stay with my girl until she goes."

"Tom, you can't be serious." Murphy banged his cane on the ground. "I sent Mrs. Porter away so we could speak freely. Stop this. This isn't you."

Anne was crying. "Tommy, please. We can't do without you."

"And I can't do without her!" He pushed Anne away, baring his teeth at Murphy as he roared, "Get the fuck away from us, both of you!"

Josie started to cough, sitting up on her own, her eyes open and glassy with fever.

"Tom?" she gasped. "Tom, who's yelling? What's wrong?"

He turned, ignoring his irate sire. "It's fine. It's fine. Here, love." He tried to get her to drink something, but the water only sprayed over the bed when she coughed again.

Murphy said, "She's mortal. You knew this when you married her."

"She's my mate," he said, not caring if Josie questioned him. She was already falling back into delirium. "Anne, get him away before I kill him myself. He don't belong here. Leave me be."

"You cannot mean to meet the sun," Murphy said, stubbornly standing at the foot of her bed. "Tom, your life is more valuable—"

"My life is not my own," he growled. "And hasn't been since I agreed to join you in this one. I cannot save her without driving both of us mad, and you've made your choice. But I tell you, I can join her when she goes. That is *my* choice. And you don't have any say in that."

"I'll lock you up."

"You plan on doing that forever?"

That shut him up, and Tom was able to concentrate on Josie again. His poor girl. She sounded like half of what she was breathing was water, but it was the fever that scared him.

"You're determined to die with her?"

Tom stroked her damp hair off her forehead. "I'll be dead already when she's gone."

He paid no attention to whatever silent arguments his sire was having with Anne. He watched Josie, watched the rise and fall of her labored breathing. Watched the fine skin of her neck where her pulse beat faintly. She'd be admitted to heaven without a doubt. He wondered if he was clever enough to talk himself in.

"Love you," he whispered. "I didn't tell you when you could hear me because I'm a fool. Thanks for loving me so well, sweet girl. You were the best part of this life."

"And who will take responsibility if she's uncontrollable?" Murphy said behind him. "Tom? He'd never be able to do it. So I'd have to, and we'd kill each other."

"It may not be necessary. She's never been a cruel person."

"She's dying and feverish. You know why there are rules against—"

"I'll do it," Anne whispered. "I love her too, Patrick. Do this, and if she is mad—if she cannot be trusted—I will take responsibility for her. You know I can."

Silence fell. Then Tom felt the touch of Anne's hand on his shoulder.

"Tom?"

"Go away."

"Tom, step away from her. Let Murphy do what he needs to. You don't need to be here for this."

He lifted his head. "What are you talking about?"

"You're sure she would want this?" Murphy asked him, tearing off his jacket and rolling up his sleeves. "She never knew the truth of who you were. You're *sure*, Tom?"

He blinked, in a daze, unsure of what he was seeing. "Positive. What are you doing?"

"What do you bloody think I'm doing?"

Anne pulled him away from Josie's bedside, and Murphy sat on the edge, brushing the hair from Josie's neck.

"Anne, find something to tie her hair back."

Tom stood gaping. "But Beecham—"

"I'm not losing my own bloody child because Beecham wants the Shaw family dead. Hang Beecham. We'll do this, and soon I'll be the lord of Dublin, but only if you're at my side. Do you understand me?"

"Yes, boss."

"She's dead to the world. Do you understand? She's not in society, mortal or immortal. She died this night. And she'll stay dead until everyone who remembers her in this life is gone. Can you live with that? Can she?"

Mad hope had finally pierced the shadow around his heart. "We'll make do. I'll take care of her. Always. I promise."

"Of course you bloody do. You're the most stubborn, loyal bastard I've ever met. Don't know why I fooled myself that you'd let her go." He tilted Josie's neck to the side. "Now tell the cook to start bleeding all the servants who haven't given in the past month and pray to God this works."

IT took Anne and Declan both to wrestle Tom out of the room, even though the big man knew it was necessary. The process of turning was not far from the process of death. Even now Anne and Declan would be spelling the few servants who didn't know of their true natures and sending them away, while the others gave blood before retreating to the safety of Murphy and Anne's house. Away from the danger. Away from the newborn who would wake.

Murphy had removed half the woman's blood when he heard Anne return. Josie's heartbeat was failing, so he drank faster. It tasted... wrong. He spit most of it into the basin beside the bed, not wanting to chance any kind of strange reaction. He'd never fed from anyone as sick as Josephine, and though he knew vampires were immune to human disease, some instinct told him too much of her blood would make him ill.

"Stop for a moment," Anne said.

He drew back and she wiped his mouth, bending down to take his mouth with hers. Then she brushed a hand over his cheek and gave him her wrist. "Take some of mine. You'll need extra since you're not taking much of hers."

"This is already so risky. I don't want to chance it."

"I agree."

He bent to Josephine's neck again. It was not such an easy thing to drain a human—especially when not in the throes of true bloodlust—but her blood had to be removed to the point of death before he gave her his own.

Minutes stretched as he held the poor thin woman in his arms, killing her to save her. Finally—when her heart began to falter—he put her mouth to his wrist.

"No," Anne said, pulling his collar down. "As much as I hate the idea, she needs to take your neck. Your wrist won't be fast enough."

"Are you sure?"

Anne was his mate, and as much as he loved Tom, his first loyalty was to her.

*"And I can't do without her! She's my mate."*

It was the pain of those words that finally convinced him, because Murphy knew Tom spoke the truth. Nothing he could do would save his dearest child if Josephine Shaw was allowed to die. No political maneuvering, no intricate plan, and no cultivated reputation would excuse Murphy in his son's eyes.

So Josephine must live.

Anne slashed his throat with her own fangs and held the girl to his neck, forcing the blood into her body. His mate held them both until Murphy felt the first stirrings of amnis in the girl, felt her own fangs lengthen and grow, latching on to his neck with vicious hunger. Amnis, the energy that would bind her to him as his immortal child, flowed over him and into her, resurrecting her, tying them for all time. She was his, but he was hers too. For as long as she lived, Murphy would be responsible for her. Care for her. With every child he sired, he gave up a small part of his soul.

He hushed her when the small groans of pain crept through. He smoothed her hair back and held her as her body began the process of turning. Anne stood on her other side, ready to help her friend's transition into immortal life.

Josephine Shaw would live. But she would never be the same.

## Chapter Eight

SHE BOLTED UP IN BED, almost throwing herself into the fire with the unexpected strength of her limbs.

"Josie!"

She screamed when she hit the floor. And she kept screaming.

The hunger.

The pain.

She was in the throes of a most horrific dream.

Her throat burned. Her mouth ached. The room burned. There was a roaring in her ears and a tumult of voices surrounding her.

"Put out the fire, it's too hot!"

"Is the bath ready?"

"Josie? Josie, try to drink."

A goblet was forced to her mouth, thick with the scent of copper and meat. Blood. It was *blood*. She choked on it until the taste hit her tongue, and then she opened her throat, howling inside from the pleasure.

"Another. Give me another, damn you."

"Bath is ready, boss."

Her body hit the water, and it was hot and cold all at once. She tried to scramble away until she felt him at her back.

"Shhh." His voice captured her and she turned to it. She blinked her eyes open before she closed them again, wincing.

"Turn the lamps down. They're too bright. Josie? Josie, love, can you hear me?"

"She needs to drink more."

The water crawled up her body, and it was her friend. It petted her as if she were a cat curled by the fire. It was a cool blanket on a warm day. Her nurse's soft touch.

"Josie?" Another goblet shoved under her nose, and she grabbed it with both hands, feeling the metal bend under her fingers.

"What?" she croaked. "What—"

"It's all right now. Just drink."

"Tom?"

"Drink, Josie."

She drank. And then she drank some more.

Liquid heat. Satisfaction.

*I'm dreaming. This is a dream.*

"You're not dreaming, Josie."

*I've died. I was so afraid to die. I left him. My lovely Tom. I left him.*

"I'm here, sweet girl. You didn't leave me. You're right here."

She closed her eyes to block the light, weeping with the pain of losing him.

And when the tears touched her mouth, they tasted of blood.

HENRY Flynn put his arm around Mrs. Porter as he showed the old woman into the room where Mrs. Murphy's body lay. He'd be grateful when all the new servants were gone and only the ones that knew the truth were left. He'd grown weary of the lies and constantly guarded words. His father had told him he'd be expected to do things like this, but he'd had no idea how complicated it would all be.

Lucky the missus was a vampire now. At least he'd no longer have to carry on one-sided conversations for hours while the master slept. But Mr. Tom Murphy was about as grand an employer as he'd ever have, so he wasn't about to complain. He was very grateful the man wouldn't have to say good-bye to his wife, who was now lying in the darkened room, the fire low and the covers drawn up to protect her as much as possible while they fabricated the story of her death.

According to his mam, she'd wake at nightfall with a driving hunger that wouldn't know friend from foe, so it was important that all the human visitors be ready to leave well before dusk.

"The poor girl." Mrs. Porter sniffed. "The poor family. Mr. Shaw gone and Miss Shaw too. All within a day. And poor Mr. Murphy."

"He's in his room now," Henry said. "He weren't in a good state last night."

"Well of course he wasn't," Mrs. Porter said. She put her arm around Mrs. Murphy's day maid. "They loved each other so. What a tragedy."

"It is," Henry said. "Though I know my master wouldn't have traded knowing her for anything."

"Oh, poor Mr. Murphy!" the maid said. "And poor Miss Shaw. It's so sad, and yet so terribly romantic, don't you think? Miss Shaw would have liked that."

"Here now," Henry said, trying not to shake his head at the maid's melodrama. "Why don't we go downstairs? There's nothing of her here. The downstairs maids will clean the room, and I know others will want to pay their respects. Let's go see if Cook has anything to eat, shall we?"

He ushered both the grieving women downstairs and into the care of Cook while he saw to the other men on the floor who were guarding the master and the missus. Hours passed as Henry began the business of faking a funeral. It shouldn't be too much trouble. His father had faked one for Mr. Declan. It'd be easier if he had a few more men, but currently, most of Mr. Murphy's staff were busy securing the day-chambers until the vampire staff rose at dusk.

Henry was hoping when they were both sorted he'd be able to consolidate security for the two of them. Guarding one day-chamber would be so much easier than—

"Unhand me!" A domineering voice rang from the ground floor.

"But Mr. Burke! Surely you can wait for tonight. Mr. Murphy is retired and he won't want to be dist—"

"I want to see my cousin! Take me to her now."

"I say, who do you think you are?" Adams, the old butler, had never been one to mince words. "Sir, Mr. Murphy is not receiving callers at this hour. You must leave."

Henry stood at the top of the steps while Mr. Neville Burke made a great show of trying to look like a worried man. Henry wasn't fooled. Burke had the gleam of greed in his eyes.

"Mr. Burke, sir," Henry interrupted his rant. "I'll ask that you don't step any further into the house."

He was in a precarious position. Henry was only a servant. As such, if Mr. Burke wanted to barge in, he'd be able to with neither of the Murphy brothers to stop him. The only people awake in the house were servants, and the last thing anyone needed was for a constable to be fetched if Mr. Neville Burke thought the servants were trying to keep him from his cousin.

"And who are you?" Burke asked.

"I'm Mr. Murphy's valet, sir."

"And where is your master, boy?"

"Grieving, sir. Mrs. Murphy died night before last."

"Oh no." Neville Burke did not look surprised. He climbed the stairs toward Henry. "My poor cousin. Take me to her. Let me pay my respects while I still can."

"Mr. Burke—"

Neville Burke grabbed him by the collar. "Take me to her."

Henry could see a stain of pink in the sky. Perhaps if he showed Mr. Burke the body, he would leave quickly. The longer it took to get him out of the house, the more dangerous things became.

"Of course, Mr. Burke."

He shook his head at the panicked face of the guards on the second floor as he escorted Neville Burke to the mistress's bedchamber. All the curtains had been drawn, and only the ghost of a fire had been lit. According to the master, she would wake after him, her younger vampire body needing more rest. Still, it wasn't as if Henry was at ease around her. He'd been told since he was a boy how dangerous it was to be in a room with a newborn vampire. He kept the door to the hallway open, ready to run.

"Oh, my sweet cousin."

Mr. Burke leaned over the bed, a bit **too** interested, by Henry's reckoning. He was holding a hand over Mrs. Murphy's face as if checking her breathing. She wouldn't be. Vampires didn't need to breathe unless they wanted to smell the air or speak.

"Now that you've paid your respects—"

"I'll sit, boy." He drew a chair to Mrs. Murphy's bedside. "I've heard some interesting rumors about my dear cousin's husband, and I'm keen to allay any suspicion he might be under."

Henry's heart began to race. "Mr. Burke, that isn't a wise idea."

"Why not?"

"Mr. Murphy... he wanted his solitude for sure. When he wakes—"

"Ah yes," Mr. Burke said. "It will be interesting to see what happens when *Mr. Murphy* wakes."

"I'm not sure interesting is the right word," Henry muttered.

"What was that?"

Henry took a deep breath and hoped Mr. Tom would be waking soon. It was usually as soon as the sun fell below the horizon.

"I'll just... watch the door, Mr. Burke."

"Good lad," Mr. Burke said. Then he sat back and waited.

Henry heard a thump down the hall and prayed it was Mr. Tom. If he would just get here...

"By God, she moved."

It was only a whisper.

Henry's heart pounded out of his chest. "A trick of the light, Mr. Burke. Come with me, please."

"No, it was no trick. My God, Beecham was right. There's some kind of black magic—"

"Mr. Burke!" Henry's voice was panicked. He'd seen the twitch. The mistress was waking early. "Come with me. Come with me now if you want to live."

"What is this sorcery?"

Henry could wait no longer. He ran to the bedside to grab Neville Burke, but by the time he reached him, Miss Josephine's eyes were open and staring at her cousin.

She glanced at Henry for only a second, and she whispered, "Run."

Henry ran.

JOSIE'S eyes took in everything. The dim light of the room was nothing to her. She saw every shadow flickering by the firelight and the unholy gleam in her cousin's eyes. She smelled him too. Onions and roast beef. The musk of his sweat and the pungent scent of oil and gunpowder. He smelled disgusting. And appetizing.

"Hello, Neville."

"What's wrong with your voice? What are you?"

The burning was still there, but not like she'd dreamed. She was Carmilla, stealthy and secret.

"I'm dreaming," she whispered, closing her eyes. "And I shall not wake again."

"Jo?"

She could hear it thrumming, his heart, like the beat of a hummingbird's wings. It called her. Her neck arched back when she felt the fangs she'd dreamed grow long in her mouth.

"Josephine? What the bloody—"

She was silent when she leapt on him, knocking him off the chair and backward toward the fire. She reared away. No fire. Fire was bad.

"Josephine!"

He was starting to scream, and that wasn't good. She put a hand over his mouth as she dragged him away from the fire.

"Shhhh," she whispered. What a repulsive creature he was. He'd broken her dolls' faces when he was a child. Cut chunks out of her long hair. And look how weak he was! Josie was dragging Neville about the room as if he were her new doll.

He fumbled for something in his jacket, but Josie stopped and dropped him, transfixed by the dust motes dancing in the air. Everything moved as if underwater. Neville's voice was murky as he pulled something out of his pocket.

It was a gun. Pointed at her.

She laughed because she heard the thundering steps coming down the hall.

Silly Neville. What was he thinking to bring a gun into Tom's house?

"I'm warning you, demon. Release my cousin. You have no power over—"

The chamber door crashed in and the gun began to swing toward it.

"Demons!" he screamed. "Unholy monsters! He was right! William was right. I'll kill you all!"

"No," she whispered. What if her stupid cousin shot Tom? He wasn't allowed to do that.

Before she finished thinking it, she had knocked Neville to the ground and batted the gun away.

"No!" she screamed, and then the anger and heat and hunger took her. She pulled his neck up and clamped her mouth over the hammering pulse in his neck. Josie drank deep, shaking Neville when he shouted, batting at his head when he tried to squirm away. Her prey fell still, and she drank.

She fed until the pull of her hunger lessened, then she let Neville's body fall and sat back, still crouched over him when she caught the edge of her reflection in her dressing mirror. She cocked her head at the strange creature she saw.

A dark curtain of hair hung around her face. Her skin was pale, but luminous in a way she'd never noticed before. Strange green eyes went wide with delight at the curious creature in the mirror. Blood dripped down her chin, and her mouth hung open as the edge of sharp white fangs sparkled in the lamplight.

She reached up and touched them with wonder, then her eyes searched for Tom, who was standing motionless in the doorway wearing nothing but his trousers and a guarded expression. She smiled when she saw he had fangs too.

"Tom," she said, lifting a dainty, blood-covered hand. "Look at me. Aren't I the pretty monster?"


SHE couldn't stop touching him, but Tom didn't seem to object. He held her on his lap, though he'd ignored her wishes and donned a shirt. Josie kept pushing things and lifting them, enamored of her new strength.

"Tom?" she asked, lifting up her arm. "If I cut myself, will I bleed?"

"Yes. Don't cut yourself."

"I was just curious." She pushed his shoulder and felt it give. "I'm so strong now."

"I know you are." His voice was everything. It was love and relief and laughter. It was the most seductive thing she'd ever heard in her life. She was hungry for so much more than blood, but Tom said they had to wait for Murphy.

"Are you laughing at me?" She stroked the creases around his eyes. He was so handsome. Well, not to everyone, for his scars and wrinkles would never make him handsome to the fools of the world. But he was the most handsome man in existence to her.

"Maybe a little," he said softly. "I'm so happy. Are you happy? Are you content with this?"

"Tom, listen." She put a hand on his chest, then she took the deepest breath she could, letting it out slowly as she smiled. "Grand. I feel grand."

"So you're not too angry with me?" Tom asked. "For not telling you the whole of it?"

Josie laughed. "I wouldn't have believed you! Who would believe this? I'm not sure I truly believe it yet."

She turned when she heard the door. She tensed until she saw it was Anne and Murphy. Her eyes filled with tears and she stood, holding her arms out to Murphy. "I love you," she said. "So much. Both of you. Though mostly I love Tom."

Murphy embraced her, then Anne.

"We love you too," Anne said. "How are you feeling?"

"Hungry."

"How about me?" Declan came in behind Anne. "Do you love me?"

Tom made a noise and Josie turned back to him.

"Was that a growl?" she asked. "Did you really growl?"

"Maybe."

"Can we turn into great cats like in the book?" She tried not to bounce. "Is that why you can growl?"

"No. That's just a story."

Declan scoffed, "What books has she been reading?"

"You say it's just a story," Josie said. "But so were vampires until I became one. I'm a vampire…" She sank into the chair next to Tom. "How marvelous."

"Boss, what are we going to do about Burke?" Declan asked Murphy while Tom stayed suspiciously silent, guarded eyes pointed at his sire.

Josie tried to stir up some guilt about her cousin, but she couldn't seem to grab onto it properly. After all, Neville was odious. And he'd been about to shoot Tom.

"I'll tell Beecham the truth, of a sort. The human invaded my home and was about to shoot one of my people. He won't make a fuss. After all, it is evident from what Josie said that Beecham has been filling Burke's head with stories. He won't want that getting out, will he?"

"And Josie?"

"I told you, as far as the world is concerned, she's dead. Josephine Shaw Murphy died two nights ago, and you're going to bury her in a grave two nights hence."

Josie gasped. "May I go? I'd love to go to my own funeral."

The answer was a unanimous and choral "No."

"We're not telling Beecham then?" Declan said.

Murphy shook his head. "We can work this around to harm him. If I attack him now, we'll lose too many people. Aggression creates enemies. I don't need enemies, I need allies. In time, we'll let it slip that Beecham was the one who told Neville Burke about us, leading the man here. The more conservative vampires in the city will shun him. They'll start looking for a replacement."

Josie smiled. "And that replacement will be you, of course. Mr. Murphy, you are an excellent plotter. Well done!"

"Thank you, Josephine." Murphy smiled. "But I think you can call me Murphy now."

"ARE you sure?"

Tom was talking again while she tried to seduce him. How irritating.

"I'm sure," she said. "Kiss me."

They'd fled to the safety of Tom's bedchamber as soon as possible. He informed her they'd only be a few weeks in Dublin before he moved her someplace more secure with fewer humans and less temptation. He only needed to stay in Dublin long enough for her funeral and to appear properly grief stricken to anyone who might be watching.

Josie decided she wouldn't mind being farther away from people. Even now, she could smell the lingering scent of blood filling the hallways, though all the mortal servants had fled to Murphy and Anne's house next door. She wanted Tom to distract her. Also, she wanted to kiss him. As often as possible.

"I don't mind," she said again. "Kiss me."

She groaned in pleasure when he stripped off her clothes. The feel of them, like anything to do with her senses, was rough and angry on her nerves. The lights were all doused, but she saw without effort. The room was cool and comfortable. And Tom...

He was temptation incarnate.

It had been a nonstop flood of information since she'd woken that night. Well, there had been the violent episode at the beginning, but that was already far from her mind. Someday, when she could think of something other than her own hunger, she might take the memory of Neville out and feel guilty.

But of course, she reminded herself, he *had* been about to shoot Tom.

*Oh, Tom.*

Her husband clamped his mouth down on her neck, bracing himself between her thighs as he teased her body to violent arousal.

"I'm stronger," she gasped. "You won't have to be so careful anymore."

"I know." He nipped at her skin. "Josie, can I…"

"What? You can do anything you like, Tom. Always."

"Be careful offering gifts like that."

"What do you want?"

"To bite you." He captured her mouth and teased her fangs, which were deliciously sensitive.

"To drink? From me? Is that… done?"

"Yes. And then you'd bite me."

Oh, her body liked that idea very much.

"Oh, yes, please," she said, writhing under him. "Now, in fact. Please do that now."

"It's a blood tie. A bond between us."

"Silly man. Are you hesitating for me? We're married already."

He pulled back and looked into her eyes. "This is permanent, Josephine. Not anything that can be broken. Not even by the Church. If I take your blood and you take mine, we'll live in each other forever."

Josie stroked his cheek and smiled. "Like I said, silly man, we're already wed. I promised to love you till I die."

"You did die."

"No." She kissed him and scraped her fangs over the thick muscle of his neck. "I lived. And you are my life now. My very proper monster. I love you, Tom. Forever."

He kissed her as he took her, and Josie felt her soul slip free. She tilted her head back and bared her throat to him. His fangs pressed and sank in, claiming her on the most elemental level as he drove them both closer to release. She held on to him until he pulled back, then he bared his own throat to her, and she tasted her lover's blood, rich with the scent of sea and salt and whiskey. She was lost in him, and he in her.

Her husband.
Her hero.
Her Tom.

## Chapter Nine

TOM WOKE THAT NIGHT with a dream in his arms. His Josie, safe. Strong. Healthy. She was a revelation. She was *alive*.

And far from resigned to her immortality. Josie seemed to rejoice in it. But then, if it was possible any human might be born to become a vampire, it would be his Josie. Her morbid imagination existing side by side with her humor and appreciation for life was unlike any other human he'd met. She reveled in the monstrous. She delighted in the macabre.

Keeping her away from her funeral was going to be a challenge.

Tom heard a knock at the door.

Leaving her in the bed they could now share, he walked silently to the sitting room. He smelled Anne on the other side of the hall door and cracked it open.

She held out several jars of fresh blood. "Fresh from the kitchens. Tomorrow she starts getting chilled. We've gone through the available staff."

"Fair enough."

He waited, wanting to close the door but sensing she had more to say.

"He wasn't being cruel, Tom."

"So you say."

"He loves you."

"And I love her."

She waited, lips pursed. "I know that. But he didn't. Not till the end. Would you have done it? Would you have met the day if she'd died?"

He tilted his chin up, displaying the marks he'd not allowed her to heal. Her own claim on him, as she bore the scars from his first bite.

Anne nodded. "I see. She truly is your mate then."

"It wasn't a bluff. I don't bluff. She's it for me, Annie. Was from the moment I saw her, I think."

Anne glanced over his shoulder. "It's early yet. There's no way of knowing how she'll adapt. She could be mad, Tom."

"She won't be." Tom was sure of it. A bit off at times? Maybe. But she had been in life too. Her genius was its own kind of madness, but her kindness had survived her death. "It's no matter to me. I'll love her anyway. Keep her safe. I promised to care for her as long as we live. I never made that kind of promise before her, and I don't plan on breaking it."

Lifting to her toes, she kissed his scarred cheek. "You're a good man, Tom Dargin."

"Maybe." He shrugged. "All I know is I'm a better man for her."

My dearest Lenore,

If you're reading this letter, it's because I have finally slipped into the dark night that has been beckoning for so long now. I hope Tom is the one delivering the news to you. I hope you have the fortune to meet the wonderful man who made the last months of my life so full of love and life. Be kind to him, dear friend, for I think he will not come to you unbruised.

He loves me. And I love him. Most desperately.

He is, and will remain, my truest hero. My most dashing knight. The most honorable of scoundrels.

Remember me, Lenore. Remember our happy days at school and our silly rambles around town. Remember my stories. I hope they continue to bring joy to you and my readers. I wish there were more to leave behind, but I suppose I'd need a hundred years or more to write all the stories crowding my imagination. Twenty-nine was never going to be enough.

I've left them to you, my dearest editor, to do with as you please. I wasn't able to finish the grand story with the airships, but as you have a most excellent imagination, I know you will imagine a fine end for your favorite heroine. After all, I've given her your name.

I hope you find your own adventure. If there is one thing love has taught me, it is that one should never wait for life. Dare to live dangerously. You never know what mysteries could be waiting in the shadows.

I remain your true friend. Happy to the end. Content. And eager for the unknown embrace of night.

Yours, always,
Josephine Shaw Murphy


THE pretty, brown-haired woman set down the letter with tears in her eyes.

"Did she go peacefully?" she asked.

"Of course not," Tom said with a rueful smile. "Not Josie. She fought it, and I held her till the end."

A small sob escaped Miss Tetley's lips, and she covered her mouth with an embroidered handkerchief. Tom recognized Josie's slightly messy stitches on the edges.

"She was happy," Tom said. "She didn't linger long. Was active and writing up until two nights before she died. I'm happy for that."

Miss Tetley smiled. "She would have liked that. She could never be idle. A homebody, yes, but not an idle one. She loved working too much. There was always another book to read or a reference to check. A story to plan."

"She had great respect for you. And great affection. She spoke of you often."

"Thank you, Mr. Murphy. I am so sorry for your loss. Yet so happy you had the time with her that you did."

He nodded stiffly. "Thank you."

"Her father... it was only a few nights before that he died, wasn't it?"

"Yes. Only two nights."

"They were so very close."

"They were."

"Did..." She fidgeted a bit. "I know she was very keen that Mrs. Porter would receive the house in Bray, along with a generous allowance. Can you see that it be done? I hate to intrude, but Mrs. Porter—"

"Will be well looked after," Tom said. "Josie was very clear. I'm happy to see that she has a good retirement."

"Thank you, Mr. Murphy. I worried that Neville would make problems for you."

"Mr. Burke, as it happens, seems to have left Dublin. There's no sign of him at his usual haunts. There were rumors he'd fallen in with some disreputable companions."

"Oh." Miss Tetley's eyes widened. "How fortunate her father's business interests were transferred to your family then."

"We do not take the responsibility lightly, miss."

A few more polite exchanges left Tom feeling adrift. He had never been one for small talk—even less so when he felt as if he was lying—so he departed soon after Miss Tetley's father and mother returned from the theater. The young woman wiped her eyes and stood, clearly wrecked from grief but with a smile on her face.

"Thank you, Mr. Murphy, for delivering her letter and the books she left me. I'll treasure them."

"I'm glad."

"Will you be all right, sir?"

Tom paused. "I will never forget her. She was the most unexpected gift of my life. But she'd want me to keep going, wouldn't she?"

Miss Tetley nodded and gave him a brave smile. "She would."
"Then I'll be fine."

He put on his hat, tipped it toward her, and walked into the foggy London night.

THE house in Kinvara belonged to Anne. It was a great old farmhouse build up from a stone cottage that stood at the edge of Galway Bay. Most importantly, it was isolated. No humans lived around them for miles.

Like Tom, Josie had an affinity toward saltwater, which was lucky as the whole of Galway Bay was available for their play.

And they played.

They roamed the ocean, Josie buoyant with the joy of unexpected vitality. Tom often caught her breathing deeply as she sat in the salt air. She'd listen in wonder at the silence of her own lungs. Then a rare joy would cross her face, and she'd leap into the ocean, dancing beneath the water as if she were a mermaid.

Josie loved the sea. She told Tom she always had, though the doctors had warned her away from ocean-bathing when she'd been human. Now she held nothing back.

Her amnis was another story.

While Murphy and Declan were busy in Dublin, Anne had traveled out with them, hoping to help her friend along with learning to control her elemental strength. But even the most rudimentary lessons seemed to fail.

"Try again," Anne said, holding both of Josie's hands. "Do you feel it?"

"I do." Josie nodded. "It's sitting on the back of my neck, moving over my shoulders, like water poured from a pitcher."

"Excellent. Now I want you to push it. Try to spread it over your skin. As if you were smoothing a stocking or pushing a glove up your arm."

Tom looked up from his newspaper, catching the small frown that grew between his wife's eyes.

"Are you trying?" Anne asked.

"I don't know," Josie said with a huff. "I can feel it, but it's not... It simply won't do what I want. I don't understand. Why is this so easy for all of you and not me?"

Anne sighed. It was their third lesson of the week, and so far, even the most rudimentary manipulation of amnis seemed beyond Josie. While a basic shield of amnis came instinctually for most vampires, it was not instinct to Josie.

"If you can't do this, you'll have no way of heating your skin," Anne said.

Josie shrugged. "Poor circulation? I can't see any humans for a long time anyway. Tom won't care, will you, Tom?"

"Course not," he grunted, trying not to be nosy. He didn't want to interfere with the lessons, after all. Just didn't want Anne to push his girl too far. She was still new at all this.

"And your skin will be too sensitive," Anne added.

"Sounds like an excellent reason to eschew fancy clothing." She winked at Tom, who only shook his head.

"Josie, you won't be able to hide forever," Anne said. "At some point, you'll have to rejoin society."

"Why?"

Tom blinked and looked up. "What do you mean, why?"

"Why will I need to rejoin society? Or at least public society." Her eyes were wide and guileless. "Will you need me to entertain for you?"

He snorted. "Not likely, love."

Anne said, "Tom's not much for company."

"Well, neither am I. I'd rather stay home and write. Perhaps read books or visit with family. Isn't that what I'll be doing for the foreseeable future anyway?"

Tom shrugged. "Sounds grand to my ears."

Anne said, "But... you'll be a hermit. You can't be a hermit. At least not forever."

"Why not?"

"Well, I..." Anne frowned. "You wouldn't be lonely?"

"I don't think so," Josie said. "We'll see. I never was much for company. And as long as I can go to the odd play or concert, walk in the park—"

"That'll be at night," Tom said. "No people around anyway."

"—and work in my garden with a friend every now and then, I think that's all I'll need. I love company, but only friends. I always hated formal parties."

Anne shook her head. "Good heavens, you two really are perfect for each other. Who would have guessed?"

"Me," Josie said with a sweet smile. "I knew we'd get on the first night he called on me."

Tom smiled and went back to his paper. Sweet butterfly girl...

"Oh?" Anne asked. "Why's that?"

"It was obvious," Josie said. "He brought me a book."

## Epilogue

*Dublin, 2015*

JOSIE DUG INTO THE EARTH, feeling the coarse scrape of grit beneath her fingernails as she moved the loose soil from beneath the honeysuckle vine. The gardenia would be too overpowering, she thought. Perhaps the rosemary would provide a soothing note to balance the honeysuckle's sweet scent in the summer.

"Josie?" Tom called from the front of the garden.

"Come hither, my demon lover!"

His amused chuckle might have been her favorite sound in the world.

"Where do you want these roses?" he asked.

She turned and watched him as he placed one large pot down, then another. He'd stripped his shirt off and the misty night air clung to his muscled torso. His damp skin caught the light from the glass house he'd built her ten years ago.

He turned to her and caught her stare. "What?"

"You're a fine specimen of a man... for a monster."

"Am I?" He shook his head, his taciturn mouth never moving, though she caught the humor in his eyes. "Don't try to seduce me, fairy temptress. You'll never deter me from my mission."

She stabbed her trowel in the dirt and sat back, elbows propping her up as she turned innocent eyes toward him. "Your mission?"

"Yes." He swiped at the dew on his forehead, leaving a smear of dirt. "My lady has given me a task, and if I fail in it..." He sighed.

"She'd be disappointed?"

"Far worse than disappointed. Her fury would burn like the sun."

"Your lady sounds harsh, sir!"

"She is." He shook his head. "A right harridan. She beats me regularly."

"Oi!"

Tom finally broke into laughter. "Where do you want the roses?"

"One on either side, please." She pointed toward the willow in the corner. "Beats you regularly... I *should* beat you, ornery monster."

Josie didn't even hear him coming when he tackled her to the grass. She rolled across the lawn, laughing in his arms as Tom growled in her ear.

"I'll show you a monster." He nipped her ear and slowly scraped his fangs over her throat. "This monster has a taste for fair maiden. And look! Here's one sitting in my garden."

They wrestled in the grass until Josie was breathless from laughter. She threw her arms out and inhaled the fragrant night air, eyes closed and a satisfied smile on her face.

Tom reached out and traced her profile from her forehead, over her nose and down to her chin.

"Did you just smear dirt all over my face?"

"Yes. I've decided you're not a fair maiden. You're a warrior goddess, and this is your war paint."

"I like it. I could definitely write a story about a warrior goddess."

"Josie..." He leaned over her, taking her lips in an achingly sweet kiss.

She smiled. "What?"

"Nothing," he murmured. "I just like saying your name is all."

"One of these days, Tom Dargin, I'm going to tell the world how sweet you are."

"No one'd believe you. Everyone knows writers are compulsive liars."

She burst into laughter again, and something about his expression, about the curve of his mouth just then, reminded her of the first time she'd seen him.

Solemn and serious, standing proud in her father's old house on Merrion Square. Telling her to stand up straight and never apologize for who she was, even if that was a rail-thin spinster with an overactive imagination and a withering cough.

And so it still was.

She adored him so much he could make her his slave. But then he wouldn't be the Tom who'd seen the quiet girl in the corner and asked her to stand tall, and Josie would be the caterpillar who never turned into a butterfly.

"I love you, Tom."

"Love you too, sweet girl."

"What a pair of monsters we are."

# —THE END—

✟
# AUTHOR'S NOTE

The book quoted in *A Very Proper Monster*—Josie's favorite story—is *Carmilla*, a vampire novella by Irish writer Joseph Sheridan Le Fanu. It was originally published in 1871 in the magazine *The Dark Blue* and later in his collection of short stories *In a Glass Darkly*.

Le Fanu's *Carmilla* predates Bram Stoker's classic vampire novel *Dracula* by over twenty-five years, and though lesser known, this influential story featured a female vampire who became the prototype for many important works in early vampire fiction and has been adapted or referenced many times in different media.

*In a Glass Darkly* is an early classic of Gothic literature and available for everyone through Project Gutenberg and major retailers.

# Gaslight Hades

(( ✦ ))

## Grace Draven

✜

*This tale is dedicated to my darling Willow who loves all things unique and eccentric, just like her.*

*Also to my intrepid editors, Mel Sanders and Lora Gasway, my saviors in all things writing-related.*

*Sincerest thanks to Antioch Grey, my favorite Brit, for her invaluable help.*

## Chapter One

FOR THE LAST TIME, Lenore gazed at her father's coffin, draped in black velvet and topped with a spray of everlasting flowers. Her mother's doing of course. Arthur Kenward would have hated the frippery, but Jane Kenward was adamant that no expense be spared, and the bouquet had been ordered and delivered for the funeral. Lenore found it repulsive. The flowers were as lifeless as the body resting beneath the coffin lid.

She did her best to ignore the ache in her chest. The weight of it had pressed against her breast bone for almost a week; her own silent grief at her father's passing. She already missed his good-natured company, the frantic workings of his mind, so filled with ideas and creations that his inventor's hands couldn't build them fast enough. He'd enlisted her help in his work since she was old enough to hold a wrench. Much to Jane's frozen disapproval, teatime was often spent in discussion of Arthur's latest improvement to a submersible's navigation system or a modification to the rudder of an airship in the Queen's dirigible fleet.

"If you'll step back, miss, we'll cover the grave." The undertaker indicated the sextons waiting nearby with their shovels.

Lenore blew the coffin a kiss and moved far enough from the grave to stay out of the sextons' way but still keep a close eye on their work. She recalled her mother's waspish indignation when Lenore refused to leave after the initial interment.

"You cannot remain here alone! You'll accompany me to our carriage this instant." The black feathers on Jane's hat quivered as the woman shook with outrage.

Lenore's blithe disregard of her mother's ire made the feathers flutter even harder. "No. You are welcome to return home and see to our guests, Mama, but I'm not leaving here until I know Papa is properly interred. I won't have some thieving resurrectionist digging him up before the earth around him is even settled."

Unwilling to engage her recalcitrant daughter in an argument in the midst of mourners and guests, Jane had flounced away in a huff. Lenore expected she'd be subjected to a fiery tongue lashing when she returned home. She didn't care.

The undertaker had instructed one of his coachmen and carriages to remain until she was ready to leave. At the moment, he kept an eagle-eye on the sextons, making certain the grave was properly covered and suitably bricked.

Lenore kept her own vigilance but couldn't quell the worry and fear. The resurrectionists were snatching bodies these days before the grave diggers had even put away their shovels. She only hoped the work involved with quietly unbricking a grave in the dead of night might deter the thieves.

When the sextons finished, Lenore nodded her approval and requested a moment's privacy. They and the undertaker tipped their hats and left to wait nearby.

The pea soup mix of fog and coal smoke thickening London's air washed in a tide through Highgate Cemetery. Through the enveloping murk, Lenore glimpsed another burial close by. Minister and family, friends and business associates, professional mutes in their mourning cloaks; they all reminded her of a murder of crows.

Many in that crowd watched her in return, their features pinched in disapproval. Despite the fact that the Royal Sea and Air Navies regularly sent women to fight alongside their male counterparts against the horrifics that sometimes broke the

Guild Wall, a young woman alone and unchaperoned anywhere, even in a cemetery still raised the disapproval of many. The temptation to offer up a rude gesture almost overcame Lenore. Nosy, gossiping biddies far more concerned with a breach of social etiquette than the exodus of a loved one from the world.

She turned her back on them to offer a final prayer over Arthur's grave when chaos erupted amongst the gathering. Much swooning and fearful cries ensued, and Lenore gawked in amazement at the sudden transformation from somber gathering to milling circus.

"Merciful God, what is that thing doing here?" A portly gentleman pointed a trembling finger at something behind her.

Alarmed, Lenore spun and peered into the murk for a glimpse at what captured every one's attention. A lithe shadow passed along the walls of lichen-covered crypts, gliding over the brown grass of late winter before finally halting near the winged statue of the archangel Raphael. Like her father, Lenore was not of a fanciful bent, but she imagined feathered wings fluttered away from the angular darkness.

More fearful cries sounded through the cemetery. She paid them little heed, stunned by the sight before her. It was rude to stare, but Lenore couldn't help herself. She'd never thought to see a Guardian. At least not this close.

All the fears one held of the dark had gathered together and stitched themselves into the shape of a man. Rumor had it that Guardians weren't human, having lost their claim to the appellation in the notorious Dr. Harvel's crazed experiments. Lenore ignored most gossip, but this rumor carried the weight of truth.

Still as a scarecrow, the Guardian stood between the stone angel and a stately crypt, oblivious to the crowd gaping at him with open-mouthed horror. The sinuous fog intermingled with his long hair, both white as a shroud.

His apparel was nothing like one might see on the streets of London, worn by commoner, aristocrat or even one of the more eccentric airship captains. Lenore doubted such garb was worn by anyone except a keeper of the dead. Ghastly and sharp, it encased his tall form in black armor reminiscent of an insect's carapace.

As if he heard her thoughts, the Guardian turned his head. The group of mourners fled en masse, including the clergyman, leaving the grave abandoned. Even the undertaker and his minions sped for the cemetery gates.

A gaze, so eerie and unlike any she'd ever seen in a human face, pierced her mourning veil. The sclera of his eyes was black as were his irises, his pupils an impossible contrast of white pinpoints as bright as a lightning flash. That long stare bore into her, stripping away layers of black crape, crinoline, flesh and muscle until it reached her soul and dissected it with pitiless scrutiny.

Lenore's stomach tumbled to her feet, and she swayed. Except for the silent dead, she was alone with this creature. She crushed the folds of her skirt in one hand and prayed she wouldn't faint.

He came no closer, content to settle next to the angel and watch her from the gloom. Lenore looked to her father's newly bricked grave, then to the one forsaken by the fearful family and took a deep breath for courage. She was no body snatcher and as such, had nothing to fear from this Guardian. She made herself take those first steps toward him, gleaning strength from the knowledge that her mother would ignite in outrage if she saw her daughter now. Her father, if he were still alive, would chuckle with gusto.

Her steps slowed as she drew closer to the marble angel and its equally still companion. The Guardian watched her approach, saying nothing until she stood no more than a foot from him.

"May I be of service, miss?"

Lenore shuddered at the words. The Guardian's hollow voice buffeted her like a cold wind off the North Sea. Rendered speechless, she could only stare into eyes that revealed an endless stretch of barren tundra. He was a study in sharp angles and contrasting colors of soot and bone. His white hair, unfashionably long, cascaded over a suit of blackened steel spiked at the shoulders, hips and knees.

She might have stood there forever gaping at him had she not caught sight of the oddest thing among the already strange. He carried a cane and leaned on it with the casual grace of any London gentleman. The affectation snapped her out of her trance.

"You are a Guardian, sir?" The question was purely rhetorical, but she had nothing else proper for which to start this conversation. She only wished her voice didn't sound so shrill.

"I am."

He fell into silence, the endless gaze resting on her as he awaited her next statement.

Butterflies battled within her, knocking frantic wings against her ribs as she grasped for some measure of calm. The Guardian hadn't twitched a muscle, yet he loomed over her, a spectral shadow.

"Yes, well...I would beg a favor of you."

His casual stance didn't change nor did her sense of being thoroughly scrutinized, but something new pervaded the air between them, that breathless hush before a storm. Lenore cleared her throat.

"The sextons have bricked my father's grave, but I fear it won't be enough to deter the resurrectionists. I'm told the Guardians protect the dead from such men. I can pay you..."

Long fingers briefly brushed her glove, halting her movements as she reached for her reticule. Enthralled by the contrast of wraith-white hand against black glove, Lenore found it difficult to look up when the Guardian spoke.

"Do not trouble yourself, miss." He glanced at the grave near her father's. "There will be no criminal disinterments in Highgate. I protect all who rest here. Your father and the others will remain undisturbed."

The hollow voice, with its hints of eternity and long night, raised chills on her arms, though now it was from fascination instead of fear. She lifted her veil to better see him and bit back a gasp. Pale as the dead he guarded, his features held a peculiar beauty highlighted by sharp cheekbones spaced wide and high, a long haughty nose and solemn mouth. He was a combination of sinister and fragile, unearthly and eerie...and familiar.

Some invisible tether anchored her to him, drew tight until she was nearly leaning into him, peering hard into those pinpoint white pupils. Her better judgment warned such a notion was impossible, yet she asked the question anyway.

"Do I know you?"

Something bright and hot ignited in that desolate gaze before guttering. The Guardian cocked his head to one side in a puzzled gesture. "Do you?"

Lenore almost leapt away, her cheeks hot with embarrassment. She yanked the veil down. "Forgive my presumption. Of course we don't know each other. For a moment, you just reminded of someone I once..." She almost choked on the words. Two deep breaths and she managed to find her voice again. "I won't take up more of your time. On behalf of my family, I thank you for your vigilance, sir."

She broke all rules of polite convention and proper decorum and held out her hand. Even through her glove, pleasant tingles cascaded from the tips of her fingers to her shoulder when the Guardian clasped her palm lightly and bowed. A thick lock of white hair brushed her knuckles. Lenore imagined she felt its softness.

"I assure you, the pleasure is mine, Miss Kenward."

Her hand twitched in his grasp, and he released her. "How do you know my name?"

His lips curved a little. "I read your father's monument when it was delivered to Highgate. I assume that as his daughter, your surname is the same as his."

Lenore almost groaned at her foolishness, but a tenacious certainty that she once knew this Guardian goaded her to push a little more despite the fact she was making a cake of herself. "How do you know I'm not married?"

"Because a husband of any worth would never leave a wife to grieve her parent alone in the graveyard."

The words, spoken in that sepulchral voice, brought greater heat to Lenore's cheeks. She'd never been so thankful for the half-blinding safety of her mourning veil and the murk of London's filthy air. "You are very observant." Thank God she sounded so collected in this strange conversation she'd impulsively instigated.

"A useful skill in my line of work, Miss Kenward."

Lenore nodded and backed away. "I thank you again, sir, and bid you good day." She pivoted, her skirts snapping around her legs, and strode toward the cemetery gates where carriage and coachman waited just outside the grand entrance.

Eager to flee the cemetery and the guardian's deathless presence, the coachman all but tossed her into the carriage before leaping onto the coachbox. The horses lurched forward in their traces, hard enough to jolt Lenore backward and knock her bonnet askew. She turned for a last look at the keeper of the dead. He'd followed her and lingered beneath the gates' stone archway, a statue himself wreathed in fog. She raised a hand in farewell. He did not return her salutation, but she fancied she heard his voice over the creak of carriage wheels.

"Until next time. My Lenore."

## Chapter Two

NATHANIEL WATCHED LENORE KENWARD'S carriage until it disappeared behind a tree-lined esplanade. His Lenore. Despair knifed through him, as cutting and painful as that first moment of recognition when he saw her alone at her father's graveside.

Her mourning veil hid her face, but he'd recognize that proud posture anywhere, the graceful curves of her body swathed in yards of black paramatta silk. He'd envied the mist that swirled over her skirts and caressed her back.

As a Guardian, he stayed hidden in the shadows of Highgate's crypts and sprawling oaks. His role was not to terrify the living but to protect their dead. He'd broken an unwritten rule amongst his kind, manifesting in the midst of the fog and frightening the clutch of mourners gathered nearby, but he couldn't stay away.

Unlike him, she had changed very little since he last saw her five years earlier. His appearance was the stuff of nightmares, his aspect warped by the twisted ambitions of a crazed and soulless man. Lenore did not run away; she blanched with fear, but she didn't run.

He drew no closer, unsure if she might yet change her mind and flee. Instead, she approached him with single-minded purpose, hesitating as she drew closer. She might be frightened, but it didn't stop her from seeking him out. He'd almost smiled. She was still as firm-minded as he remembered.

When she spoke, the cane on which he leaned nearly snapped beneath his tightening fingers. He might not have forgotten her stubbornness, but the cadence of her voice had dimmed in his memory. Soft and sure, it caressed him as surely as if she reached out and stroked him with her hand, bringing back breathless recollections of a lost time. When she raised her veil to better see him, he'd almost dropped to his knees.

Some would say Lenore Kenward was an unremarkable miss of strong intellect and banal looks—the perfect recipe for a bluestocking spinster. Her brown eyes, dark hair and regular features didn't conform to fashion's definition of great beauty. Yet Nathaniel had been struck dumb at first sight of her in her father's workshop almost a decade earlier, his bewitchment complete as he came to know her mind and character.

Even now, when no one would call him a man any longer, he remained ensorcelled, entranced, and deeply in love with a woman who once rejected his proposal and now thought him dead.

*"Do I know you?"*

She'd rammed the knife home and twisted it for good measure with the simple question. Nathaniel thought himself no longer capable of emotions beyond the blunt satisfaction in killing resurrectionists or the equally dull grief in his existence. He'd been wrong. Those four words kindled a living fire in the empty places where his soul and heart once resided—a fire of anger and regret.

*"I was your friend and your lover,"* he wanted to say. *"I would have been your husband had you not rejected me."* Instead he uttered none of these things, answering her with a question of his own. Even if she'd truly known him, the Nathaniel of five years ago no longer existed. Only his spirit remained, still bound to earth by unnatural means in an unnatural form.

He almost stopped her from pulling down the veil that hid her eyes and soft mouth—a mouth he'd kissed and tasted many times. He didn't stop her from leaving. Lenore didn't belong here with the dead and their keeper.

The undertaker and sextons lingered at the cemetery gates, hesitant to venture any closer but unwilling to leave an open grave uncovered. Nathaniel melted back into the concealing fog, a phantom among other phantoms. Another half hour passed before the second party returned to the grave. Unlike their work on Arthur Kenward's grave, they carelessly shoveled dirt onto this casket until a loose mound formed. All three looked over their shoulders every other minute until Nathaniel thought they resembled confused pigeons. They would never see him unless he chose to reveal himself a second time, and it amused him to watch their antics.

He was not so amused when they tossed the last shovel of dirt onto the mound, packed their supplies and left Highgate. Neither bricked nor warded with the simplest protection spell, the grave was ripe picking for the body snatchers. Either the family didn't care enough for their deceased to pay for the additional protections, or the undertaker had pocketed the extra coins for his personal use.

"I shall have visitors tonight," Nathaniel whispered to himself. "Regrettably, there is no tea."

Afternoon faded to twilight and then to evening in Highgate, casting crypts and headstones into the silhouettes of a macabre cityscape. London glowed from the contained fire of gas lamps, and Nathaniel watched the *HMA Pollux* sail the path of her nightly run. She was once his home, her crew his family. Now both were as far out of his reach as the star for which she was named.

Tonight the airship hovered low over the cemetery, her propellers humming a mechanical dirge as steam and aether pumped from her engines. He'd wondered if she might make an appearance tonight to bid farewell to the man who had made her the most formidable dirigible in the fleet.

A cascade of white flowers spilled from the open windows of the control and wing gondolas. They floated to earth, a snow drift of petals and stems settling on Kenward's grave and the neighboring headstones. A series of flashes from a beacon light—two, two, two and two—and the ship sailed on, rising higher to ride the celestial currents.

Nathaniel beckoned with two fingers, and flower petals near his feet rose from the ground, spiraling into an ivory ribbon that twined around his arm before settling in his palm in a mound of fragrant slips. He held them to his nose and breathed. Rose and lilac, lily and violet. These were from Lenore's garden. Only the Kenward women grew such lush flowers in the heart of winter.

The screech of metal from the oldest part of the cemetery shattered the quiet. Nathaniel didn't move, his eyes closed as he savored the heady perfume of white roses and listened to the spectral voices of warning that rose around him.

*"They are here. They are here."*

The wrenching iron sound was as familiar to him as birdsong--rails bent to create a gap in the fence enclosing the graveyard. His visitors had finally made their appearance.

Resurrectionists usually traveled in packs of no less than four, and tonight there were a half dozen. The Guardian followed them as they fanned out among the headstones, scuttling over markers, kicking aside carefully laid bouquets and charms. Considering the noise they made and the haphazard destruction they left behind, Nathaniel wondered why they bothered to stay hidden behind crypts and trees.

Emboldened by the lack of guards or a confrontational caretaker, the men's voices rose from furtive whispers to casual conversation. One pointed to the spot where Lenore's father rested and the unprotected grave nearby.

"'ere, lads. We got a naked one and one in stays. Easy enough work tonight with two on the dirt and four on the bricks."

Another chimed in. "The doctor'll be 'appy. Two blokes should keep him busy for a fortnight or so."

"May I suggest a good book instead?"

Nathaniel smirked at the startled shouts and curses that followed his remark. Moonlight glinted on steel, and he neatly dodged the thrown dagger that whistled past his ear and struck the oak behind him with a hard thunk.

"You missed." He casually circled their little group as they tightened into a defensive cluster.

They'd dressed for an evening of thieving, tool belts slung across their hip, picks on their backs. One man bared yellow, broken teeth at Nathaniel and raised his arm. He clutched one of the new mercurial disrupters for sale on the black market. He aimed it at Nathaniel's heart, and his cracked grin promised murder.

"We'll make it three blokes then, mate. I'll bet Doc Tepes would pay 'andsomely for a bone keeper seein' as 'ow you're muckin' up 'is business these days."

The de facto spokesman's bravado lent the others courage. They snickered and two more brandished sidearms. Nathaniel braced his weight on his cane and shrugged.

"Shoot then, and let's have an end to this. I grow bored." He closed his eyes for a moment and shifted, feeling his armor come alive and slither across his skin. As with the time before this, and the dozen more before that, yelps of horror and the predictable lock and whine of a disrupter just before it fired met the action.

He knew what they saw—a white haired, pale-eyed demon clad in armor that writhed and hissed and snapped fanged jaws in a Medusa dance around his body.

A miasma of green light filled his vision before a blunt force smashed into his chest. Nathaniel stumbled, the breath rushing out of him in a hard gasp. He righted himself with the aid of his cane. Mercurial rays that would have killed a normal man ricocheted against his rib cage and darted through his altered veins in a shower of razor-edged splinters. The living armor pulsed with verdant luminescence, shifting back to rigid angles and points that set him aglow like an ethereal gasolier.

"For God's sake, shoot it again!"

More blasts, more green light. Nathaniel shuddered from the agonizing shock of the blows but remained standing. All his focus centered on containing the energy suffusing his body, shifting and shaping it until it emerged from his chest in a rotating sphere of fire. The orb hovered between him and the resurrectionists, tiny bolts of lightning arcing along its surface.

"Dust thou art." Nathaniel blew gently and the sphere exploded, blasting outward in a blinding surge.

It enveloped the men in radiant flame. Their screams cut through the night breeze, dampened to whimpers by the rays' effects. Fabric and flesh melted away from bone that darkened to coal and finally disintegrated altogether until what were once six men became nothing more than the scrapings from a dirty fireplace.

Nathaniel ran the tip of his cane through one of the ash heaps, pushing aside the melted scraps of destroyed disrupters. "And unto dust shalt thou return," he whispered.

The sepulchral chorus chanted in his ears once more. *"They are gone. They are gone."*

"Yes, and good riddance." He suffered no guilt for dispatching the vile creatures that desecrated the dead and turned them over to men who would make them lurching horrors. He wiped the cane on the dew covered grass. And people called *him* monster.

He left the ashes where they'd fallen. Wind and rain would wash them away until they became part of cemetery earth and the gardeners would dispose of their melted tools. He paused at Kenward's grave. "Be at peace, friend." He scooped up another handful of petals. Frail slips drifted between his fingers as he carried them through the graveyard to the caretaker's cottage.

There would be no more thieves tonight. They were a territorial lot and staked their claims on certain burial grounds on certain nights. Once others discovered this band no longer offered a challenge, a new group would take their place to do the nefarious Dr. Tepes's work. Nathaniel snorted derisively at the pompous pseudonym.

A carafe of wine awaited him at the house, left by the wife of the rector who attended the adjacent chapel. No amount of wine or ale would ever dull his senses again, but he found some lost measure of humanity in the simple act of enjoying a libation.

The cottage had once been a homey place, despite its location. Now it reflected the cemetery's hushed solemnity. Nearly empty of furniture, the rooms lay in darkness, broken only by bars of moonlight filtered through panes of cloudy glass. Dust drifted across Nathaniel's feet and rose in a murky cloud when he sat at a rickety table in what was once the parlor and poured wine into a pewter chalice.

Cool on his lips, the wine was sweet and tasted of summer—or what he remembered of summer. An image spun before his eyes, of a brown-eyed girl with an easy smile and long dark hair that glinted red in the sun.

"Lenore." White rose petals danced across the table, and the name echoed in the void.

## Chapter Three

"WOULD YOU THINK POORLY of me if I confessed to the temptation to drown my mother in her koi pond?" Lenore eyed her hostess over the rim of her pint glass and wiggled her eyebrows.

Nettie Widderschynnes, captain of the *Pollux*, grinned and raised her glass in a toast. Lamplight winked off the bits of beads, shell and ribbon entwined in her blonde braids. She'd greeted Lenore's sudden arrival on the ship with a spine-cracking embrace and the offer to share a pint in her quarters. "I'd think you were your father's daughter. I'm surprised he didn't do it years ago."

A fundamental traditionalist, Jane Kenward had loathed Nettie at first sight and considered her a low-class, immoral strumpet who dirtied their doorstep each time she appeared at Kenward's workshop to do business. Nettie returned her contempt in equal measure.

A formidable woman of unknown age and even more obscure birth, Nettie Widderschynnes had risen from the gutters of the Abyss to become one of the airship fleet's most experienced captains. She ran her ship with a strict hand and carried a reputation as a fearless captain and even more ruthless business woman. She had no patience for traditionalists like Jane and told her so in no uncertain terms, forever earning the other woman's enmity.

Lenore adored Nettie for all the reasons Jane abhorred her. Encouraged, albeit on the sly, by her father, she had pretended to be Captain Widderschynnes when she was a child, guiding the *Pollux* on her many runs, capturing cargo and enemy dirigibles for the king. She'd dreamed of joining Nettie's crew, but her mother's stringent disapproval and the progression of her father's illness had insured it remained a dream. Until now.

She put her glass down and folded her hands in her lap, once more silently rehearsing what she planned to say. A golden tide of ale rocked in the glass as the airship gently yawed at its mooring mast.

Nettie eyed her, one eyebrow lifted. "Now this should be good. Every time you do that, I know you're about to spin some scheme. Spit it out, girl."

Lenore took a deep breath and spilled her words in a torrent before she lost courage. "Papa was a great inventor but no banker. There's debt—a lot of it. The creditors will seize his workshop and everything in it to pay what is owed." She took a quick sip of beer before continuing.

"He left some funds so that Mama may live comfortably but not enough to support us both." Arthur Kenward had expected his only child to be married by now, and if Lenore was honest with herself, she once assumed the same thing. "I want to join the crew. Your crew. I'll take any spot—messman, rigger, mechanic, ground crew even—whatever is open. Papa taught me soldering and welding. I can read blueprints and am familiar with propulsion and the concepts of thrust vectoring. I haven't much experience for telegraph or navigation, but I can learn. What do you think? Would you take me on, Captain?"

She inhaled after her long spiel and stared at Nettie, willing the woman to say yes. Unfortunately for Lenore, Captain Widderschynnes' distinction as an intrepid adventurer didn't include an impulsive nature.

The terraced lines at the corners of the captain's blue eyes deepened, and she set her glass on a nearby table. She braced her elbows on her knees and scrutinized Lenore as thoroughly as the Guardian had done two months earlier at Highgate.

"Your father," she said in a far more formal accent than Lenore had ever heard before, "bless his departed soul, would have my guts for garters if I had you flutterin' in the wind from a mooring mast or runnin' about stringing yaw guys to cables and pulley blocks."

Lenore's heart threatened to pound out of her chest. "I don't have to be a rigger." She loosened the death grip she held on her own fingers. "I can work in the mess or the laundry. There's no danger in sweeping and washing dishes. Or I can post to the main engine room. I know machinery. I assisted Papa with several of the improvements installed on this ship, including the incendiary shield."

Nettie graced her with a disgusted look. "Don't play stupid, Lenore. The *Pollux* is bristlin' with cannon, machine guns and bombs, as well as other nastiness you're best not knowing about. You know any post on an airship, especially a runner, is risky. If Nathaniel's death didn't teach you that lesson, nothing will."

Five years, and the grief was as crushing as the day she received word of Nathaniel's death. Lenore closed her eyes for a moment, forcing the sorrow back to the shadowed parts of her soul. It was enough she mourn for her father. She knew the pain of that loss would lessen with time; she'd shoulder the pain of the other until she died.

She opened her eyes to find Nettie's expression had gentled to one of sympathy. "It's not my way to be cruel, Lenore. I think you just need remindin' this isn't a game or some great adventure. There's danger and costs in this business. Nathaniel paid the 'ighest price, and you paid with 'im." She frowned. "Your papa was one of my best mates. I'd be no friend to 'im if I put 'is girl at risk. You're better off hiring out as a governess or lady's companion."

Jane Kenward and Nettie Widderschynnes agreed for once in their lives, much to Lenore's dismay. Jane had suggested—insisted—on the same thing. A position as governess or companion was Lenore's best course. Respectable, safe, soul-withering. Lenore blanched at the idea of years stretched out before her, trapped in households where she was isolated from everyone except spoiled, difficult children or bitter widows whose idea of a companion was synonymous with whipping boy. Her father might disapprove, but he wasn't here to tell her no.

"Nettie, I know the risks, but I've wanted this all my life—before I met Nathaniel, before Papa's death. You saw me when I was a child, how I'd pretend to be you." Lenore didn't miss the faint blush warming the older woman's cheeks and pressed her advantage. "Other women serve under you on the *Pollux*. Will you not consider it?"

Nettie took a long swallow of her beer and wiped her mouth with the back of her hand. "Brilliant with his inventions, your papa. Not much of a sailor or crewman. Got airsick each time he went on a night run with us, but he loved it all the same. Said you would too had you been old enough to accompany him." She scowled at Lenore. "I'm not sayin' aye, but I'm not sayin' nay either. I want to think about it."

Lenore's shoulders sagged, and she slumped in her chair with relief. "Thank you, Nettie. For what it's worth, you might well save me from a slow death of needlepoint, alphabets, and smelling salts."

"And put you in harm's way with a quick death from a stray bullet." Nettie pointed an accusing finger. "Don't play the savior card with me, missy. If I say no, you keep your dignity, accept my decision and walk out of here without argument. Understood?"

Lenore saluted. "Aye, Captain." She didn't dare smile.

"We sail in three days' time for the Redan, providing escort for the *Andromeda*. It's a month out and a month back. You'll have your answer then. No sooner."

The Redan. Lenore's heartbeat stuttered. She'd been raised on tales about the defensive perimeter. Bordering the length of Atlantic coastline from Hammerfest in Norway to the Strait of Gibraltar, the buffer protected the continent from the horrifics that sometimes erupted out of the dimensional fissure. Many airships, along with their crews, had been lost fighting at the Redan. Nettie had almost lost the *Pollux*, and Nathaniel had died there. If she joined the crew, it was a guarantee she'd see it first-hand.

"You'll be careful, won't you, Nettie?"

Nettie shot her a reproachful look. "Not much choice. We're playing nanny to a cargo lifter loaded with flyers and munitions." She gestured to Lenore's untouched glass. "You might not want to let that get too flat. It turns bitter."

Accustomed to the captain's pragmatic view of her job, Lenore didn't expound on her concern over this latest mission. She rose from her chair. "No more for me. I'm off to visit Papa, then home. I need my wits sharp to face Mama's tirade. She won't soon forgive me for sneaking away." She didn't hide her distaste. "I missed Aunt Adelaide's weekly one o'clock visit, along with her atrocious piano playing."

Nettie's chuckle was less than sympathetic. "Better you than me, ducks. I'll take a good battle at the Redan over that nonsense any day." She stood with Lenore. "You'll give my best to your papa when you visit, yeah?"

Lenore gathered her shawl and reticule. "Always." She paused, remembering the funeral and the Guardian who vowed to protect her father's grave. "Did I tell you I met the Guardian of Highgate?"

The other woman's eyes widened. "Did you now? And how did you manage that? They're not known for socializin' with the living."

"He revealed himself once the sextons bricked Papa's grave. I approached him..."

Nettie's bark of laughter interrupted her. "You've a backbone tough as those corset steels you wear, girl. Guardians scare the lights out of most people."

Lenore's cheeks heated at the compliment. "He had a fearsome aspect. Tall, dressed in black armor—and the strangest eyes, as if he looked back on eternity."

"You make him sound like a right 'andsome bloke."

She shrugged. "He was, in an odd way. Very gentlemanly as well. He promised none would disturb the grave, and he's kept that promise. The bricks are as they were laid." She didn't mention the sense of recognition that struck her at their first meeting. Even now, weeks later, his image burned darkly in her mind's eye, along with the unwavering certainty she knew him. "I haven't seen him since then, and I go to the cemetery weekly."

"A good thing, I think." Nettie escorted her out of the captain's quarters and into the corridor that ran the length of the keel. "He's one of Harvel's experiments. Who knows what terrible things those poor souls suffered and how much it changed them—for the worst I'll wager."

They bid each other farewell at the gangplank. Donal McCullough, Nettie's master rigger, escorted Lenore to the omnibus waiting at the depot. "Sure you don't need me to take you to the station, miss?"

"I'm certain, Mr. McCullough. Thank you." She boarded the omnibus and found a seat next to a woman cradling an infant. She returned McCullough's wave as the driver pulled away and settled in for her journey to the train station.

## Chapter Four

NATHANIEL GROANED UNDER HIS BREATH at the sight of Lenore strolling down one of the cemetery paths to her father's grave. Hidden by an ancient elm bedecked in ivy, he consumed her with his gaze, taking in the bombazine gown of unrelenting black, the upswept hair that revealed her pale neck and highlighted the line of her jaw.

She tortured him with these weekly visits to her father's grave. Pulled from the opposite side of the sprawling cemetery as if by a lodestone, he sensed her presence the moment she passed through the entrance archway. Coves of hanging ivy and the shadows cast by crypts kept him hidden from view as he admired her profile and listened to the easy pitch of her voice.

She conversed with her father at each visit as if he were standing before her, his eyes bright with the avid curiosity he'd passed on to his only child. Nathaniel could have told her that Arthur's spirit didn't linger the way some did, that it had crossed the ethereal barrier; the body beneath the bricks had been an empty vessel at burial. Nathaniel was not, however, a cruel man. He recognized her need to hold onto some remnant of her loved one, to accept her sorrow and gradually let it go. Other mourners did the same. The difference was he didn't eavesdrop on their conversations with the dearly departed.

Many might say he breached every form of courtesy in listening to her one-sided conversations with her father. He invaded her privacy, but he couldn't stop or bring himself to feel any shame. He'd thought his love for Lenore Kenward had been ripped out of him along with his humanity. His first glimpse of her at her father's graveside had re-ignited emotions once lost in the hazy memories of a distant life. Seeing her again had been an ecstasy. Knowing she was forever out of his reach an agony. He concentrated on her words and closed his eyes as a wave of homesickness washed over him.

"I visited with Nettie today, Papa. She sends her regards. The *Pollux* will be in port at Maldon for a few more days, then Nettie is taking her out. I'm to understand she will act as escort for the *Andromeda*. They will face the Redan."

The Redan. The dimensional fissure. Images flashed behind Nathaniel's closed lids.

*He'd never get used to seeing it, never lose the terror that churned his guts and sucked the air from his lungs. The black tide of roiling clouds pounded the protective barrier, searching —always searching—for the one weakness that would allow it to breach the wards woven by Her Majesty's best guild mages and rip the fissure even wider.*

*The nebula writhed and twisted, illuminated by flashes of sour yellow lightning that revealed the monstrous things surfing its waves—colossal maws baring teeth the length of cathedral spires, segmented legs of insectile abominations bristling with spiky black fur, and slick tentacles that whipped from the fissure to tongue the wards with a barbed stroke.*

*Wind, flecked with ice crystals and smelling of ozone, blasted across the* Pollux's *gun batteries and glazed the* empyrean-*loaded carronades in a thin sheet of ice.*

*The gunnery crew shouted as one when a tentacle lashed out of the obscuring cloud, the curving claws stretched across its underside extending and retracting as it reached for the* Pollux. *The ship dove, narrowly avoiding the shredding appendage. The tentacle retreated into the miasma.*

*"Steady, men," he called out to the other gunners.*

*"Look sharp, lads."* Nettie's command traveled through the speaking tube, as bracing as the wind threatening to freeze his hands to the battery shield.

Despite the numbing cold, sweat trickled down his ribs beneath his heavy woolens. The fissure contorted and labored as if trying to whelp the unearthly life squirming within it.

Three tentacles burst out of the nebula and struck the ship.

*"Fire!"* he roared into the link. *"Fire!"*

Crimson light filled his vision as the carronades belched empyrean from their barrels. An explosion deafened him. The Pollux squealed and yawed hard to starboard. Wood shrapnel and broken tether lines exploded into the air. A wash of heat splattered his face. Blinded, he wiped at his eyes and came away with a glove smeared in blood. Something heavy struck his shoulder and bounced across the gunnery deck—an arm, shredded at the shoulder joint, and no body attached to it.

The Pollux suddenly pitched back on her rudder, sending him careening into the nearest cannon. His tether cable jerked taut, smashing his stomach against his backbone. Scorched wool filled his nostrils. He clutched at a broken railing to stay upright. Hot metal burned through his glove, searing his palm. He gritted his teeth against the pain and held on. The agonized screams of men rent to pieces filled his ears.

He looked up—far, far up to the boiling sky where an arching nightmare laced with curving white claws hurtled toward the wounded Pollux. The deck bucked hard beneath his feet. He lost his grip on the railing and jittered across the slick surface like a marionette dancing to the tune of the shuddering ship...

...the shuddering ship.

Nathaniel's eyes snapped open. He inhaled a strangled breath. A voice, achingly familiar, cut short its casual monologue.

"Who's there?"

He blinked, desperate to clear his mind of the images that seized and held him fast in frozen horror.

"Who's there?" The sharp tones of Lenore's repeated question, didn't quite disguise her fear. She peered into the ivy shielding him from view, poised to take flight at the slightest motion, her brown eyes wide in her pale face.

Nathaniel breathed deep, willing away the terror, the memory of the churning nebula, the whipping tentacle.

...*the shuddering ship.*

"Forgive me, miss," he said in a smooth voice and stepped from the ivy's concealment. "I didn't mean to frighten you."

Despite his knowledge of her character, he still expected to her run. She didn't. Instead, she wilted, her stiff shoulders relaxing in obvious relief. It was a first for him in this new incarnation. Guardians weren't persecuted outright, but they were shunned and feared. Most people avoided them as if they were plague-ridden. Lenore wasn't most people.

She drew closer, head tilted. "The Guardian."

He acknowledged her designation with a low bow but said no more.

Her somber features softened a little, and her eyes warmed. "You've done a fine job taking care of Highgate's citizens." She gestured to Arthur's grave. "Not a brick moved. Even the flowers I placed here last time are as they lay." She bent to trace the discolored edge of a wilted white rose with one fingertip. It had taken all of Nathaniel's willpower not to claim the small bouquet for himself or at least the ribbon that bound it together.

"It isn't safe to be here alone, miss. Have you no companion?" Some things never changed. The one time he'd remarked on Lenore's penchant for taking solitary jaunts, she'd arched an eyebrow at him and tipped her chin in such way that he braced himself for a setdown. She wore the exact same expression now.

"This isn't Whitechapel, sir, and we're in broad daylight with many perfectly respectable people nearby taking the air." She shrugged. "Besides, had I a maid or companion with me, she would no doubt have abandoned me to my fate the moment you made an appearance." The eyebrow lowered, and she offered a faint smile.

He tipped his head. "While I might argue the wisdom of taking the air of London, I cannot refute the last. Guardians aren't sought after for their charming wit and illuminating conversation."

"True, but there is a difference between avoidance and fear." A puzzled line creased the smooth skin of her forehead. "People flee when they see Guardians, as though their lives are in immediate danger if they so much as glimpse you, yet I've never heard of a Guardian doing harm to anyone."

That was because he and his brethren made certain there was nothing to investigate or report when they did away with resurrectionists. The only evidence left of the ones Nathaniel had immolated were soot marks on the grass, and those had washed away with the next inevitable rain. All but one body thief's soul had crossed the Veil, and Nathaniel ignored that ghostly voice which joined the chorus of others. He admitted none of this to Lenore.

"We're frightful sights to look upon, and our choice of employment far too macabre to discuss over tea."

Her mouth tightened, a sure sign she was settling in for an argument. "Those aren't adequate reasons to flee as if the Dartmoor Hound were snapping at your coat or dress hem."

"For some, those are perfectly acceptable reasons." He suspected people would be more inclined to linger and stare if they saw the Hound. It was a creature far removed from themselves in every way. He, on the other hand, was still a little too similar for comfort. After Harvel's experiment, and with *gehenna*-tainted blood in his veins, he was no more human than the Hound and a hundred times more terrifying. Like those fearful folk, he'd once been an ordinary person. Now he represented the horrors that might have happened to any one of them but by the grace of God had not. In his observations, people feared the *almost* far more than the *what if*.

The ever-present pall over London deepened. Clouds, heavy with rain, lowered even more. Drizzle that had threatened all afternoon finally fell to beat an arrhythmic tattoo on High Gate's crypts and verdant landscape.

Lenore snapped open the umbrella looped on her wrist and swung it over her head. She raised an eyebrow. "Improper or not, it seems hardly fair that you become drenched while I remain dry. I'm willing to share."

Nathaniel smiled a little, as charmed by her offer cloaked in challenge as he was by the memory of her subduing a belligerent pack of butchers boys on a Camberwell street with the same umbrella.

Rain didn't bother him. He acted as sentinel here in all weather, had even survived a lightning strike once with only the acrid smell of burned hair to mark the event. Still, her offer tempted him beyond words. To be close to her once more, breathing in her scent of bergamot and lemon water and hearing the gentle rise and fall of her breathing...

"Your offer of shelter is kind, miss, but it's only water. Everything dries in time." He noted the continually darkening sky. Once the rain stopped, the fog would roll in, blotting out what little light still remained and turning the city into a murky sea. "You should return home. Even the hardiest person doesn't stroll through a pea-souper if they can help it." He frowned. "And it isn't safe for those alone, even when you aren't in Whitechapel."

A soft whirring sound overhead forestalled her reply. Nathaniel followed her gaze to watch one of the many airships dotting London's sky drift past them. It flew low under the cloud ceiling, the whirring noise that of the two rotating disks that spun around its girth at bow and stern. Nathaniel recognized the ship; so did Lenore.

"After the *Pollux*, my father was always partial to the *Merope*. Her design made it easy to retrofit her engines for adiabatic demagnetization." Her smile was wistful. "He was almost as proud to see her inaugural flight after the upgrade as he was to watch the *Pollux* after retrofit."

Rain sheeted off the ship's sleek exterior as it glided past them. Nathaniel had sailed on the *Merope* once years ago when Nettie brought him with her to inspect the gun batteries for ideas on how to improve upon her own ship's arsenal. He'd come away unimpressed. The engines were indeed a marvel, no longer subject to overheating from the volatile *empyrean* used to fuel them, but the *Pollux*'s firepower remained superior. The *Merope* was built for transport, the *Pollux* for war, and their designs reflected their different purposes.

"She's a good ship for a thermal and her pilot one of the best. He'd have to be to keep her from porpoising every time the throttle settings change."

The weight of Lenore's measuring gaze rested heavily on him. "You know something of airships," she said in a voice both curious and admiring.

"A fact here and there," he replied. The common knowledge they shared—his through experience as a deckhand, hers through design and theory—had provided him with the perfect excuse to talk with her when he visited her father's workshop. She'd seduced him as much with her passionate descriptions of membrane structures and buoyancy ratings as she did with her beauty.

She asked him a question that made the breath die in his chest. "Would you like to sail in one in the future?"

Of everything he'd lost since the *Pollux*'s near disaster at the Redan and Dr. Harvel's experiments, the greatest—besides Lenore herself—was his post on Nettie's ship. Any ship for that matter. He strove to keep his voice even and free of bitterness lest she sense it and question him, as had always been her wont.

"I'm neither a creature of air nor ocean, miss, but of earth." He swung an arm to encompass the cemetery with its wide field of headstones, crypts and mournful angels. "My place is here."

Despite his best efforts, something of his regret must have colored his words. Lenore's pitying gaze turned his stomach. He steered the conversation back to her. "And you, miss? Would you like to see the world from an airship gondola?"

Her expression lightened, but his delight in the change was short-lived. "I would, and I may yet have the chance. I've requested a post on the *Pollux*, serving under Captain Widderschynnes." She grinned, unaware of Nathaniel's growing horror. "I'll know in a few days if I have a place."

Nathaniel stared at her, no longer seeing a woman clothed in black under an equally dark umbrella silvered with rain, but the gunnery deck of the *Pollux* slippery with ice and blood.

"Sir, what troubles you?"

He blinked, refocusing on Lenore's pale features and the puzzlement clouding her expression. He shook his head. "I beg your pardon, miss. I'm more familiar with the ships than I am with their captains." A lie as white as his hair. "But Widderschynnes is well-known."

Lenore's shoulders straightened even more with pride, as if the accolades were hers instead of Nettie's. "She is a fine skyrunner captain—the best in the fleet, I daresay."

He couldn't agree more, and the second he laid eyes on Nettie Widderschynnes again, he'd wring her neck like a Christmas goose. What was she thinking to even consider allowing Lenore on a battleship?

Rain fell harder, and Lenore huddled tighter under her umbrella. "Forgive me. I've trapped you out here for a good soaking."

Nathaniel shrugged. "As I mentioned earlier, miss, it's merely rain. I'm in no danger." He gestured toward the cemetery entrance. "You, however, could catch your death out here. Allow me to escort you to the gates and hail transport."

Her soft laughter almost blunted the terror riding him at the thought of her on the *Pollux*. Almost. "You're very kind, but as we've both witnessed, you…intimidate most people. I think a driver would whip the poor horse to a faster pace if he saw you and abandon me to my fate." She held up a gloved hand to thwart any argument. "You may accompany me to the gate and wait there if you wish until I've caught a hackney or omnibus. Agreed?"

He nodded, and they started toward Highgate's grand entrance. Twice he gripped her elbow to keep her from slipping on the wet lanes. Her arm rested delicate and warm in his too-brief grip. What would she do were he to take her in his arms, not as Nathaniel Gordon, but as the deathless Guardian, armored and strange?

God, he missed her.

She bid him goodbye at the gate. "Until next time, sir, should I see you again when I visit my father."

"Safe journey, miss." *Come back to me, Lenore. I'll be waiting.* The words flowed through his mind and remained tightly behind his teeth. He doffed an imaginary topper at her and bowed.

His ordinary action somehow startled her. Badly. She gasped, her eyes wide beneath her bonnet. The umbrella shook above her, and the cloth of her glove stretched tight across her knuckles where she clutched the handle in a death grip.

"Miss Kenward?" he inquired and almost reached for her. He dropped his hand at the last moment, fingers twitching with the desire to touch her.

Lenore blinked and shook her head before offering him a rueful half smile. "Forgive me. I remembered..." She shook her head a second time as if to clear her thoughts. Nathaniel wondered at the sudden glossiness in her eyes: tears.

They exchanged farewells a second time before parting; he to linger in the gate's shadow and keep watch, she to stand at the edge of the road.

She'd been right that he intimidated others, but any driver attempting to bypass Lenore as she stood in the rain waiting for a ride would have found himself suddenly off his high seat and on his backside in a puddle while Nathaniel himself took her home. Fortunately, for all involved, an empty omnibus halted a few minutes later, for which he was grateful, and carried her away from him.

He waited until he no longer heard the clop of hooves on cobblestone before setting off eastward to the Bishopsgate station. His reputation as a vigilant, lethal Guardian served him well. Resurrectionists hesitated to rob Highgate of its newly buried citizens during daylight, and Nathaniel didn't think they'd try again anytime soon—at least not now when he abandoned his post to seek the person who once commanded his most devout loyalty.

The streets were almost empty of people. Most who hadn't found shelter indoors huddled in doorways, and none accosted him. He avoided the main roads, keeping to side lanes and squalid alleyways ankle-deep in water. If any saw him pass, they said nothing, wishing no acquaintance with an apparition possessing eyes that resembled gateways to Hell.

Nathaniel made quick time to the train station, unencumbered by crowds. The station itself offered numerous places for him to blend or disappear, concealed by shadows and a Guardian's unique talent for being overlooked by even the most observant gazes.

He avoided the passenger trains. Stowing away was easiest on the freight lines run by freight guards instead of the more eagle-eyed conductor guards. He hid in an empty car on a freight bound for Maldon and its vast mooring field of airships, tapping his foot impatiently and cursing his former captain under his breath the entire journey. The trip took a little more than an hour, and he was off the train and out of the station before anyone noted his presence.

Maldon's airfield stretched over a flat of land next to a farmer's fields, but this one's crop flew instead of fed. At least a dozen airships of every size and design rocked gently at their tall mooring masts. Nathaniel paused for a moment to admire them. The sweet ache of recollection filled him. These majestic lasses had occupied his dreams since he was a boy and caused the rift between him and his family. He never regretted his course of action—to serve in the fleet instead of on the family estate—even when he fell from the *Pollux*'s deck and into the Atlantic's frigid depths.

The ache grew when he spotted his previous mistress docked at her mast tower. He knew every inch of her as intimately as he did Lenore's own supple frame and loved both with equal ferocity. The ship's thin metal envelope sparkled in the wet gloom, beckoning him to stroke her once more with an affectionate hand.

He'd happily stand all night staring at her, but he came with a purpose, and it didn't include hours of forlorn, lovesick gazes that put a green lad to shame. Mud sucked at his feet, and the fog rising off the fields didn't wait for the rain to stop. It rose to his knees to swirl around his legs, creeping ever higher. By the time he reached the mast tower, a gray shroud enveloped him completely.

A pea-souper only worked in the favor of thieves and murderers, and in this case, Guardians as well. The fog lapped over the *Pollux*'s keel, obscuring the control room gondola windows and any occupants. A clearer day and alarms would have sounded across the field, along with the warning crack of rifle shot, at the sight of him shimmying up the tower like a spider on a skeleton.

The long spike attached to the tip of the airship's nose aided in tethering her to the mooring mast and, much to Nettie's disgust, earned her the nickname the Narwhal. Despite the ridicule, the steel horn had saved the *Pollux* numerous times, generating a buffer shield that protected her from attack by both enemy ships and the otherworldly monstrosities lurking in the dimensional rift.

The shield was powered down, and Nathaniel used the spike as a death-defying bridge to cross onto the airship's broad back instead of the platform the crew used to enter the ship's interior. Rain made the metal sheathing slippery as ice. His balance was exceptional, but he grasped the cable that ran the length of the ship like a sliver of spine from some prehistoric beast and raced toward the stern. Halfway there, he used the line to sling downward, snagged a second cable stretching from one of the engine gondolas and caught his footing on the ladder leading from the gondola to an opening in the ship's hull. He slipped inside unseen to drop silently onto a narrow catwalk.

He breathed a longing sigh at the familiar view. The belly of the beast. Longitudinal and transverse girders filled his vision-- the rigid frame that gave the ship her streamlined shape. Corded and wire netting ran from girder to girder, completing the massive metal spiderweb. The catwalk he stood on ran perpendicular to the much longer gangplank that stretched from the *Pollux*'s bow to her stern, suspended above the ship's helium and *empyrean*-filled gasbags.

Many a trip out, he had walked these narrow planks and climbed the girders. His fingers danced across a section of framework, following a span of varnished duralumin tubes riveted together. He imagined the *Pollux* sang to him down the weave of wire bracing, her metallic serenade welcoming home a much-missed, if wayward son. It was good to be near her, inside her and see her whole and undamaged once more.

Voices originating from the rear gondola spurred him toward the ladder that spanned the distance between gasbag deck and keel corridor. He wasn't fast enough.

"Oy! Did you see 'im?"

"See what?"

The first voice, exasperated, grew louder. "Looked like a vicar climbing into the keel!" Disbelieving laughter followed the remark, but the chase was on.

Nathaniel dropped from the ladder into the narrow corridor. Gaslights attached to long tubing flickered overhead and ran parallel to the speaking tube and water line. His familiarity with the ship served him well. Unless Nettie had builders gut the *Pollux* and change everything—which, knowing Nettie, seemed unlikely—he'd find her quarters near the ship's bow. He just needed to reach her without encountering more of the crew.

His luck didn't hold. A crewwoman almost cannoned into him as she emerged from a berth doorway. Her surprised shriek set his ears to ringing as he swung around her at a dead run toward the bow. Were he truly a vicar, her colorful curses would have set his ears alight.

He raced past crew quarters and storage rooms containing water ballasts, weaponry, fuel and food. In different circumstances, he might have laughed at the shouts behind him.

"There's a churchman on the ship!"

"See? Mary saw him too!"

"Why's he running away?"

"Ain't no soul on this ship can be saved that fast."

Others joined the pack as more of the crew sought out the source of the commotion.

A voice rose above the rested, its tone one of revulsion. "Bloody hell, that ain't no vicar. It's a bone keeper!"

Nathaniel paused to glance briefly over his shoulder. That alone brought the foremost pursuer to a sudden halt, causing the line behind to crash into him. They went down like pins in a nine pin match. The resulting chaos bought him a few moments of reprieve but cost him his goal.

He turned to flee again and found himself staring down the business end of a double-barreled Howdah pistol. The woman holding it in a steadfast grip resembled a ragged and beaded trull straight out of a Whitechapel crack. The cold gleam in her eyes warned she'd put a bullet in him if he so much as twitched an eyelash.

"Mate, you're either very lost or very stupid. This ain't a graveyard yet, but to back-slang it onto my ship is a sure way to see you end up berthing next to the dead you watch over."

Nathaniel exhaled a slow breath and bowed, never breaking eye contact. "Captain Widderschynnes," he said softly, his great affection for her surging into his voice. Surprise flickered in her flat stare. "It's been far too long."

Her aim never wavered. "You'll pardon me if I don't recall our association."

He knew that tone. Step lively or be shot. "I wish to speak with you." The crew gathered behind him, a silent, breathing beast ready to tear him apart at its mistress's signal. "Alone."

One of Nettie's eyebrows lifted in a doubtful arch. "Is that so? I'm not in the habit of having chinwags with Guardians."

"I'm here regarding Lenore Kenward."

Nettie's finger flexed on the trigger, and Nathaniel's body reacted. Fabric transformed to steel, encasing him from head to foot in black armor. Various cries calling upon the Almighty filled the narrow hallway.

"'Oly mother o' 'Baub!"

"Blue damn, it's a demon!"

To her credit, Nettie didn't blink, even when the only thing she saw of Nathaniel were his eyes behind a mask of plate steel. She gave orders to her crew. "Back to work and carry on proper."

A chorus of reluctant "Aye, Captain," answered her, and Nathaniel listened as the crewmen backed reluctantly down the corridor, in no rush to leave Nettie alone with him.

Her stoic expression grew annoyed. "Move it!" she snapped, and this time the running thud of boots filled the space. Nathaniel himself had to squelch his own reaction to the order and not race after them.

His armor softened, changing back to cloth and the ensemble that many mistook as a vicar's. She might still shoot him, but her trigger finger had relaxed. She gestured toward the door at the bow. "Walk on," she said. "I'll follow."

Once inside her quarters, she motioned for him to sit in one of the chairs facing her desk. Nettie's quarters were exactly as he remembered, even down to the heavy silk coverlet folded neatly at the foot of her bed—a gift from the crew a decade earlier. The comfortable chamber reflected a mix of both her rank and her personal tastes—books, maps, souvenirs from her many travels, some beautiful, others macabre.

She settled into her own chair opposite him and laid the pistol down within easy reach of her right hand. Her left hand, hidden from view, rested idle in her lap—or so she liked her visitor to believe.

Nathaniel knew better. The danger to himself was no less now than when he stood in the corridor staring cross-eyed at the Howdah. He had no doubt Nettie's index finger caressed the trigger of the loaded 12-gauge break-action shotgun mounted and braced under the desk, its sawn-off double barrels guaranteed to put down anyone sitting in the chair he now occupied.

"You've always been a suspicious sort, Captain." He hid a grin when her eyes narrowed to slits. "I'm no danger to you or anyone else on the *Pollux*."

"Then I suggest you crack the bell, mate, and make it quick, or I might just shoot you for playing games and wasting my time." Her lips tightened, and she spoke the words through her teeth. Lamplight bounced off the beads in her wild hair and cast her sharp features in partial shadow.

He nodded. Nettie never issued idle threats. "Miss Kenward told me she requested a post on this ship."

Nettie cocked her head to one side, puzzlement replacing hostility. "And why would she say such a thing to the Highgate Guardian? I knew you two spoke, but I didn't think you chums."

The bottom of his stomach dropped out at her statement. "She mentioned me to you?" He closed his eyes for a moment, relishing the idea.

"Just today in fact. You've watched over her father's grave." Nettie's fingers tapped out a drumming rhythm next to the Howdah. "And now you're here, making her affairs yours. Why is that?" She perched on her chair, a harpy ready to rip his face off with her talons if she didn't like his answer.

"The *Pollux* is a risky mistress to serve on, a battleship suitable only for the most experienced crewmen. Her architect's blue-stocking daughter has no place on such a ship, even if serving under so able a captain."

Nettie snorted, her suspicious gaze stripping him down to bone. "Be that true or not, what business is it of yours?"

He struggled with how to adequately convey his fear without revealing why. "Her safety is of utmost importance to me." He tried another tack. "I knew her parents. Jane Kenward will disapprove and Arthur Kenward's spirit will be troubled."

Nathaniel knew the first to be absolute. The second--he wasn't so sure. Arthur had given his only child a great deal of freedom when he was alive, encouraging her various exploits and thirst for adventure. His spirit might well applaud the idea of his daughter serving on the ship he designed and Nettie captained.

"The chance to watch Jane Kenward pop a stay-lace isn't the best way of convincing me Lenore shouldn't come aboard." Nettie's hand, as free of jewelry as her hair was heavy with it, played across the Howdah's grip. "As for Arthur, either you just told me a lie or you didn't know the man at all." The dead flatness returned to her voice. "I don't like liars."

Clearly, almost dying once wasn't enough for him. His fate demanded he waltz with the Reaper twice. He forced back the warning crawl of armor on his skin and leaned forward to rest his elbows on the desk in a casual pose. "Do you want her to meet the same end as Nathaniel Gordon?"

Nettie's eyes blazed. He barely heard the cracking echo of the shotgun before a round of shot pummeled him point-blank in the stomach. The chair rocked under him, and he bent over with a low wheeze, certain he'd just been kicked in the gut by a pair of Shire horses. Wet heat streamed down his torso, and silvery blood painted the strands of his loose hair where they dragged through the growing pool of gore in his lap.

"Damnation, Nettie Eliza Whitley," he said between gasps. "That hurt!"

## Chapter Five

A HOUSE IN MOURNING WAS more dismal than the cemetery where the dearly departed rested. Lenore hung her wet cloak and bonnet on the rack near the front door and paused to listen. Except for the steady click of the pendulum in the grandfather clock occupying one corner of the foyer, the house was quiet, shuttered in a pall of gloom.

The soft glow of the low-burning gasolier allowed just enough light to prevent a person from tripping on the rug or the nearby stairwell in the dark. When her father was alive, it had blazed like a star caught in chains. Arthur's death wrought many changes in the Kenward household, none of them welcome.

The flicker of firelight danced across the surface of the parlor's partially open door. Lenore stepped inside and spotted her mother in her usual place—one of three chairs furthest from the fireplace to prevent any stray coal dust from falling on her hem. A nearby lamp provided illumination for the stitchery on which Jane industriously plied her needle. She glanced briefly at her daughter, features pinched, before turning her attention back to her needlework.

Lenore sighed inwardly. Tonight would be as the many nights before it—awkward conversation saturated in resentment that slowly built to a hot argument. "Hello, Mama." She swept across the room and sat down opposite her mother.

Jane didn't look up or return Lenore's greeting. "You almost missed supper."

"Then Constance is serving earlier than usual. It's not yet half past five." She reached out and pressed her fingertips to the teapot. Cold.

The needle whipped ever faster through the cloth, a sure sign of Jane's agitation. "Your aunt inquired after you. You were missed."

Lenore poured herself a cup of the tepid tea, foregoing the milk and sugar. "Mama, Aunt Adelaide does not like me. I very much doubt I was missed."

Adelaide Evenstowe, a galleon of a woman, didn't like children in general but reserved most of her contempt for her niece, whom she deemed headstrong and inappropriate. She'd done more than her fair share in convincing Jane to send Lenore off to boarding school, an interference for which Lenore had never forgiven her.

She sipped and made a face. The tea had grown bitter as well as cold. She set it aside. "Did you enjoy your visit?"

Jane's mouth compressed into a scowl as bitter as the tea. "Yes."

The heavy silence between the two women grew, and Lenore waited for her mother to fire the inevitable first volley. The housekeeper's appearance offered a temporary reprieve.

"Miss, I didn't hear you return." She gathered up the cups and set them on the tray along with the teapot and accompaniments. "A fresh pot for you? It's miserable outside."

Lenore nodded. "Thank you, Mrs. Harp. That would be lovely."

Once the housekeeper left, Jane spoke. "Even Constance disapproves of you gadding about this late in this weather."

Lenore picked up her own sewing, a handkerchief with a complicated embroidered border whose completion had so far eluded her. Maybe because she found it duller than watching grass grow. "Mama, I don't think Constance's remark on the weather bore any connection to whether or not she approves of me being out and about."

Jane's needle flashed and flew, the taut fabric popping with each jab of the pointed tip. "It's both improper and dangerous for you to be on London streets alone."

"I brought flowers for Papa's grave." She remained silent regarding her conversation with the Guardian.

The whip stitching slowed for a moment before picking up speed once more. "And visited that airship harlot in Maldon." Jane finally looked up at her daughter, her eyes, as dark as Lenore's, reflecting the flames from the fireplace. "Your duty is to your family, Lenore, not her."

Lenore groaned. "Mama, what duty is there in sitting for hours listening to Aunt Adelaide abuse our poor pianoforte and complain that the tea is cold or the fire too hot or the room too drafty? And Nettie is a respected captain, not a harlot."

Jane hissed at the sudden snarl in her thread. "I've never understood why your father tolerated that woman." Her eyes narrowed. "You realize she's no longer welcome here?"

"So I assumed. Why do you think I went to Maldon instead of inviting her here?"

"Why do you even associate with her at all?"

This had ever been a point of contention, not just between Jane and Lenore but between Jane and Arthur. Lenore had once thought her mother feared the association between her husband and the airship captain was one of a more conjugal nature. As she grew older and observed the repartee between Arthur and Nettie, she abandoned the idea.

While their friendship was unusual and likely perceived as something else, the inventor and the captain were nothing more than professional colleagues of like minds. Had Nettie been a man, Lenore still didn't think Jane would have approved of the friendship. The class divide was too wide and too deep, and one Jane believed never should be crossed.

Much to Jane's disgust, Lenore didn't agree and embraced her father's more egalitarian views. "I associate with her because she is my friend as much as she was Papa's."

Simmering silence fell between them again and lasted through supper. Lenore wished with all her heart that she and

Jane might one day reach past the endless squabbles and arguments and meet on common ground. With no other siblings and Arthur gone, they only had each other, and Lenore stared into the heart of that fact, both sad and frightened.

Jane finished her last course and excused herself from the table, the heavy slide of her skirts audible in the dining room as she ascended the stairs to her bed chamber. Lenore pushed aside the remains of her pudding and drained her wine glass, happier with the solitude than with her mother's disapproving presence across from her.

Mrs. Harp entered to clear away the supper remains, and Lenore rose to help her. Constance Harp had been in service with the Kenward family since Lenore was still on lead strings, and more than a few times it was Constance she was tethered to in those early childhood years. Her grief over Arthur's death was as profound as that of his wife and child.

She offered Lenore a sympathetic smile. "How was your papa, Miss Nora?"

Lenore followed her to the kitchen with the remains from supper. "Regrettably quiet. His manners regarding civil conversation have lapsed abominably."

The housekeeper chuckled. "It's good you visit him as often as you do. Good for you both."

Lenore didn't argue that. It was true. Visiting her father's grave eased the grief. Her brief conversations with the fascinating Guardian presented their own charm as well. She said nothing of this to Constance. "I hope to convince Mama to accompany me next time."

Constance took the dishes from her and stacked them near the dry sink. She dusted her hands and gestured to the door with a thrust of her chin. "It's never been her way to reveal what's inside. Give her time, miss. She grieves for him in her way."

Lenore followed the direction of her gaze. Not once had she witnessed Jane shed a tear since her husband's death. "I'll trust your word on that, Mrs. Harp."

When the housekeeper refused her help with the dishes, Lenore left the kitchen with promises to rise early to start the Friday ironing.

It was far too early for bed, and she was too restless to read or sew. The windows on the stairwell's first landing revealed a back garden made bleak and bare by the winter cold. The rain had stopped, leaving the branches of cherry and apple trees Jane lovingly tended through every season to drip in the deepening evening.

Lenore had inherited a little of her mother's skill with plants, but it was nothing compared to Jane's innate magic. Her father often joked that his wife was the only person he knew of outside the Guild mages who could plant a broken stick in a coal heap and watch it flower into a great oak.

The greenhouse Arthur had built for his new wife nearly three decades earlier glowed softly in the darkness, lit not by candles or gas but by the numerous blossoms of white roses, lilacs, lilies and violets housed inside. Their soft luminosity reminded her of the Highgate Guardian, as pale as a new marble headstone draped in black weeds.

Each time they met, he drew her like a ship to a shore beacon and sent flutters through her belly. So oddly beguiling. Truth be told, his was a visage one might see in a *danse macabre* mural—spectral and strange as if bound to earth by the thinnest of threads.

*Quod fuimus, estis; quod sumus, vos eritis - What we were, you are; what we are, you will be.*

She shook her head to clear her grim thoughts and padded softly to her room so as not to disturb her mother. Dwelling on the legend of the Three Living and the Three Dead guaranteed nightmares, and she had no wish to lay awake half the night imagining skeletons dancing with the terrified living.

The temperature in her room made the rest of the house seem warm by comparison. Cold air drafted in from the partially open window, bringing with it the fresh scent of air cleansed by rain and a touch of the damp. She shut the windows and pulled the drapes closed before lighting an oil lamp with shaking fingers. The shawl she draped over her shoulders offered some warmth, and she added another from her wardrobe for good measure.

A book on steam engine design lay next to one of poems by the poet laureate Tennyson. Lenore traced the poetry book's cover design. A finely made book with its gold-tooled leather and gilt-edged vellum pages. A beautiful book. An expensive one given to her by a man who'd likely spent three months' hard-earned wages to obtain it.

Lenore made a mournful sound in her throat. Nathaniel. She closed her eyes, remembering his ready smile and eyes as blue as bachelor's button. She thought of him every day, but lately, in the weeks following her father's death, he was constantly on her mind.

She knelt before the chest at the foot of her bed. Inside were stored various keepsakes—sketches her father created for her, letters from Nathaniel posted from Madrid and Provence, St. Petersburg and Milan. Bound to the London suburb of Camberwell, where her longest adventure away from home had been the annual trip to rainy Bath, Lenore had traveled the world through Nathaniel's letters.

He never spoke of the Redan, and the few times she'd asked him about the dimensional rift and the horrifics, he turned pale and taciturn. Whatever he witnessed during the barrier battles, it was as far removed from the beauty of lavender fields and marble palaces as one could get.

She found what she sought beneath the stack of beribboned letters and books of pressed flowers. Lenore carried the muslin-wrapped package to the table, unwrapping the cloth to reveal a folding case containing her most precious possession. The lamp's yellow light bathed the ambrotype photograph, highlighting the hand-tinting the photographer had added to enhance the photo.

A man posed next to a desk, dressed in his Sunday finery, elbow resting casually on the desktop as he stared at the viewer with a solemn expression. Sandy-haired and broad-shouldered, he was a fine specimen guaranteed to catch the eye of any woman from fifteen to fifty. He had certainly enthralled Lenore at their first acquaintance. That Nathaniel Gordon seemed equally enamored with her still left her in a state of wonder. And deep sorrow.

She outlined his figure under the protective glass with one finger, recollecting his wide smile and the way he made her laugh with his witty remarks or go round-eyed at the stories of his travels. He had a way of wishing her good day that made her blush and Jane growl under her breath if she chanced to witness it—a flirtatious tipping of his pot hat that managed to convey both humor and keen interest.

A memory superimposed itself over the one of Nathaniel. The tall, elegant Guardian tipping his imaginary hat in a manner that made Lenore's stomach jump into her ribs. An uncanny mimic; a strange coincidence surely. Lenore frowned, staring into the distance.

It was more than the hat tip. The way he shrugged or tilted his head as he listened to her talk, even the smile—gracing a face that looked nothing like Nathaniel's—seemed familiar. How did two men, so vastly different, exhibit such similar movements and expression? Or send butterflies whirling through her chest?

Lenore shook her head, frowning harder. She was spending too much time at Highgate cemetery; it was making her daft and even more melancholy. Despite the puzzling hold he had on her, the Guardian was nothing like Nathaniel Gordon.

She shuddered at the thought of what her mother might say if she knew of Lenore's fascination for the keeper of the dead and the reasons behind it. A spinster bemoaning her unmarried state so much that she imagined the behavior of a lost love on a being who walked two worlds. That Lenore had no interest in marrying after Nathaniel's death wouldn't change Jane's opinion.

She kissed her fingertip before pressing it to the ambrotype. "My darling boy, you are the husband of my heart. I will love and miss you until they lay me in hallowed ground. There is no shame in that."

It was still early for bed, but Lenore had promised Constance help in the ironing, and that meant awaking well before dawn if they had any hope of completing the chore the same day. Lenore wrapped the ambrotype in its muslin envelope and carefully returned it to its place in the chest.

The kitchen was deserted, dishes cleaned and put away. Lenore blessed Constance's name under her breath when she spotted two hot water bottles resting on the stove's still-warm surface. She wrapped one in a towel to take back to her room and warm the sheets.

A ribbon of light crept under the library's closed door. Lenore paused in the dark foyer. She hadn't noticed it on her trip downstairs. The comforting crackle of a fire reached her ears as she drew closer, along with the crisp turning of a book's pages.

Her breath grew short, dark fancies engendered by hours in a cemetery and conversations with bone keepers. She eased the door open slowly, half certain she'd find the ghost of Arthur Kenward lounging in his favorite chair by the fire, a book in his lap, his pipe in his hand.

What met her gaze made her throat close and her vision blur. Jane, not Arthur, sat in the favorite chair. A book rested in her lap, and in her hand she held a glass of port instead of a pipe. Firelight caressed her hair, bronzing her long braid where it draped over one shoulder. She had changed for bed, her white gown partially concealed by her robe. She wore Arthur's dressing gown over the robe. Dry-eyed and expressionless, Jane stared into the fire, sipped her port and raised the dressing gown's cuff to her nose for a long inhalation.

Tears dripped down Lenore's cheeks, and she eased the door shut before making her way to the stairs. The spinster wept; the widow did not, but more than one woman grieved the loss of a loved one in the Kenward household.

## Chapter Six

"BRANDY OR BLACK STRAP?" Nettie held up one decanter of brandy and another of port.

"Brandy." Nathaniel rubbed his aching midriff, still sore from the round of shot she'd fired into him.

Nettie's hands visibly shook as she poured a dram of brandy into each glass. She passed one to him before taking a seat in the chair opposite his. Her ruddy skin was still pale from shock, and she eyed him as if not quite believing he was real much less the man he claimed to be. "After what you just told me, I need something stronger. I'd pour meself chain lightning if I kept it stocked."

Nathaniel scowled at her. "Stay away from the stuff, Nettie. It's poison in a glass, and I've seen more families bury a poor lad baned by it."

They clinked glasses in a silent toast, and Nathaniel sipped his brandy under his former captain's piercing gaze. Her quarters were peaceful now, completely opposite from the riotous chaos a half hour earlier.

Nathaniel had pressed a hand against his riddled midriff, coughed twice and spat a mouthful of bloody shot pellets into his palm before spilling them to the floor. The wounds made by the ammunition closed up, and the silvery blood flow slowed to a trickle before ceasing altogether.

Nettie watched the entire thing with eyes slitted with fury and her hand steady on the Howdah she aimed at his head a second time. Even when half the ship's crew threatened to pound her door down, her stare never wavered.

"Cut that racket and go about your business!" she'd bellowed over the noise. The pounding abruptly stopped, and Nathaniel recognized the worried voice of her long-time boatswain.

"Are you all right, Captain? We heard the shot."

"I'm fine, Mr. Sawyer. Just a little mishap with the trigger." She cocked an eyebrow at Nathaniel and the smooth expanse of his coat, no longer peppered with shot or silvered in his blood.

The silence on the other side of the door stretched for a moment before the boatswain spoke. "Aye, Captain." A chorus of grumbles and questions followed, and from the sound of it, Mr. Sawyer was having a difficult time herding the crew away from Nettie's door.

When it grew quiet again, Nettie gestured with the pistol. "How dare you," she snarled through clenched teeth. "How dare you use my lost lad's name as a weapon!"

Nathaniel's already sore gut clenched at the agony in her voice. "Forgive me, Nettie," he said, contrite. "That was unfair of me."

"Who are you? *What* are you?"

He dared a slight smile. "Promise you won't shoot me again if I tell."

She matched his smile with a hard scowl of her own. "I promise to you shoot you if you don't, and I doubt you can put your skull back together after I put a pair of slugs between your eyes."

She had a point. He was inhumanly strong and fast, with an uncanny ability to heal wounds that would kill a regular man, but a shot to the head from a pistol used to hunt tigers—well, he was tough, but he wasn't invincible.

"You once had a lover named Tom Black," he said. "A coster you ended up killing before he killed you. Widderschynnes is the name you took when you first signed onto the fleet. You sport a tattoo of a swan on your left hip, gotten in Algiers on a helium run." Her eyes rounded as he recited fact after fact of a life none but a close few knew. His voice softened. "You had a sister named Ruth who died of the cholera in '33. Your only child, an infant you christened Margaret, is buried in Abney Park. You carry a scrap of her gown in your pocket at all times along with a curl of her hair in a watch locket. They are the most precious things you own."

The pistol wavered infinitesimally to the right. Nettie blinked, and her voice was hoarse and low. "How do you know all of this?"

The ache in Nathaniel's chest had nothing to do with Nettie's shot. "Because you were once my commanding officer, and I am still your devoted friend. It's me, Nettie," he said gently. "Nathaniel. Believe it or not, but please don't shoot me again."

A weaker woman might have fainted. Nettie Widderschynnes did not. She gazed silently at him for several moments before laying the Howdah on the desk. Nathaniel knew he'd won a small portion of her trust when she handed him a handkerchief to clean his hand and partially turned her back to pour them drinks at the sideboard. Now they sat across from each other, sharing a dram of brandy.

Nettie tapped a finger on her tumbler, her fingernail making a soft *pink-pink pink* sound in the silence. "My eyes are tellin' me you're a liar, but you know things only Nathaniel did. You move like him too, even if you're thinner than a rasher of wind by comparison."

The part of him wound up tighter than a new spring drive clock loosened. Nathaniel swept a hand from his chest to his knees. "This body once belonged to a knockabout droll named Jack Preston."

Jack's soul had departed his body before Harvel played God and rammed Nathaniel's own dying spirit into it. While the soul was gone, some of Jack's memories remained. An acrobatic comic who played the stage and entertained the low brow crowds of London, he'd lost his life to a thief with a knife and a fatal aim. The mad doctor had saved the body if not the man and bequeathed it to Nathaniel whose own physical form had been beaten beyond repair by war and the harsh Atlantic waves.

Nettie shook her head. "How is that even possible?"

He shrugged and swallowed half the brandy in his glass. "I don't know. Galvanism combined with *gehenna* and whatever strange magic Harvel cooked up in that torture chamber he called a laboratory. All I remember are lights and the burn of liquid hell running through me."

Liquid hell and lightning. The magic pairing that allowed dead men to live again. They lost most of their humanity in the process, turning the colors of ghosts and shadow. The seven men Harvel turned possessed extraordinary qualities beyond the abilities of normal men. Their blood ran silver instead of red, and like Nathaniel, all were much closer to the dead than to the living.

"I heard one of Harvel's creations killed him." Nettie arched an eyebrow. "Was that you?"

He only wished he could lay claim to that achievement. "No. His first experiment, Gideon, killed him. And rescued the rest of us." All Guardians owed a life debt to Gideon.

Nettie slapped the arm of her chair. "Good. He deserved it for what he did to you and the others." She cocked her head, her sharp gaze noting every detail of his appearance. "Do you have the droll's memories then, as well as your own?"

"Vague ones. More like shadows of memories. My own returned to me over time." The first one had been that of a woman's face. Smooth skin and brown eyes. Dark hair and an enigmatic smile. Lenore.

Nettie's knuckles whitened where she gripped her glass, her features drawn and stiff. "You should have come to me," she said in a low voice that quavered faintly. "The second you remembered, you should have come."

Nathaniel rose, placed his glass on the desk and knelt in front of the woman who had been more a mother to him than the one who birthed him. He reached for her free hand, lacing his fingers with hers, trying to ignore the ghastly difference between the natural hues of her skin and his own deathly pallor.

"And you would have believed me just like earlier?" he said. "Look at me, Nettie. You just said it yourself. It's difficult to accept this is the Nathaniel you remembered."

Her fingers tightened on his. "Lenore doesn't know."

"No, and you can't tell her."

Her brief smile lit her eyes for a moment. "No worries there, lad. You have to be the one to bell that cat."

Nathaniel shook his head and stood to resume his seat. "And I never will. Nathaniel Gordon is dead. My appearance alone should make that obvious."

"Don't be a fool. You might be keeping company with cold meat now and wearing some dead bloke's body, but under all that you're Nathaniel Gordon, and Lenore misses you as hard now as she did when she first heard the news of your dying five years ago."

He crushed the swell of hope threatening to engulf him. "She'll forget and love someone else."

Nettie rolled her eyes and snorted. "Obviously your little journey to the underworld and back has made you a touch beefheaded."

"I'm not here to talk about Lenore," he snapped.

Another disbelieving snort. "Is that so? 'I'm here regarding Lenore Kenward,' she repeated in an affected accent. Your words, lad, not mine."

Nathaniel ground his teeth. "You know what I mean. Your crew members are experienced fighters. Each one has fought at the Redan at least twice. None of them are sheltered inventor's daughters whose only close call with death was an accidental fall into the Surrey Canal when she was four years old."

Nettie sipped her brandy, licking her lips in approval of the taste. "More than a few mites have drowned in the Camberwell Death Trap."

"Even more have been rescued from it by vigilant nannies and parents." He raked a hand through his hair. "That's a ridiculous rebuttal and not at all amusing."

Her chortle echoed in the room. "It's funny as hell, lad." She set aside her glass and leaned back in her chair, arms crossed.

"By my lights, you're asking a great deal and giving nothing in return. You don't want Lenore knowing you're alive because you don't want to what? Interfere? Hope she'll forget and turn her affections to another? Yet you travel from London to Maldon just to tell me not to allow her on the *Pollux*. You're sounding just like a husband—alive, well, and dictating what Lenore Kenward—not Gordon mind, Kenward—should be doing."

Nathaniel scowled. "You missed your calling. You should have been a barrister."

Nettie gave an unapologetic shrug. "Not likely. I look terrible in a wig."

He might have laughed if he weren't so frustrated. He leaned forward, forearms on his thighs and sighed. "I wanted more than anything to have her as my wife. She rejected my suit."

Nettie straightened in her seat. "I've a strong suspicion that had nothin' to do with her not loving you."

"But everything to do with her not trusting my character." Five years earlier, he'd sworn to himself he'd return from his trip to the Redan and beg her to explain her rejection of his proposal. But he hadn't returned, at least not as he'd left, and that chance was lost to him now. "Ours is a permanent estrangement," he said. "I can accept that as long as I know she's safe."

Nettie scrubbed at her eyes. "Lad, any number of things can kill us at any time without ever leaving our doorsteps. The churchyards are full of people dead from consumption and the Irish fever. However, if it eases your mind, I'll tell you what I told Lenore. I'll think about it. The *Pollux* sails with the *Andromeda* to the Redan. I have time to make my decision." She paused and frowned.

Curious, Nathaniel leaned closer. "What is it?"

Nettie shook her head. "I'd not be telling this to anyone else, mind. This request for a post? It isn't a lark for her. Arthur was a fine man, but he left his family with crushing debt and almost no income except a pittance inheritance for that starched up widow of his. Lenore must seek out service. Governess, companion. Airship crewman."

Nathaniel reared back in his seat, shocked. Nettie's revelation cast a different light on Lenore's request and his own stringent objections to it. The Kenwards were a middle class family of means. Their house in Camberwell, with its many rooms and spacious front and back gardens, was the envy of its neighbors. Arthur's funeral had been a lavish affair. No one could accuse Jane Kenward of besmirching her husband's memory on that front. What had Arthur done to place his wife and daughter in such dire financial straits?

"Her knowledge of design and repair would be wasted trying to teach a baronet's brats their letters and numbers." He ignored Nettie's knowing smirk.

"Aye, it would. Besides, she's a bricky girl and learned plenty from her papa about engine design. She'd be easy to teach the hands-on stuff, and apprenticeship under a good mechanic would make her valuable to any airship crew."

Nathaniel closed his eyes for a moment, recalling those final moments aboard the *Pollux* before the whiplash of a barbed tentacle bit into his flesh and flung him off the deck. *The shuddering ship.* He opened his eyes and met Nettie's steady gaze. "If you take her on board, would you take me as well?"

Her face drained of color, leaving her almost as pale as he was. Her blue eyes sheened with unshed tears. "Oh Nate, my boy," she said softly. "I just got you back." Her rueful smile made his heart ache for her. "A little peaky and odd looking for sure, but alive. I don't think I can bear to lose you a second time. Besides, I'm not sure having a bone keeper onboard will sit well with the crew.

Nathaniel clasped the chair arms in a white-knuckled grip. "Please, Nettie."

She glanced at his hands, then at him and blew out a sigh. "Like I told Lenore, I'll think on it."

It would have to do for now. He knew her well enough to know if he kept pushing, she'd flat out refuse and then bodily throw him out of her quarters to hammer home her point. He stood when she did. "I imagine you never thought I'd end up guarding a bone yard."

"Better that than lying in one." Nettie reached up to cup his jaw. Nathaniel pressed his cheek into her palm. "If you need me for anything..." she said.

He held her hand and kissed her callused fingers. "Likewise." He bowed and headed for the door, her goodbye to him eliciting a laugh.

"Quit robbing the barber and cut that mop!"

## Chapter Seven

TWO MONTHS EARLIER LENORE had prayed and crossed her fingers that Nettie Widderschynnes would see her way of it and give Lenore a chance to join her crew. When the airship captain returned from the Redan, she countered Lenore's offer with one of her own. Her letter arrived in the post a week after the *Pollux* docked in Maldon, drafted by one of the fleet's secretaries.

*Dear Miss Kenward,*

*This post is addressed to you on behalf of Captain Nettie Widderschynnes of the* HMA Pollux. *Your request for a post aboard this airship has been reviewed and a counter consideration offered. Temporary post as cabin boy aboard the* HMA Terebullum *is currently available. Captain Widderschynnes will lead a training crew on a test flight of the* HMA Terebellum *to Gibraltar, Spain. Total flight duration is seven days to begin 12th of February, departing from Maldon Airfield. At the end of the stated flight, consideration for a more permanent post will be discussed.*

She scanned the remainder of the letter, noting the deadline for a reply and immediately set to scribbling her acceptance letter. Cabin boy wasn't quite what she'd hoped for, but it was the perfect post for someone with no experience aboard ship. Nettie could just as easily have said no and put an end to it. Lenore had no intention of questioning her good fortune.

Temporary and of lowest rank it might be and on a ship not the *Pollux*, but she had a post.

Gaining Nettie's short-term approval was the easy part, defying a furious Jane Kenward, a battle hard-fought and costly.

Jane read the letter, crushed the parchment in her hand and glared at Lenore over her spectacle rims. "I forbid it," she announced in tones low and seething. High color scorched her cheekbones, and the jet beads draped over her collar juttered against each other from her rapid breathing.

"You can't forbid it, Mama," Lenore replied in what she hoped was a serene voice. "I've already posted my acceptance and received both my travel instructions and ticket. I leave for Maldon Tuesday next."

Jane's nostrils flared, her outrage palpable. "I am your mother," she bit out. "I demand your respect."

Lenore's patience began to fray. "You have it, but this isn't about respect. This is about survival. We must retrench." The second wave of creditors had already cleaned out Arthur's workshop down to the last gear and pencil.

"I'm well aware of our circumstances, Lenore. However, that doesn't mean you abandon all propriety and expectations of your class to go sailing off with some ragged lot of Shoreditch outcasts." Jane rose from her chair to pace before the parlor window. Her skirts swept the floors in an agitated swish. "There are many positions available for an unmarried woman of your station."

"And they pay one-third or less the rate of an airship crewman." Lenore had made some effort in seeking out other employment possibilities. Even were she not so eager to avoid the slow, stifling death as a paid companion or harried governess, the pay of an airship crewman offered its own attraction.

Jane retrieved her fan from one of the side tables, its many ribs snapping in time each time she opened and closed it. "It's vulgar to speak of money."

Lenore clenched her teeth and prayed for patience. "It's even more vulgar to starve."

"A crewman's pay is greater because the danger is significantly greater. As a governess, the most you might suffer is a recalcitrant child or his demanding mother. I doubt either of them will shoot at you, blow you up or try and devour you."

Lenore couldn't help the chuckle that escaped her lips. "Have you seen some of those children? Don't be so sure."

Jane bent a hard glare on her. "Lenore," she warned.

Lenore exhaled a frustrated breath. "Mama, I love you with all my heart, but I am twenty-seven years old and capable of making independent decisions. We may argue this to death, but I'm not changing my mind. Let me help you."

The two women clashed in a silent battle of wills, before Jane turned her back and found refuge on the nearby settee. She stared out the window onto the front garden washed in fragile morning light. "Were you married, we wouldn't have this discussion." Her voice had lost none of its edge, but Lenore sensed she'd given ground.

She sat, facing Jane. "As I recall, you were at first against me marrying Nathaniel Gordon."

Jane's frosty gaze didn't thaw. "Foolish boy tossing away his birthright as if it were scrap. I wish you had never met him."

Lenore refused to apologize. "I'm so very glad I did," she said softly. She rose and smoothed her skirts.

Her mother's eyebrows rose, and she frowned. "Where are you going?"

"To visit Papa."

"That's the second time this week."

And if Lenore had anything to say about it, it wouldn't be the last. "I go for us both. You're welcome to join me." She knew Jane's answer before she made the offer.

The older woman stiffened and turned away, her voice a little more hollow this time. "Not yet," she said. "Not yet."

Lenore clasped her shoulder briefly before rising to leave. "I will return by tea."

"Take Constance with you," Jane called just as Lenore curled her hand around the door knob.

Lenore raised her eyes to the ceiling. "Mama, Constance is taking deliveries today and waiting for the washer woman. She's far too busy to play nursemaid to me. I promised her I'd stop by the markets and pick up supplies for her as well."

A muttered "Stubborn girl" followed her into the hallway, and Lenore closed the door behind her with a relieved "whew."

Despite the hints of sunlight breaking through the clouds, the day was brutally cold, the only blessing the lack of a wind to cut through clothing. Lenore wrapped warmly in layers of wool coat, mittens and scarves. She'd rolled on her thickest stockings and donned her heaviest petticoats in a futile bid to stay warm. Only the crowded omnibus that transported her and others from Camberwell, across London Bridge to Camden and Swain's Lane offered some relief and a little warmth. She pitied those who rode on the open upper deck.

Most would think her mad if she admitted to the nervous anticipation that sent her stomach in a tumble once she stood outside of Highgate's grand entrance. A visit to a cemetery usually elicited tears or in many instances, much appreciated moments of peace and reflection on a Sunday afternoon. Lenore had not lied when she told Jane she planned to visit Arthur. She simply didn't mention the hope she dare not acknowledge out loud that she might see and speak with the Guardian.

She passed the Lebanon Circle vaults, following a narrow path to where Arthur's grave lay undisturbed. No longer a target for body snatchers, his remains rested beneath bricks turning green with lichen. Sometime between now and her last visit, someone had placed a bench close enough to the grave so she might sit and chat with her father's spirit in comfort. The butterflies swirled in her belly. Had the Guardian been responsible for the thoughtful gesture? Those otherworldly eyes revealed nothing of his thoughts, but he had always been courteous to her, and kind.

Lenore set the basket she carried on the bench alongside her ever-present umbrella. Constance had slid it onto her arm before she left. "A bit of lunch for you should you have need of it."

Lenore would also use the basket to bring home those items the grocer didn't deliver to the house.

Sunlight filtered through the bare trees and thick ivy, golden and alluring with its false promise of warmth. The flowers she laid on the grave three days earlier were already a black slimy mess. She retrieved a new bouquet from the basket, scraped the dead one aside with her shoe and placed the fresh flowers in its place. Like her, they shivered in the cold.

Lenore returned to the bench and perched on the edge. Huddled deep in her coat, she listened for the footfalls of any nearby visitors. Only the silence answered. Her breath clouded before her when she spoke.

"Good morning, Papa. I have news. Nettie has not yet agreed to me joining her crew permanently, but she has allowed me to join them on a test flight. Not the *Pollux* mind, but a new one—the *Terebellum*. Do you remember her? A cargo lifter. We saw her plans four years ago. The Vickers Armament modified Sir Smithson's design so the engines will generate more horsepower with the possibility of speed at 61 knots. They've installed them on the *Terebellum*. Nettie has been offered the chance to test-fly her before she's formally assigned captain and crew. A short run to Gibraltar and back. No more than a week out. I'm to play cabin boy."

Lenore didn't mention her argument with Jane or the fact that creditors had seized everything of value from his workshop and were now eyeing the furnishings in the house. Such things were the burdens of the living, not the dead. She spoke instead of the latest scandals posted in the scandal sheets and conjectured over what the secretive Guild mages might do to strengthen the barriers at the coast.

A faint whine interrupted her one-sided conversation. Lenore went silent, listening. Another whine followed the first, and she peered into a cluster of ivy to her left. A dog, thin and quaking, emerged from the foliage, wary but no doubt drawn to the scents wafting from her basket. Its fur, dark with caked mud, did little to hide its bony hips and ribcage.

Careful not to cause a scare, or worse, have her fingers bitten for the kindness, Lenore broke off a small bit of cheese from the wedge Constance packed and tossed it to her visitor. The mongrel sniffed before wolfing down the tidbit. It didn't come any closer, but there was no mistaking the pleading look on its canine features. Just one more bite, please.

Lenore reached further into her basket and pulled out the rest of the cheese, slices of cold, boiled ham, a bun, still warm in its wrapping and a square of moist parkin. "Poor dog," she crooned to the pathetic creature. "When was the last time you ate?" By the look of it, a long time ago. She tossed more of the cheese along with pieces pinched from the bun. The ham and the cake soon followed until there was nothing left of Constance's carefully packed meal.

"I'm sorry, friend," she said in response to the expectant look it gave her, along with a timid tail wag. "You've eaten everything. Hopefully, that will last until your next meal."

She blew on her fingers, frozen even in the mittens she wore. "I've sat too long," she said aloud. "My blood is turning to ice chips."

She looped her umbrella over her forearm, grabbed the empty basket and rose from the bench. The dog lingered nearby, too shy to approach but unwilling to leave this newly discovered source of food. Lenore shooed it gently away with her umbrella. "I'm sure you'd make a fine companion, but I cannot take you home with me. My mother would get one look at you, and we'd both be on the streets hoping for handouts from strangers."

The umbrella worked as a deterrent for two seconds at most. The dog simply skittered out of the way, only to return as Lenore's tail-wagging shadow.

She sighed. For years, she had begged her parents for a pet, specifically a dog. Jane couldn't abide them, and in this matter, Arthur bent to her wishes. Now, when Lenore was older and far more in control of her life, the timing didn't suit. She had no doubt that were she to leave a rescued street mongrel with her mother while she went sailing off to Spain, she'd return to find the animal had mysteriously vanished.

Woman and mutt gazed at each other for a moment before Lenore gave in. "Care for a walk among the dead?" she asked. The dog cocked its head to the side as if considering her proposal before trotting a little closer, tail snapping back and forth even faster than before.

The unlikely pair traveled an ordered path through the cemetery, pausing periodically for Lenore to read the various headstones or admire the lavish memorials sculpted in marble and granite commemorating various people wealthy or famous or both. At each pause, she glanced over her shoulder or sought the shadows that played behind penitent angels in the hopes of seeing the white-haired, black-garbed Guardian. She refused to admit her disappointment to herself when he made no appearance.

She gave a start at the sudden rise of voices and clink of metal. The dog, her silent companion, laid back its ears and retreated farther behind her. Alerted by the animal's wary behavior, Lenore crept softly toward the sounds and peeked around a marble cross.

Two men, dressed in ragged coats and tool belts bent to their work over a small grave. Mangled wreathes of fresh flowers lay strewn in haphazard chaos, pelted by the dirt the men shoveled off the new mound.

Lenore clapped a hand over her mouth, frozen in horror . Resurrectionists! In full daylight. The realization of what they dug for made blood roil in her veins in a red fury. They were defiling a child's grave.

One of the body snatchers spoke. "I don't like it. We shoulda done this at night."

The second thief flung a shovel full of mud at his compatriot. "Shut your gob and dig," he snarled. "Daylight means the bone keeper won't be watchin' for us."

Lenore's anger made her careless. "You vile bastards," she said aloud before freezing in place.

Both thieves spun to face her, shovel handles gripped in dirty fingers—weapons as a last resort to be used on anyone unfortunate enough to witness their crime.

Lenore was the first of the three jolted from their mutual surprise. She opened her mouth, drew a deep breath and screamed for all she was worth. The sound, fueled by sheer terror, exploded from her lungs and carried across the cemetery with the force of an enraged banshee. Both men dropped their shovels to cover their ears, and Lenore used that moment to turn and flee.

Her basket and umbrella lay somewhere in the shrubbery where she dropped them, and she sped down the path, skirt and crinoline hiked up to her knees. A cry went up behind her, much too close.

"Catch that bleedin' trollop before we both end up ridin' in the Black Maria!"

Lenore's breath roared in her ears, even as her feet flew over the ground. Even when she veered from the path to race past headstones and over wild patches of vegetation not yet killed by winter frost, the main gate remained out of reach—as far away as the moon, especially with the resurrectionists hot on her heels.

A snarl sounded behind her followed by a surprised curse. "Stupid mutt!"

Lenore's eyes filled with tears at the canine yelp of pain. Her erstwhile companion and unexpected protector. She prayed that sound had not been a death cry.

The hard thud of booted feet grew closer along with coarse panting. She didn't dare look back, and her lungs burned as if she drew fire into her nostrils instead of air.

Fingers touched her shoulder. Lenore screamed and wrenched away. The movement proved her undoing. Her ankle gave, and she fell toward a headstone. She twisted sideways to avoid it, her outstretched hand saving her from splitting her skull open on the unforgiving marble. She hit the ground on her back, pain exploding in both her palm and the back of her head. Black spots burst across her vision, interspersed with colors that blurred and bled together.

A triumphant cackle sounded in her ear, only to be cut short by a gurgle and a snap, as if someone had stepped on a frozen twig. Lenore tried to raise her head only to watch the blurry world turn topsy-turvy. Her stomach heaved in reaction, and she lay still as the sky carouseled madly above her.

Darkness blotted out the anemic sun only to give way to twin stars that blazed white in a black ocean. Someone spoke, and she recognized the voice. Achingly familiar. Oddly hollow.

"Lenore. I have you, my sweet."

"Nathaniel?" That wasn't possible. She'd hit the ground a lot harder than she thought.

Icy fingers caressed her face, soothing despite their chill. "All is well, love. You're safe with me."

White stars. So distant. So beautiful. Lenore smiled, even as darkness encroached into her whirling vision. "I should make a wish" she said, wondering why the words felt as thick and sticky as treacle in her mouth. "Two wishes."

She floated above the ground, light as a feather, pressed against velvet woven from night. A steady heartbeat drummed against her ear, and Nathaniel's voice teased her once more. "What will you wish for, my Lenore?"

Lenore nuzzled her cheek into the soft fabric. "That you come back to me so I can tell you..."The words weighed heavy on her tongue, and a high ringing filled her ears.

The soothing voice rose it above it all. "Tell me what?"

"Tell you yes instead of no." The white stars disappeared and the voice and ringing with them until she was only the feather, and even that faded to nothing.

She awakened to the pungent scent of cheese mixed with dog breath and the lap of something wet and warm sliding across her cheek. She groaned and covered her face with her arm. "Hello, dog." The greeting earned her a soft bark and another damp lick, this time near her ear.

Lenore lay still for several moments, resting on her side, and struggled to find her bearings. Someone had removed her bonnet. It rested in the cove of her body, one side misshapen.

The pain in her head had lessened from a tower bell's clamor to a hand bell's chime. Her right hand still throbbed, and she raised it for a better look. She'd lost her mitten, and the illumination from an unknown light source revealed the lacerations across her knuckles and the swelling in both her ring and smallest fingers. An experimental wiggle assured her nothing was broken.

She rested on a wooden floor, facing a dark wall of linen fold paneling gone gray with dust and years without a proper oiling. An equally forgotten fireplace interrupted the expanse of wood, the ashes in its grate long cold. Winter sunlight forced its way through the cloudy panes of a nearby window and battled for dominance against the flame of a lit oil lamp on a small table.

Except for the table and two chairs that looked in imminent danger of collapsing if someone dropped so much as a tea cozy on them, the room was bare. Stark and abandoned and colder than a crypt.

The dog pressed against her back and rested its chin on her waist. Lenore welcomed the shared warmth if not the reek of canine exhalations. "Good dog," she murmured. "Thank you for trying to help."

She recalled its hurt yelp, the body snatcher's curses and her sadness that violent death had been the poor creature's reward for its bravery. She herself might well have perished, not from a thief's attack but from her own clumsiness. Lenore would have laughed if her head didn't pain her so much. What a ridiculous eulogy that would be. Lenore Kenward, unfortunate spinster taken far too young by the malevolent machinations of a headstone. She did chuckle then, the sound cut short by the return of the tower bell thrum between her temples.

"Laughter is always a good sign."

Lenore gasped at the sight of a paler shadow separating itself from the darker ones clotting the chamber's doorway.

The Highgate Guardian stood in the entrance, holding a basin and pitcher, linen towels draped over one arm. "Don't be frightened, Miss Kenward. You're safe."

*"Lenore. I have you, my sweet."*

She blinked. He had called her Lenore, not Miss Kenward and sounded like her beloved Nathaniel. Good God, how hard of a knock to the head did she suffer? "I fell," she said.

He glided across the room and set his burden on the table by the lamp. "Yes. Fortunately, your quick reflexes saved you from worse injury. Had you struck the headstone, I doubt we'd be having this conversation now. You still managed to strike a tree root when you fell, and you've a cut on your scalp. If you will allow me, I'll tend to your wound."

"Unfortunately, my clumsiness nearly got me killed in the first place." She tried sitting up, only to pause as the room swam before her eyes. When her vision cleared, she stared into the Guardian's porcelain features.

"Peace, Miss Kenward. Let me help you." He bent and scooped her effortlessly into his arms.

Lenore placed her hands on his shoulders, feeling the flex of muscle as he shifted her weight. Unlike the hard black armor he wore when she first met him, he was garbed in the sober apparel of a vicar, minus the brimmed hat or white collar.

He set her gently down on one of the questionable chairs. Lenore waited a few tense moments for it to collapse under her and send her sprawling in a heap of skirts, petticoats and crinoline.

She offered the Guardian a small relieved smile when the chair held, wondering if his kind not only heard the whispers of the dead but the thoughts of the living when he told her in a wry voice "It's sturdier than it looks."

He seated himself across from her and waited patiently while she removed the pins from her hair. Lenore's cheeks burned hotter with every pin she laid on the table, and the silence in the room thickened. The last time she performed this small intimacy in front of another person, she had been standing before Nathaniel in his bedroom, dressed in nothing more than a blush.

The Guardian busied himself with filling the basin with water from the pitcher and wetting one of the towels, his gaze on his task. Yet Lenore felt the weight of his scrutiny, intense and admiring.

The thought made her pause. Did Guardians feel as other men felt? Know affection and passion for another? Or had Dr.

Harvel's gruesome experiments left them so transformed that they retained only the shades of emotion?

*"I have you my sweet."*

Her breath caught in her throat. Whatever horrors this Guardian had suffered under the mad doctor's hands, he still possessed the ability to show kindness and express sympathy. And feel desire. She was certain of it, knew it right down to her bones.

With the removal of the last pin, her hair fell around her shoulders, thick and straight. She'd have a devil of a time taming it back into a neat bun, especially with her scalp hurting the way it did.

The Guardian stared at her, pale features expressionless. "Lean forward, please. I'll tend that cut."

Lenore did as he instructed and bent toward him so he could better see the crown of her head. She closed her eyes at the light touch of his fingers parting her hair.

The tree root she struck had left a nasty gash, and she hissed when he applied the wet towel to the wound.

"Forgive me," he said. "I will do my best to be quick and careful."

"I know you will," she replied. "I trust you." Those gentle hands rested briefly on her head before continuing their work.

To ease the silence and take her mind off her stinging scalp while she stared into her lap, Lenore asked a question. "Did you see them? The resurrectionists? I thought they were like rats and only scurried out at night."

"They're either growing bolder or more desperate."

Her mind raced. Desperate for what? "I think they escaped."

"No, they didn't." The gloating satisfaction in the Guardian's voice was palpable.

Lenore recalled one of the thieves crowing triumphantly when she fell, its abrupt end followed by a brittle snap. She didn't ask her rescuer to expound on his statement.

He took up the fallen threads of conversation. "Who is your companion?"

Lenore glanced at the dog from the corner of her eye. It held sentry duty not far from the table, tail thumping when she met its gaze. "Some poor stray. It tried to protect me when the resurrectionists gave chase."

"Cleaned up and fed, she'd make a fine companion."

Lenore tried to straighten and regretted the action. "Ouch!"

The Guardian's voice held a touch of amusement. "Patience, Miss Kenward. I'm almost finished."

"The dog's a girl?" Not that Lenore had looked closely, but for some reason she had assumed her canine friend was male.

"It's hard to tell, as emaciated as she is, but I believe she's still a pup, not yet whelped a litter. If her paws are anything to judge by, she'll be a large bitch hound. A good hunter or guard dog."

This mysterious, deathless being possessed more layers than Lenore imagined, and similarities to someone else that made her reel. They at least explained why she was so drawn to him. "I once knew a man with a keen eye for a good dog. He would have liked this one."

The Guardian dropped the last bloody towel into the emptied basin. His hand on her shoulder prompted her to straighten. The stoic mask he wore hadn't altered, but something flickered across his face—a yearning. "Then I suspect he also had a keen eye for dauntless women." He gestured toward her forehead. "I've cleaned the gash and washed away the blood in your hair. I don't think you need stitches, but once you're home, I implore you to call out a physician. Let me see your hand."

She offered him her scraped hand, squeezing his fingers when he instructed. Her two fingers ached, but were far less painful now.

"Nothing broken or sprained," he announced. "That hand will be good as new by tomorrow."

Lenore reached up to touch the laceration on her scalp, halting when the Guardian shook his head. "Resist the temptation," he said. "And you may wish to forego both hair pins and bonnet for now, improper though it may be."

She shrugged. "I've often thought the rules of society to be both inconvenient and illogical at times."

A wide smile curved his pale lips. "Why does this not surprise me?"

He stood and retrieved her cloak from where it lay on the floor. "It's still damp, but I have no coal for a fire to dry it or warm you. Not even a kettle for tea. But I have wine if you wish to partake."

She accepted the cloak and his offer of wine. He gathered up pitcher, basin and towels and left her alone with the dog to disappear into the dark hallway from which he emerged earlier. No longer muzzy-headed and huddled in her damp cloak, Lenore abandoned her seat to travel a circuit around the room—a parlor once, from the look of the paneled wall on one side and the remnants of faded wall paper on the other three. Grime hid much of the decorative plaster work that edged the ceiling and filled the medallion from which a chandelier or gasolier once hung. The window, cloudy with dirt, looked onto a garden choked with dead weeds and surrounded by a low stone wall in tumbled disrepair.

The Guardian returned, this time bearing two goblets and a decanter of wine the red of faceted garnets. He placed them on the table. "Enjoying the view?" he asked as he poured the wine.

Lenore joined him at the table. "This was once a lovely home. With a little repair and a lot of scrubbing, not to mention a few more sticks of furniture, it could be that way again." She accepted the glass he passed to her. "Do you live here?"

He shrugged. "I take sanctuary in here from the elements when needed." Again that fleeting smile that so charmed her. "And minister to injured ladies."

There was nothing suggestive in his remark, yet Lenore felt her face heat yet again as if with fever. The Guardian's smile melted away, and she rushed to coax it back once more. "Then you are a very busy man," she said. "Consorting with the departed, chasing off resurrectionists, rescuing women with clumsy feet. When do you find the time to socialize?"

Her teasing worked its magic, and his smile returned. "I'm doing so now, Miss Kenward." He raised his glass in toast. "Not a rare vintage. A home brew made by the neighboring rector's wife. I hope you like pomegranate."

His features turned serious again, though not from awkwardness this time. "I don't want to compromise your reputation. I've left a note with the rector's housekeeper. Both he and his wife are currently out but will return soon. Due to my position and my appearance, I can't accompany you home, but I won't allow you to return alone, not with that head injury. Mr. and Mrs. Morris will see you safely home."

Lenore shook her head, prepared to protest, until the room's axis tilted a little. She stumbled and reached for the Guardian who steadied her with a hand at her waist. A scowl darkened his pale visage. "I must agree that yours is a proper plan," she said.

His hand, pressed against her ribs, no longer feeling chilly but scorching. She felt the heat all the way through layers of black wool, corset and shift. Neither wine nor wound made the blood surge through her body like this or made her so exquisitely aware of each breath this man took, each subtle slide of his coat against her skirts or the way the lamplight carved out the deep hollows beneath his cheekbones and made his long fall of hair shimmer in the gloom.

His fingers tightened before sliding to spread across her back and urge her closer. A glass fell to the floor. Hers or his, she didn't know, nor did she care. Propriety be damned. For five years, she had lived a half life, numb to all but the darkest emotions. Now, in the arms of a man no longer considered one, she came alive. A gift of Mercy or Fate, she had no intention of squandering it.

Corded muscle tightened under her touch as she slid a hand from his elbow to his shoulder. "We've shared conversation and now wine," she said softly. "And you've played both rescuer and nurse to me, yet still I don't know your name."

A smear of wine darkened his lower lip like blood on an Alba rose petal.

"Colin" he replied in equally subdued tones. "Colin Whitley."

She startled, and his hand fell away.

"What's wrong?" he demanded. "Are you dizzy? Do you need to lie down again?"

Lenore grasped his sleeve, refusing to allow the distance between them. Colin had been Nathaniel's middle name. She didn't believe in trickery of mediums or claims of reincarnation, but this was uncanny. "No, I am well." She reached for his hand and returned it to her waist. "Thanks to you." A lock of snowy hair caressed the back of her hand. "I am in your debt, Colin Whitley. Many times over."

Once more his fingers splayed along her ribs before sliding to her back, urging her closer. He was taller than Nathaniel had been, sinuous as an adder and seemed to coil around her as well as loom over her. "There is no debt, Lenore," he whispered.

One hand stroked a path up her arm, leaving hot trails on her skin through the black wool of her sleeve. It lingered at the slope of her shoulder before gliding over the stiff crape edging her frock's high collar.

She arched her neck, inviting him to climb higher and stroke the skin bared to his touch. They were pressed together from shoulder to hip, confirming for Lenore that these beings of stark light and shadow still experienced the same sensual pleasures as other men.

The hand on her back ascended her spine to bury itself gently in her hair. The one at her shoulder accepted her invitation to curve around her throat before settling under her jaw. The Guardian's black gaze with its white-sun pupils, held her captive. He lowered his head, breaking the spell. Lenore moaned softly as the tip of his nose glided down the bridge of hers.

"Come in to the garden, Maud," he recited in a voice guaranteed to lead Eve out of Eden. "For the black bat, night, has flown."

Her legs buckled at the suggestive verses, and she leaned hard against him.

"Come in to the garden, Maud. I am here at the gate alone." Cool lips, damp with wine, tickled a path along her jaw.

Her arms twined around his narrow waist so that her hands clutched the fabric covering his back and shoulder blades.

"And the woodbine spices are wafted abroad."

She tilted her head back, the ache behind her eyes nothing compared to the stunning pleasure of his mouth tracing a path over the arch of her throat to the hollow under her chin.

"And the musk of the rose is blown."

His tongue slid into her mouth in a kiss deep, and hot, and possessive. A groan vibrated low in his throat when Lenore returned his caress by stroking her tongue along his.

It was glorious, this passion that awakened her after years of a deathless sleep. She would love Nathaniel Gordon all her life, but Colin Whitley in her arms eased the pain of her loss and made her remember joy.

He tasted of pomegranates and smelled of cinnamon. His lips were firm, coaxing, teaching her how to kiss him back. Lenore learned quickly, instinctively understanding how the tip of her tongue sliding along the underside of his upper lip might make his knees buckle as hers did or make the hand in her hair fall lower to clutch her buttocks with kneading fingers.

If he rucked her skirts at this moment, she'd urge him on with her legs around his waist. His kiss, his touch, everything about him drew her, and she went willingly. He could take her on the dusty, unforgiving floor in the frigid parlor, and she'd cry out his name. The carnal images accompanying those thoughts made her squirm in his arms, and her hips bucked hard against the erection pressed into her skirts and crushed crinoline.

A knock at the front door dashed Lenore's fantasies. Colin broke their kiss with a gasp. His chest rose and fell like the bellows in a forge, and silvery color dusted his cheekbones. He pressed his forehead to hers.

"I would give all of eternity for one more hour with you," he said. A second knock. He kissed her forehead. "But today, it's not to be."

Still dazed by what transpired only seconds before, Lenore let him help her with her cloak. Her senses slowly returned to normal, along with an unwelcome surge of embarrassment.

Colin grasped her chin. "Don't," he ordered in a stern voice. "You'll not let those society rules you so abhor sully what's between us, Lenore."

She nodded and tucked a lock of her hair behind her ear with a trembling hand. "What do you want me to do?"

He kissed her briefly, as if unable to help himself, and pointed to a spot by the hearth. "Lie down and pretend to sleep. I'll tell them you were already unconscious when I found you and never awakened while I tended to you. They'll invent some tale to explain how you ended up here."

"You mean they'll lie. Not very clerical-like."

Colin smirked. "All in the service of guarding an innocent's virtue. They'll assure themselves Heaven will grant forgiveness for so noble a cause."

Lenore covered her mouth to stifle her laughter and lay down by the hearth. She watched through slitted eyes as he scooped up the fallen wine glass and decanter and once more disappeared into the corridor.

Low murmurs punctuated by horrified gasps echoed through the empty house. Lenore closed her eyes as footsteps drew closer and crossed the parlor to where she lay.

A woman's soft hand pressed against her cheek before parting her hair to check the gash on her scalp. "He did a fine job of cleaning the wound, but the poor dear is feverish. Look at her cheeks, Robert. Rosy as a Christmas stocking. We need to return her home as soon as possible."

The rector nearly stuttered in his outrage. "Vile body snatchers. Digging up children and attacking innocent women who come to grieve their parents. Highgate should have crawled with police once someone heard this girl scream. We can't just leave this solely to one man, no matter how exceptional he is. His role is to protect the dead; now he must also protect the living? Something more must be done!"

His wife was far more practical. "For now my dear, that something is to get this young lady home to her family." She lightly patted Lenore's cheek, encouraging her to wake up.

Lenore played the role of confused victim, fuzzy with her memory and relieved to see the rector and his wife. She let them help her stand and leaned a little on the rector's arm as he escorted her out of the abandoned house; it was the old rectory according to Mrs. Morris. A slender shadow, no more substantial than smoke, lingered at the edge of a stand of overgrown shrubbery and raised a hand in farewell.

She rode home between her escorts, assuring Mrs. Morris that she was on the mend and expected a full recovery within the week. The woman's constant pressing of her cold hand on her cheek tested Lenore's patience, but she only smiled and thanked her for her help. These were kind, well-meaning people, and she was grateful for their care. She only wished the Guardian had not solicited their aid quite so soon.

To her credit, Jane Kenward didn't fly into hysterics when the Morrises explained events at the cemetery. She questioned Lenore as to how she felt, summoned a physician and packed her daughter off to bed to wait. The rector and his wife stayed for tea, served by a rattled Mrs. Harp who took every spare moment to poke her head into Lenore's room and inquire after her health.

The doctor examined her scalp, pronounced the wound well-cleaned and prescribed steps for preventing infection. He also left a bottle of dark liquid by her bedside. "For your fever," he said. "Two drops in a cup of tepid tea, once in the morning and once before bed time."

Suspicious of whatever snake oil lurked in the smoked glass bottle, Lenore smiled her thanks and promised herself she'd dump the contents down the privy the first chance she had.

By the time the house quieted for the night, she was both exhausted and restless. Her head ached, and her body hummed with need. She closed her eyes and touched her lips, still tingling from the memory of the Guardian's kiss and the pale caress that had ignited the fire burning inside her.

She closed her eyes, praying for sleep. Nathaniel's face rose before her mind's eye, Colin's superimposed over it. Their features melded in a strange patchwork amalgamation, two beings attempting to merge as one.

Lenore opened her eyes. Moonlight spilled through the room, unblocked by the drapes neither she nor Constance remembered to close. The silvery light illuminated her bedside table and the books she'd left there. Her heart tripped a beat at the sight of her book of verse—Nathaniel's gift to her.

The Guardian had recited Tennyson while he kissed her.

## Chapter Eight

NATHANIEL FOLLOWED HIS MOST CURRENT nighttime visitor to Highgate past the towering obelisks flanking Egyptian Avenue and on to the Circle of Lebanon. Lenore's stray mongrel padded silently beside him, ears forward and alert.

This intruder moved like a cat: silent and fleet with hardly a footprint to mark their passing. Nathaniel's only clues to their presence were a sixth sense of recognition and the sweet scents of tobacco, licorice and honey.

He tracked his quarry to the steps leading to the inner circle of crypts. A figure sat casually on the bottom step, smoking a cheroot. The thin cigar's burning tip glowed cherry-red in the darkness. A pair of eyes, black as the Chislehurst caves, with white pinpoint pupils, regarded him through a haze of smoke.

Whomever Nathaniel expected to find here, it wasn't another Guardian, especially not this one. He gave a short bow. "I think you've wondered into the wrong bone yard, my lord. Kensal Green is a leisurely stroll south of Highgate." He cocked his head. "Or are you visiting in hopes of a hunt?"

His brethren drew deeply on the cheroot, inhaling smoke and exhaling revenants that swirled and silently beseeched before fading into oblivion. His voice was raspy and held a thread of amusement. "Kensal Green swarms with gardeners at all hours. Tripping over one isn't nearly as entertaining as confronting a body snatcher, though I begin to wonder which of the two is more ubiquitous in our cemeteries these days." He gained his feet in one smooth motion and joined Nathaniel at the top of the steps.

Nathaniel clasped the other's offered arm. "Good to see you, Gideon."

Like Nathaniel, Gideon possessed the physical attributes of all Guardians: long, snowy hair and equally white skin, spectral eyes and the ability to protect his body in a hard shell of armor by simply willing its presence. He was the first of the Guardians and the deliverer of the other six from enslavement to a madman who fancied himself a god.

Gideon returned the welcoming clasp. "How are you, Nathaniel?" He offered the cheroot.

Nathaniel declined. "I thought you abandoned that vice."

Gideon shrugged, and with a graceful sleight of hand, made the cheroot disappear. "Only in the house. I don't wish to incur my housekeeper's wrath."

Nathaniel recalled a tall, elegant woman with hair the color of summer wheat, smiling eyes and soothing hands. Newly rescued by Gideon, and delirious with pain from the *gehenna* flowing through his resurrected body, he'd thought Rachel Wakefield an angel at first as she bathed his face and crooned soft assurances to him. "How is Mrs. Wakefield?"

"Quite well I suppose. She's engaged to be married." Gideon's voice held a bitter edge, even while his expression remained studiedly bland.

He and Gideon shared a warped and twisted history. They were the alpha and omega in an exclusive club of a select, unfortunate few. They were not, however, close friends, and Nathaniel sensed the other's reluctance to speak more of the woman who managed his household and aided him in rescuing the other Guardians. "Please offer her my regards and my congratulations," he said.

Gideon nodded and eyed Nathaniel's companion who eyed him back from behind her master's legs. "Who is this?"

Nathaniel sighed. "It seems I've been adopted," he said. No matter how often he turned the young hound over to Mrs. Morris for bathing, feeding, and coddling, the dog always returned to the abandoned rectory. Even Mrs. Morris's tempting offers of bowls of food hadn't lured her away, and the rector's wife finally gave in, leaving the bowl with Nathaniel.

His visitor's brief smile fled almost as soon as it appeared. "A good protector if trained right, and useful these days. Word's reached me that resurrectionists attacked a woman here in Highgate yesterday morning."

The admission surprised Nathaniel. He often employed the Morris couple to deliver messages for him. None had yet been dispatched to Gideon. "Word travels fast," he said dryly. "I was intending to send you a message to request a meeting."

Gideon chuckled. "You'll learn over time that ghosts are the worst sort of gossip-mongers. Not much else to do when you're trapped on the earthly plane except note the comings and goings of the living." He sobered. "How is the young lady in question? Or have you heard anything?"

The scent of lemon still clung to his fingers from the letter Lenore had sent to Mrs. Morris, assuring her of her improving health and thanking her and her husband for their assistance. The rector's wife had thoughtfully brought the letter to him just this morning so he might read it for himself. Its citrusy smell teased his nostrils when he unfolded the missive and silently read the words written in Lenore's precise hand. He resisted the temptation to raise the letter to his nose and inhale, halted only by Mrs. Morris's presence and her gaze on him as he read.

"According to the rector's wife, she is recovering and in good spirits."

He wished he could send a letter in return. What would he say?

*I no longer sleep, but I still dream. You consume my thoughts, Lenore, and soothe my spirit.*

He would write more, so much more. Wax rhapsodic over the feel of her in his arms, the taste of her in his mouth...

Nathaniel shook away the recollections shredding his focus and returned his attention to Gideon who watched him with a raised eyebrow. "Did your gossiping specters tell you what she caught the thieves doing?"

Gideon shrugged. "The usual, though doing so in the middle of the day is out of the ordinary. I assumed Tepes has raised his bounty. First thief with the prize takes the purse."

"She caught them digging up a child's grave."

He'd told Lenore the elements didn't bother him, though he felt their effect—the wetness of rain, the heat of the sun. And right now, the cold buffeting his skin lowered from frigid English winter to frozen Arctic tundra.

Gideon's features had thinned to a skull's mask, and his eyes narrowed to abyssal slits. "When I find the good doctor—and I will find him—I intend to allow him to fully embrace the history behind the name Tepes and nail his hat to his head," he vowed in flinty tones.

There were no witnesses to the first Guardian's execution of his creator, not even the other Guardians. Nathaniel suspected that whether swift or slow, Dr. Harvel's death had been brutal and Gideon without mercy. He would show none to Tepes either.

The two men strode to the Lebanon Circle to stand beneath the ancient cypress tree. Nathaniel scanned the acres of tombstones, searching for the tell-tale flicker of dim lamplight or the metallic clink of grave-digging tools. Only the occasional wandering spirit roamed the cemetery. "Why does Tepes want dead children?"

The thought made him ill. Nathaniel held little affection for men of science. Admiration, yes. Guild mages and their ilk manipulated the world's mysteries, scientists its wonders. But the quest for knowledge sometimes bred madness, and the men who lost their humanity were more often those who chased wonder and embraced brutality.

Gideon clasped his hands behind his back and paced. "Rumor has it he's experimenting with an elixir, something that will turn those shambling dead he likes to puppeteer into something more than corpse automatons."

A waning moon spilled feeble light onto the patch of dead grass under the Lebanon tree. Nathaniel's veins throbbed under his skin. "*Gehenna*," he said softly. "He's trying to remake *gehenna*."

Gideon nodded. "Whatever concoction he's brewed right now is probably expensive and difficult to reproduce for experimentation. A smaller body needs a smaller dosage."

"My God."

"It was just a matter of time." Gideon changed directions to wear a different path into the grass. "I destroyed all of Harvel's notes. Everything down to the grocer's bills he stashed in an herbal cabinet. If Tepes is making liquid hell, he's doing so on his own from the ground up."

Nathaniel's heart pumped his own *gehenna* blood through his body at an ever quickening pace. "If he manages to make a Guardian of his own..."

Gideon's hollow laughter lacked any mirth. "He won't. Harvel's mistake was in keeping our minds, and therefore our free will, intact. He paid the price. Tepes won't take that risk. Whatever he tries to animate will be nothing like us." Brittle grass crackled under his feet. "As much as I dislike drawing the Mage Guild's attention to us, we'll need their help. We're seven Guardians with acres of graves to watch over at all times. Tepes has significantly raised his bounty if resurrectionists are willing to exhume a body before the rest of London has sat down for dinner. The cemeteries will swarm with the bastards. A handful of second-tier mages working with each Guardian can provide enough oversight to prevent complete chaos."

"I've already contacted the Mage Guild. Five second-tiers arrive here at dawn next Tuesday." Nathaniel might have laughed at Gideon's stunned look if things weren't so grim. "I didn't know about the doctor's latest machinations. My request for help stems from a personal matter. I leave for Gibraltar and will return in a fortnight. I intended to include that news in my message to you."

The Morrises had been an invaluable help to him the previous day, delivering Lenore safely to her home in Camberwell and a message from him to the Guild House in the City of London.

Gideon's eyebrows rose. "Taking a holiday?"

He wished such were the case. In his previous life, he often dreamed of whisking Lenore off to places beyond gray London. Her traveler's soul would have gloried in such sights as the blue Mediterranean and sun-kissed Greek isles or the lavish gardens of the Alcazar de los Reyes in Cordoba.

"Nothing so delightful," he replied. "I will be on an airship once more."

Gideon turned a gimlet stare on him. "Not the *Pollux*?" He scowled. "Why would you put yourself through such an ordeal?"

In the early days of Nathaniel's rehabilitation, memories of his life—and his death—threatened to overwhelm his fragile sanity. Spilling them out in long, rambling screeds to Gideon had kept him anchored, able to merge each one back into its place without shattering his mind. The recollections of his last battle on the *Pollux* still sent tremors through him.

"Not the *Pollux*," he said. "A new ship. The *Terebellum*. A harmless training mission for her new crew. I will be a...guest on board."

Gideon patted his chest as if a pocket hid somewhere behind his armor. "I need another cheroot." He gave up on the pocket and put Nathaniel back in his sights. "You've answered my first question but not the second. Why?"

*"I should make a wish. Two wishes. That you come back to me so I can tell you...tell you yes instead of no."*

Those words had wrought more life inside him than all the voltage Harvel once slammed into the cold body that now housed

Nathaniel's soul and memories. They revived a hope he thought long dead, offering a second chance—once improbable, then impossible, and now within reach—to reclaim Lenore as his. He'd sail a skiff to Hell if necessary.

"To assure another's safety," he said.

Gideon's stygian gaze intensified. "The inventor's daughter will be on that airship."

Nathaniel nodded. "She will."

"Does she know yet who you are?"

"No."

"It's probably best she remain ignorant of your identity."

Gideon gave him a puzzled look. "I am curious as to how you managed to get yourself invited aboard an airship. Guardians are usually only welcomed at burials, and only if they stay out of sight."

Had it been any other captain besides Nettie, such a miracle would never have occurred. Even now, there was a chance she'd change her mind. Nathaniel had already figured out a way to stow aboard if necessary. "I can be very charming when I put my mind to it."

Gideon snorted. "Obviously." He held out his hand to Nathaniel who shook it. "When you return, contact me. I will call a gathering of all Guardians. We'll meet with the Guild Counsel to discuss what's to be done about the rats defiling the cemeteries."

Nathaniel noticed Gideon made no mention of Tepes. The good doctor's fate was sealed regardless of whatever the Guild decided. The only thing Gideon might still have yet to determine was which type of nail he'd choose—French horse or ox shoe.

He bowed once more, this time in farewell. Gideon paused before descending the stairs to the circle vaults and catacombs. Moonlight painted a silver nimbus on his hair. "Nathaniel, Spain isn't the Redan, but any flight is dangerous as you well know." His pupils were almost incandescent in the darkness. "How often can you ride the pale horse and fall? You may not rise again."

Nathaniel had no answer for him. "Farewell, friend. Expect my message upon my return."

The other nodded and was soon embraced by the shadows that always welcomed the Guardians.

Nathaniel returned to the tree and the dog whose eyes gleamed as brightly as Gideon's had. The pup's tail thumped the ground. She pressed against his hip when he sat at the tree's base, her head between her paws. She cast an odd shadow across the grass—that of a great hulking mass with a ridged back and muscular shoulders, a beast of Herculean proportions that protected the dead alongside her master.

A thought tickled Nathaniel's fancy. She still had no name. He grinned and stroked two fingers down the dog's head. "Spot," he said. "I think I'll call you Spot."

## Chapter Nine

LENORE DECIDED THAT DESPITE being a few thousand feet in the air, tasks for an airship cabin boy were very much like those of a housemaid on terra firma—except for the four hour watches of course. Her lips twitched at the idea of Jane handing Mrs. Harp a set of field glasses with instructions to keep a lookout for apple thieves in the back garden at three in the morning.

She entered the *Terebellum's* compact galley and spotted the cook in his usual place before the stove. No scent of wood, coal or gas filled the air in this kitchen. Airship stoves and ovens were fueled by *empyrean*, that almost mystical essence discovered by the British Mage Guild. *Empyrean* gave rise to the age of dirigibles and consolidated the Guild's power and influence.

The galley was situated behind the control room and next to the telegraph room, with a breathtaking view of the eastern horizon from its starboard side windows. The sun, a blaze of volcanic orange began its steady climb in a sky still dotted with fading stars.

"Good morning, Mr. Smith." She tucked herself into a corner to keep out of the way while the cook busied himself at the burners.

He nodded. "Likewise, miss. And how is the captain this morning?" He poured a dark stream of liquid into a vacuum flask. The smell of hot coffee filled the air.

Lenore inhaled an appreciative breath. "Not exactly in the sunniest of dispositions. I hope you brewed the coffee strong." Lenore had quickly learned why several of her new crewmates had given her pitying looks and good luck wishes once they found out one of her many tasks aboard the ship included bringing "Dragon" Widderschynnes her morning coffee.

Mr. Smith closed the flask and snapped a cup on top. "Strong is the only way to brew it, miss. Otherwise, it's not fit for drinking." He handed her the flask. "Best step lively. You've learned by now, the longer her Nibs has to wait, the more dangerous it gets."

"Indeed it does, Mr. Smith." Lenore backed out of the galley. "I'll return as soon as possible to help Clark serve breakfast."

The *Terebellum's* keel corridor bore a similar design to the *Pollux,* except bigger and more modern. Nettie's temporary quarters were only a short jaunt down the gang walk from the control and radio rooms. Lenore exchanged morning greetings with crewmen changing watch or on their way to the crew mess for breakfast.

She knocked briefly on the captain's door, easing it open at Nettie's abrupt "Enter."

"I have your coffee, Captain. Mr. Smith promised..." The rest of her sentence faded when she caught sight of Nettie's visitor. Black garb and white hair. As with every other time she saw the Highgate Guardian on the *Terebellum*, her heartbeat doubled. Thank God, she wore her corset looser than usual, or she'd probably faint from lack of breath. "Forgive my interruption," she said. "Good morning, Mr. Whitley." Lenore hoped the wide smile curving her mouth didn't look as foolish as it felt.

He bowed, his features more guarded but his voice as warm as his hand had been on her waist when he kissed her in the abandoned rectory. "Always a pleasure, Miss Kenward." The way he uttered the salutation heated Lenore's cheeks and made Nettie's eyebrows climb.

She passed the flask to Nettie without taking her eyes off Whitley. "My apologies. I didn't know you'd have a visitor. I only brought one cup. I can bring another."

"No apology necessary," he said. "I was just leaving." He glanced at Nettie who watched them both with a wry gaze. "If I see anything else, I will inform you."

She toasted him with her flask. "I'll pass that bit on to the gunners."

Lenore had the very strong sense she had walked in on a particularly important discussion.

He bowed and doffed his imaginary hat. "Captain. Miss Kenward." The action guaranteed to startle Lenore every time she saw him do it. He looked nothing like her Nathaniel, yet a great many of his behaviors and speech patterns reminded her of him.

Both women stared at the door after he left. Lenore jumped when Nettie snapped her fingers. "Ah damn! Lenore, catch him. I forgot to tell him to meet me after supper for a report review."

Lenore saluted. "Aye, Captain."

Why Nettie had to discuss such things with the Guardian of Highgate—or why he was even on this ship in the first place—remained a puzzle, but Lenore dared not ask. On this ship, social class didn't matter the way rank did. Here, Nettie was Queen and Lenore a minion. To ask such questions broke a rigid protocol.

She caught up with him just as he climbed the ladder from the keel corridor to the hull. "Mr. Whitley, wait!"

He halted to peer down at her before descending the ladder back to the keel deck. Nettie had introduced him to the crew as an "official observer" on their flight. She didn't elaborate beyond that short statement, and no one asked the question they all thought: why was a bone keeper aboard an airship?

Lenore's shock at first seeing him on the *Terebellum* had given way to excitement. The memory of his kiss still made her lips throb. She had lost count of the many times she replayed those moments in the empty rectory, held close in his arms as he made love to her first with verse and then with his mouth.

Despite the airship's close quarters, she rarely saw him. Her numerous tasks as cabin boy kept her busy from the second she rose to the second her head hit the pillow on her bed. Whatever the Guardian observed, he did so in near invisibility. Rumors ran rife about him in the crew quarters, conjectures over why he was aboard this ship and if restless spirits followed wherever he walked, whispering forgotten tragedies and bitter deaths in his ears.

For now, he observed her. Closely. She shivered, not from the pervasive cold, but from the pleasure of his scrutiny. "Nettie..." She paused and started again. "Captain Widderschynnes asked that I deliver a message. She wishes to meet with you at three bells concerning a report review."

He narrowed the space between them. The harsh overhead lights, so unflattering to everyone else, sharpened the contrast between the white and black of his visage. Lenore indulged in the fanciful notion that he looked like a revenant caught under a searchlight. The smile he held back in Nettie's quarters blossomed across his lips. "How are you, Lenore? Or am I allowed the liberty of such address?"

She liked his face—ethereal, with a touch of melancholy. "It seems ludicrous that we use our surnames in private, considering my questionable and improper behavior with you last week."

"I prefer the term iconoclastic over improper."

Lenore chortled, delighted at his repartee. "You're very charming," she said. Charming, fascinating, bewitching.

Two pale fingers traced the air at the side of her upturned face. "And you are extraordinarily beautiful," he replied.

She couldn't help it; she leaned into him just as she'd done in the rectory. "If you recite Tennyson, I shall be lost," she said softly.

A low sound rumbled in his throat. His hand lingered at her neck, fingertips teasing the exposed skin above her coat collar. "If you kiss me, I will be made whole."

He was so close, so very close. Her body ached for him while her mind repeated words in the cadence of prayer. *One kiss, just one. I'll capture lightning for you for just one.* She swayed toward him.

They jumped apart at the sound of a door opening and closing in the direction of the control room. Lenore gasped, amazed at how fast the Guardian moved. One moment he stood so near, his soft hair tickling her cheek when he bent to kiss her. Now he perched on the ladder he climbed earlier. He held out hand, beckoning. "Come with me," he whispered.

She sighed. "I can't. I'm helping the steward deliver breakfast to the crew in the mess. I'm already late." She backed away before the temptation to grasp his hand and climb the ladder overcame her.

His shoulders slumped in obvious disappointment. "Are you free this evening?"

Her task list was long and didn't end after supper, especially this night. "I'm standing the lookout watch tonight."

Footsteps sounded on the metal gangplank, coming closer. Lenore peered down the narrow corridor but saw nothing yet. When she looked back, Colin had disappeared off the ladder. Only a pair of white pinpoint stars above her hinted at where he stood in the clot of shadows gathered beneath a girder. "Another night perhaps," he said in his sepulchral voice.

Lenore held up a hand. "Wait!" She lowered her voice. "I have last dog watch, eight bells. Join me. Please."

The two bright stars faded along with his voice. "Until eight bells then. My Lenore."

She spent the remainder of the day in a fog, absurdly eager for the late-hour watch and the brutal cold that came from standing at an open gondola window two thousand feet in the air with ice frosting the glass. In the interim, she delivered messages for Nettie, made notes in the official log book, inventoried medicines and surgical instruments in the surgery compartment, ironed sheets for the crew bedding and helped the steward deliver meals to the crews' quarters from the kitchen. Lenore hoped that by the end of the trip, she might get a chance to visit one of the engine gondolas to see the newly modified engines at work.

She didn't see her Guardian until she'd taken up her post at the watch, bundled against the freezing temperatures, field glasses clutched in her stiff fingers. The land below was a wide shadow of valleys and hills, broken periodically by clusters of yellow lights—towns and villages gleaming in the darkness like fireflies in summer. In the distance, the jagged line of the Alps marched across the horizon, dark silhouettes against a night sky layered in shades from velvety indigo to mourning black.

They were alone up here, no other beacon light flashing amongst the stars to indicate another ship. "I wish you could see this, Papa," she said. "It's magnificent."

The door to her watch post slid open, and an umbra shape slipped in on silent feet. Unlike her, the Guardian wore his usual garb, without coat or scarf or gloves. He held a metal flask that gleamed dully in the low light of an *empyrean* torch. His hair fluttered in the draft swirling through the window until it lifted away from his face, a white banner offering surrender.

He passed the flask to her. "Tea," he said. "Still hot. Courtesy of the boatswain's mate, though she doesn't know it." He winked.

Lenore placed the field glasses on the ledge in front of her to wrap her hands around the flask. "Mrs. Markham, bless her. And you for bringing it to me. It's chilly tonight."

He leaned casually against the gondola frame, pale mouth curved in amusement. "That's understating it a bit, don't you think?"

Content to simply hold the flask and let the hot tea inside thaw her fingers, Lenore shivered. "A little." She envied his imperviousness to the temperature. "No tea for yourself?"

"I'm more partial to a good brandy on a cold night."

She frowned. Another small detail that reminded her of Nathaniel. *Stop it, Lenore. Many men prefer brandy over tea. You're seeing a ghost in the guise of a bone keeper.* A beautiful bone keeper with a sorcerer's touch but not Nathaniel.

"Such burdensome thoughts. What are you thinking, Lenore?" He uttered her name with a priest's reverence for the sacred.

"You're not bothered by cold or rain. Do you hunger or thirst?"

He straightened away from the window. A bright moon plated one half of his body in silver light. "For food or water, no, though I can eat and drink if I wish. But I'm like any other man regarding certain things. I crave friendship, comrades..." He reached out to tug the edge of her scarf closer to her cheek. "Affection." His voice was deep, soft, as was the half smile he offered her. "The dearly departed who speak tend to be a little repetitive, with limited topics of conversation."

The scarf muffled Lenore's *tut*. "Trust me when I say the living can be just as afflicted by such character weakness. That or everyone who visits my aunt's drawing room hasn't yet realized they're actually dead."

His laughter warmed her far better than any coat. "And there you are, trapped in the drawing room with the walking dead until all the tea is gone."

What a delight it was to laugh and tease with this man. Not since Nathaniel's courtship of her had she been so enthralled.

"I shouldn't be so harsh," she admitted. "I'm certain the boredom was mutual. Many of them dreaded engaging me in conversation, terrified I'd rhapsodize over the efficiency of a Daimler engine design or how Sir Hugh Carver once again improved the impact shields on the ships. I, however, will restrain myself from falling into that trap tonight. I've no wish to lose my intrepid companion who can withstand the cold but possibly not the ennui of my company."

Colin's expression sobered. His fingers glided over her gloved hand where it rested on the ledge by the field glasses. "You have nothing to fear on that score, Lenore. Trust me."

She laced her fingers with his, regretting the barrier of her glove between his skin and hers. Once more they stood only inches apart, the space between almost shimmering with tension. Lenore met his gaze, a Shakespearean dichotomy of dark and bright.

"Is a post on an airship what you thought it might be?" He spoke in tones reserved for lovers, as if the innocuous question was meant to be asked while he nuzzled her breasts or drew invisible murals on her bare belly with his fingertips.

He held her mesmerized. Only a blast of icy wind through the window cleared her head. She blinked but didn't let go of his hand. "Yes and no," she said, waving her free arm to indicate the wide sky. "This. This is beyond the ability of the most eloquent poet to adequately describe. Great men dreamed through the ages to fly like birds, and here we are above the world, counting falling stars."

She gave a rueful shrug then. "Mostly, it's like home. There's tea to be made and supper to cook, laundry to wash, accounts to settle and beds to tuck in." She winked at Colin. "The adventurous life of a cabin boy. Or girl if that better suits your sensibilities."

"It's how many captains started and rose through the ranks. You learn the ship's language and her song until she becomes more familiar than the mother who bore you."

There it is, she thought. A hint of the life before his transformation. "You speak as if this isn't your first time on a ship."

A wistful expression played across his elegant face. He tapped his chest. "Before I became this, I served aboard an airship."

His admission didn't surprise her. For a "guest" and observer, he moved with surprising ease and familiarity aboard the *Terebellum*, as if sailing high above the earth were an everyday thing. She still gazed at her surroundings in open-mouthed wonder, unspoiled by the drudgery of everyday chores. "No wonder you seemed so at ease and unafraid of great heights or the *Terebellum's* movements," she said.

"Some things you don't forget."

She wanted to ask him more, but a flash of light caught her attention. She grabbed the field glasses and peered through the eyepieces. She passed the glasses to Colin and pointed to the light. "There. Do you see her?"

He looked through the glasses before returning them to her. "If I'm not mistaken, that's the *Danika*, a Russian skyrunner.

Likely on her way to the Redan." He slipped behind her and tucked her gently against his body. "Now this," he said, "is resoundingly improper."

"I should strike you in outrage," she agreed in a mild voice and leaned back against his tall frame. No coat or cloak, and still he radiated a delicious heat that seeped through her woolens to warm her from the inside out.

"And I should beg your pardon and release you," he replied, his arm sliding around her waist until she stood snug in his embrace.

"We won't do any of those things, will we?"

"I certainly hope not," he whispered against her temple.

Were she not at her post, she'd turn in his arms and bring his head down to hers for a kiss.

They watched the *Danika* for several moments, Lenore noting her flight pattern and that it vectored safely away from the *Terebellum*. Once more the sky curved empty around them except for the moon and stars and those they watched as well.

Were it up to Lenore, they'd stay like this for hours, silent, unmoving, content to relish each other's nearness. Colin's warmth, however, worked better than a sleeping tonic, and she fought off a warning yawn.

Colin's blunt inquiry snapped her wide awake. "Why aren't you married, Lenore?"

Had he pushed her head out the window for a bracing blast of icy wind, she doubted it would have worked any better at obliterating her somnolence. Lenore stood silent in his arms for a moment, remembering the surprise visit from a dignified marchioness with a kind face and sad eyes. The tea had been bitter that day, almost as bitter as the choice presented to her.

"You need not answer if you wish." He was strong and lithe against her back, a literal pillar of strength.

"I don't mind," she said. "I was almost married. Well, almost engaged." A shooting star arced across the sky before disappearing into the horizon. "Unbeknownst to me, the man who courted me was the youngest son of a marquess, a lord. Because there was already an heir to the title and another brother in line after the heir, his family tolerated his 'eccentricities'."

As aware as she was of his every touch and breath, Lenore didn't miss the slow stiffening in Colin's body as she spoke. "Like you, he served aboard an airship. The *Pollux* to be exact. He loved it, embraced it, risked scandal over it.

"You understood his passion."

She nodded. "I did. I think we're born with a love for a particular thing that calls to our souls. To ignore it reaps unhappiness."

"What happened?"

Five years on, and it still hurt to recall that meeting and the events which followed. "I didn't know it at the time, but my almost-fiancé had lost both brothers to cholera in the space of a week. He became the heir to the marquisate. His duty was to the estate and providing the next generation of heirs to succeed him."

"And you were an inventor's daughter." Colin's voice sounded clipped and cool, even as his hand stroked a comforting rhythm along her ribs.

Lenore swallowed, willing down the clot of tears trapped in her throat. "Indeed. A mésalliance not to be borne. Once they discovered his intention to propose, his mother paid me a visit. She presented a sound argument. Accept his offer and consign myself and any offspring we produced to the status of outcast." She sighed. "I would have suffered it gladly. I have no interest in or fondness for the nobility. My children, however, and their children as well would be burdened by our selfishness, ostracized from Society the moment they were born."

"You refused him when he asked."

She wondered at the odd flatness in Colin's tone. "I did and will regret it all my life. We parted on bad terms. He was killed while fighting at the Redan."

Colin's arms tightened around her, his embrace both comforting and strangely desperate, as if he sought solace in her nearness as much she found it in his. They held each other for a long time, Lenore lost to her memories.

Her creeping melancholy threatened to cast a pall over this lovely but oh-so-brief time with the Guardian, and she resolutely shook it. It was best to speak of other things, lighter things.

"I was at first disappointed that my inaugural voyage would be on a ship other than the *Pollux*," she said. "But I think now it was for the best. Adjusting to my role aboard ship is much easier when it's a peaceful journey on a cargo lifter. I'm not certain how well I'd do on a skyrunner in the midst of battle."

Colin pressed his cheek to the side of her head. "Every crewman feels that way on their first flight," he whispered near her ear. "I think you'd learn quickly enough to hold your own if put to the test."

Either Fate played some great joke on her or had chosen to bestow some great beneficence. Colin Whitley might look like a ghost himself, tethered to this earthly realm by the most gossamer of threads, but to her, he was almost too good to be true. He heard the dead speak and protected their remains by means both mysterious and sometimes violent. People ran from the sight of him, even if dogs didn't, proving what she'd always thought—man's four-legged companion was often a lot more insightful regarding another's character than its master.

That last thought made her recall the intrepid little dog who'd tried to rescue her from the resurrectionists. "What happened to the hound who kept me company when I was unconscious?"

Colin exhaled a slow breath. "She's currently in the care of the rector's wife who spoils her relentlessly. She, however, fancies herself my dog."

The news lightened Lenore's heart. "And why wouldn't she? I imagine you make a wonderful master." No doubt, he'd make an equally fine spouse. The thought startled her almost as much as the peal of the bells that signaled the end of her watch.

She did turn then, still held in the cove of Colin's arms. "My watch is over," she said and wondered if any watchman ever regretted departing his post as much as she did.

The Guardian brushed his lips across hers in a tantalizing hint of a kiss. "I must go before your relief arrives."

She traced the arch of his eyebrows with her finger. "Thank you for your kindness in keeping me company." One eyebrow twitched under her touch.

"It wasn't kindness, Lenore," he said in that low, sensual voice. "It was selfishness, and temptation, and need." He kissed her a second time with the sweep of his tongue across hers before setting her from him.

Lenore's breath streamed from her nose and mouth in small clouds. For the first time since she'd boarded the *Terebellum*, she wanted to shed her layers of clothing and cool off her overheated skin. "I don't know why you're on this ship," she told him, "but I'm glad of it. So very glad you're here with me."

He gazed at her in a way that made her heart pound as hard as his kiss did. "I am always with you, Lenore." A pause. "Good night."

He was gone before she had a chance to raise her hand in farewell, a wraith embracing the darkness beyond the door.

"Good night," she whispered to the empty room.

## Chapter Ten

THE RETURN JOURNEY FROM GIBRALTAR to London was proving as uneventful as Nathaniel hoped. The *Terebellum* was a fine ship and so far hadn't suffered a single problem. He was both relieved and suspicious. Some might accuse him of an unnecessary paranoia, however, since the woman he loved was currently aboard, he'd argue for his caution. Nothing ever remained problem-free, and judging by the look on his former captain's face as she handed him a snifter of brandy, she was about to prove him right.

They stood together at a pair of windows, staring down at the Portuguese coast. The city of Lisbon perched on the Atlantic, its imposing Sao Jorge Castle overlooking a cluster of white buildings with red tile roofs that marched down the hillside to the beach and gleamed under a cold winter sun.

Nettie swirled the brandy in its snifter, her expression grim. "I'm telling you first before I gather the crew for the announcement. We're sailing to the Redan."

His stomach wouldn't have lurched any harder if she'd cocked back her arm and gut-punched him. Nathaniel stared, silently willing her to correct her statement. He surprised himself with the calm in his voice. "Why?"

"I received a cable from Fleet command. The fighting has been fierce. Two ships lost to the horrifics, four others crippled with a number dead and injured crew on board." She abused the brandy, tossing it back as if it were gin. "The *Terebellum*, the *Bellatrix* and the *Gatria* are to alter course and offer assistance in both ballistics and transport."

Nathaniel took a bracing swallow of his own, welcoming the burn of alcohol down his throat. The only sounds in the captain's quarters were Nettie's soft breathing and the constant background whir of the *Terebellum's* propellers. Inside his head, the clamor was deafening with the wrench and squeal of broken girders, the screams of the dying, the gunshot snap of rivets popping out of steel.

*The shuddering ship.*

He closed his eyes to clear the images and opened them again to Nettie's knowing, pitying gaze.

"The *Terebellum* isn't built as a skyrunner," he said.

She lowered her chin and gave him a don't-play-stupid-with-me-lad look. "I think we both know she isn't just a cargo lifter either. I've seen you inspecting her. Her middle gun deck alone has enough cannon and gun batteries on her to make the *Pollux*'s arsenal look like a child's toy chest. Her engines can put out three times the horsepower for speed if pushed, and her shield is powerful enough to withstand a full broadside from the biggest horrific."

Nathaniel shivered. He doubted anyone living had yet encountered the biggest horrific lurking in the dimensional rift. "That's true, but her principal firepower is in that keel-mounted weapons platform. Completely unsuitable for fighting in the Redan. She's a nautilus killer, Captain. Her guns are meant to blow holes into submarines and sea pirates. The rail ties can move the platform out a distance, but without a port or starboard rotation, the guns can't target anything directly above the ship."

"Jonas Tibbs is a first-rate helmsman," she said. "I'd have poached him off the *Serpentis* years ago if Captain Narada hadn't threatened to put a canon ball up my arse if I tried it. God rest his poxy soul." She pinned Nathaniel in place with a sharp gaze. "A good helmsman paired with a good gunner can make the clumsiest ship do cartwheels on a high wire and hit a fly at a hundred paces."

Nathaniel returned the look she'd given him earlier. "That is either the most spectacular exaggeration I've ever heard, or the most ridiculous. I've not yet decided which."

She shrugged and downed the rest of her brandy before setting it on the nearby table with thump. "It doesn't matter. What I want to know, lad, is if I need you to shoot at something, will you do it? *Can* you do it?"

His stomach jerked taut against his backbone, leaving him queasy. *The shuddering ship.*

The Nathaniel Gordon of five years ago had earned a reputation within the airship fleet as a gunner both accurate and precise with his shots. The Nathaniel Gordon of now hadn't fired so much as a slingshot in five years. For all he knew, he couldn't hit the back end of a coster's cart.

"You already have a senior gunner aboard with three juniors under his command. You don't need a second senior."

"Who says I have to ration gunners? Why limit myself to one senior when I have two on board?" She raised a hand to halt his reply. "I don't need you telling me how rank protocol works. I've been doing this a lot longer than you have, mate. Owens is a capable gunner with a good eye, but you have more experience in a turret, not to mention fighting at the Redan."

That Nathaniel would agree was a foregone conclusion. Short of assassinating Lenore for her, which was a ludicrous idea, he'd do anything Nettie asked of him. "I'm rusty," he said. "I might miss."

Her disbelieving snort made his lips twitch. "They're horrifics, Nathaniel, not hummingbirds."

The reminder of the peril they'd face when they reached the Redan killed what little humor Nettie's sarcasm had kindled inside him. "Lenore..."

"Is a crewman aboard this ship. No better, no worse and no different from anyone else serving." Nettie squeezed his forearm, her lined features softening. "Lad, don't think I don't worry for her. For both of you. Arthur'll haunt me until I'm dead if something happens to his daughter, and I still wake up in a sweat some nights remembering when you fell from the *Pollux*."

She was pale but resolute—the Nettie he'd always known. "But I'm not stopping or turning around to let one crewman off. Besides, Lenore would refuse. You know that."

Nathaniel abandoned his half full snifter next to Nettie's empty one and scraped his hands through his hair. "This is a nightmare." His great relief at learning that Lenore would sail on the *Terebellum* on a peaceful test flight and supply run had shredded with the wind rising off the ocean waves.

Nettie nodded. "It is and no avoiding it," she said flatly.

He stood in the shadows as Nettie informed the crew of their new orders, his gaze on Lenore. The blood slowly drained from her face, leaving her ashen. Her pupils had expanded with her fear, turning her brown eyes black. Some of the brasher crewmen whistled and cheered at the chance to taste battle. Others less cocky and more experienced stared at their captain with grim, determined faces. Nathaniel suspected if someone suddenly held up a mirror to him, he'd see that same expression stamped on his features.

Nettie answered several questions from the crew before dismissing them. She sought out Nathaniel's gaze and jerked her head toward Lenore's retreating back. *"Follow her, idiot,"* couldn't have been clearer if she'd yelled it in his face.

He tracked her to the berth she shared with another female crewman. Only Lenore occupied the space at the moment, and Nathaniel closed the door, locking it behind him. She didn't startle or even look at him. Instead, she stripped the sheets off her tidy bed and began remaking it.

"Are you frightened?"

She paused at his softly uttered question and stared down at her pillow. "A little," she replied. They both stared at the hand she raised. Her fingers twitched and trembled. Lenore's smile was sheepish. "A lot."

He gathered her into his arms, words hovering on his lips. He was frightened as well. They would face something that made even the most hardened crewman's stomach drop through the floor. The horrifics' colossal size alone induced open-mouthed terror, their appearance straight out of an opium-eater's hallucination of Hell. Nathaniel had fought at the Redan in more than a dozen battles, and each time he'd nearly pissed himself at his first sighting of a horrific.

Lenore shook in his arms, her face pressed into his shoulder. She mumbled something he couldn't make out. Nathaniel leaned back and tilted her chin to look at him. "What did you say?"

"Do you think me weak for being scared?"

Her skin was hot satin under his fingers, her body a sliver of paradise in his arms, and he wished her anywhere but here aboard this ship. "No. Fear can be a good thing. It keeps you sharp and alert. It isn't a weakness when it benefits you."

She cupped either side of his jaw with slender hands. He bent at her coaxing, his moan low when her lips gently teased his open and her tongue slipped inside his mouth. He lifted her in his arms, reveling in the feel and scent of her as *gehenna* blood roiled and bubbled in his veins.

Lenore's fingers slid into his hair to massage his scalp. She ended their kiss with a soft sucking tug on his lower lip. Her breasts pressed against his chest in a shallow rise and fall. "When this is over and we're home safe again, I would like another glass of pomegranate wine."

He set her down and loosened his embrace. The ashen pallor from earlier had faded. Her cheeks were rosy and her mouth full and red from his kiss. "We will share a glass in a winter graveyard," he promised.

"And you will recite verse to me." Her lips turned up, and the corners of her eyes crinkled.

"Then kiss you under the moon." He traced the contours of her corset stays beneath her bodice.

"It will be terribly improper." Her hand glided down his arm.

He captured her hand and kissed her fingertips. "We won't care."

"No, no we won't."

A last kiss, urgent and hot enough to send the blaze of a blush from Lenore's cheeks to her neck. Even her ears were pink. She left the berth before Nathaniel, her work boots tapping a quick rhythm on the gangway as she headed for sick bay to help prepare for receipt of the injured from the crippled ships.

He watched until she turned a corner, disappearing from view. He would share the wine and recite poetry and for a second time, put his heart on a plate before her. "This time, Lenore, tell me yes instead of no."

They reached the Redan in record time, the *Terebellum's* engines proving their worth and Nettie's statement proclaiming the ship's impressive speed. None cheered over their speedy arrival. Crewmen stood at their posts, faces tight with resolve or slack with disbelieving horror.

One crewman spoke, his voice high and thin as if he squeezed the words out of a constricted windpipe. "Blood o' Christ, would you look at that."

Nathaniel's gut was a snarled knot that churned and twisted itself around his ribs. He forced down the fear and made himself stare into the great, lightning-fractured wall known as the Redan.

Twenty-seven years earlier, a renegade group of outcast guild mages, greedy for limitless power, met in a secret convocation and proceeded to rip a hole in the universal fabric that separated worlds, a small tear but one that grew like a lesion on a plague victim. What squirmed and crawled through made the worst nightmare conjured by a human seem a sweet daydream by comparison.

The Guild responded, using a magic similar to that which made the dimensional rift to build a barrier wall called the Redan. Half the guild mages in service to the Queen died in the effort. Since then, countless airships and crews from every nation defended the wall and the countries it shielded against monstrous abominations known as horrifics. In Nathaniel's opinion, Hell's levels didn't go deep enough to hold these spawn of some dark, pustulant god.

The *Terebellum* swung to port, and he got his first look at the crippled ships. Two were missing engine gondolas or propellers, another a portion of the control room gondola. They hung in the air, the catastrophic loss of power turning them into helpless prey unable to avoid or flee a strike from rift's abominations. A fourth ship spewed black smoke from its forecastle engine. The bow section of its steel envelope was flensed away from the hull from top to keel.

Lightning flashed across the Redan, illuminating a kraken-like thing with multiple bulbous eyes, tentacles edged with barbed spines like harpoons and three mouths. Those gaping maws were big enough to swallow the *Terebellum* whole and ask for more. Fangs filled the mouths like sharpened menhirs, eager to shred anything that drew too close.

The thing crowded against another equally giant horrific that raked a seven-finger clawed hand along the Redan. The barrier held but tore in spots. Before it could heal itself, a claw inserted into one of the tears and casually gouged away the control gondola from the airship spewing black smoke. Bodies plummeted toward the ocean below. The broken airship yawed first to port before pitching back on her stern to follow those who sailed her.

Nathaniel's knees turned to water at the sight. The *Terebellum* was too far away to hear the screams of the falling, but he heard them in his head, memories of his last minutes on the *Pollux*. They made his ears ring. The weakness didn't last. Rage, with a hard thirst for revenge, took its place, incinerating every fear and hesitation. No one aboard this ship would die like that. Not the crewmen, not him, not Nettie, and most definitely not Lenore.

Nettie's voice crackled down the receiver tubes issuing orders. A burst of activity followed her commands. Nathaniel didn't wait for her to request his help. He bolted for the ship's center, bypassing the ladder connected to the B deck where the keel-based weapons platform was located. The newly made spirits of crewmen from the other ships flowed behind and in front of him, their ethereal chorus firing the already hot *gehenna* inside him and making his armor sizzle and smoke.

"*Shred them, gunner. Destroy every last one.*"

A junior gunner standing by the turret's entrance gaped at him. Nathaniel halted in front of him. "Where's the control room speaker tube?" The gunner pointed to a tube attached to a girder.

Nettie's long pause traveled the entire length of the tube when Nathaniel told her "Captain Widderschynnes, this is the Guardian requesting permission to enter and man the weapons platform."

He waited, muscles thrumming in anticipation of seating himself behind the pair of Dahlgren guns to blast away at the horrifics lurking in the rift.

"Permission granted." Nettie's voice held an odd note—of both pride and a touch of fear. Despite her assurances that he'd have to be the one to bell the cat, she did it for him. "Nathaniel Gordon, if you die again, I will take your sorry carcass and hang it from my ship's shield spike!"

## Chapter Eleven

LENORE CLUTCHED AT ONE of the bed frames bolted to girders in the sick bay as the floor beneath her feet vibrated from the canon fire the *Terebellum* spewed into the Redan from her gunnery deck and the rotating turret housed in the weapons platform under the keel.

*"Nathaniel Gordon, if you die again..."*

The shock of Nettie's statement booming across the entire length of the airship made her reel.

Nettie had lost her mind. Too many years fighting in the Redan had done this to her, made her see ghosts of loved ones aboard her ship. Lenore was certain of it. Nathaniel Gordon had died five years earlier. No one died twice, not even him.

It can't be. It can't be. Horror battled with hope inside her.

Everyone knew the renegade scientist-doctor who called himself Harvel had created seven Guardians—men brought back from the brink of death by unnatural experiments, made inhuman and forever changed.

The Guardian of Highgate had fascinated her from the first moment she met him. And he looked nothing at all like her lost Nathaniel.

He tipped his imaginary hat just like Nathaniel. He'd called her Lenore when he thought her unconscious or too far away from him to hear.

He told her he once served aboard an airship.

He recited Tennyson right before he kissed her and brought her numb spirit back to life.

Anyone could chalk those things up to coincidences or her seeing and hearing what she wanted to hear, a woman still grieving for her lost lover. She might have even agreed except for one thing.

*"Do I know you?"*

She'd asked the question by her father's grave, confused why such a thing might fall from her lips when logic dictated that acquaintance with a Guardian was an event none would forget. Lenore's soul had instantly recognized what her eyes had not.

Oh God, Nathaniel. He'd come back to her—resurrected by methods she could only imagine and that made her shudder. Now he courted death again, housed in a gun turret under an airship's belly, taking aim at the abominations that had ripped him away from her.

A hard bang sounded over the thunder of artillery fire, and the ship jolted sideways. Lenore fell against one of the metal medicine cabinets. She righted herself and searched for the doctor. The impact to the ship had knocked him to the floor. He clambered to his knees before gaining his feet with the help of his white-faced assistant.

"What was that?" the other man asked in a quavering voice.

The doctor, equally pale, straightened his coat and adjusted his skewed spectacles on his nose. "I don't know, but it can't be good." He gestured to the cabinet behind Lenore. "And there's nothing we three can do about it. Kenward," he ordered," see to the contents in there and make sure nothing is broken or spilled."

"Yes, sir." She caught the key he tossed her and unlocked the cabinet doors, hoping all the bottles and vials of medicines and chloroform were intact.

Before she could begin her inspection, the sick bay door banged open and a crewman rushed in—a junior mechanic judging by his close-fitting cap, goggles and boilersuit. His gaze locked on the doctor. "Where's Kenward?" he asked in a breathless voice, as if he'd run the length of the ship.

"Here," she said.

He motioned frantically for her to join him and was halfway out the door already when he told her "Mr. Jupiter needs your assistance in the forecastle. We have engine trouble."

Lenore gawked at him for a moment before glancing at the doctor who waved her out. She raced to keep up with the crewman as they flew down the gangway, up a ladder to the deck above the gasbag deck and across the hull to where an exterior shaft connecting hull to gondola allowed the mechanics access to both places during shift changes. Bless Nettie for insisting her female crew members dress like pit lasses—trousers under skirts tucked at the waist—otherwise she'd never been able to keep up.

The mechanic stopped her before the shaft's entrance. From her place at the top, she had a good view of the gondola. Part of its housing was torn off, exposing some of the engine to the elements. She wondered if they'd been hit by either friendly fire or a horrific's strike.

The wind blasted an icy howl up the shaft, nearly drowning the mechanic's shout. "Do you have a cap?" He tapped his head, encased in the tight-fitting cap everyone entering an engine gondola wore. She shook her head, and he stripped his off to hand it to her. "You'll need it," he bellowed. "That braid of yours will get you killed down there."

Thanks to her father, Lenore understood engine design, even if she'd never been allowed to work on a physical one. Jewelry, hair, ties; anything hanging loose in an engine gondola was dangerous. Getting hair caught guaranteed a fatal scalping.

She tucked her braid into the cap and buckled the strap under her chin. He steadied her as she got her footing on the shaft ladder and descended toward the gondola. The wind that had blown into the shaft now gusted hot and smelled of burning metal.

Artillery fire and wind howl were nothing compared to the mechanical roar of the engine in the gondola's tight, enclosed space. Mr. Jupiter, the *Terebellum*'s master mechanic motioned her to where the engine's crankshaft spun in fast rotation. The acrid metal smell was especially prevalent here.

With the noise and her cap covering her head, his shouts directly into her ear were the thinnest whispers, and she had to strain to hear.

"You know this engine's design from your father."

She nodded and yelled her reply. "Yes, but I have no hands-on experience." She couldn't imagine why the master mechanic had summoned her for help when he had a junior mechanic waiting at the top of the shaft.

He enlightened her posthaste. "One of the other ships took damage from a horrific. Sent out a shrapnel blast that tore off some of this gondola. A metal splinter lodged in a gear in the speed reduction unit and froze it up."

Lenore inhaled sharply. These mechanics were lucky to be alive and not sliced to bloody remains. It was one small thing to be grateful for in the face of impending disaster.

She glanced around the engine toward the propeller exposed by the rip in the gondola's side. The massive blades spun much faster than they should have. Without the propeller speed reduction unit working, the powerplant's rotations per minute would rise to critical failure levels. What damage a horrific didn't manage to inflict on a ship, her engine's torsional vibration would.

"Why is the engine still running? You'll lose the prop if it keeps going or break the crankshaft." Her voice was a thin echo felt more than heard. She wondered if Mr. Jupiter could read lips.

"Orders from the helm."

He was halted from saying more by canon blast from under the keel. The ship dipped into a steep yaw, slamming him and Lenore both against the gondola's undamaged wall. A high unearthly shriek made Lenore cover her ears, even beneath her protective cap. Mr. Jupiter did the same, his craggy features drawn in until they were a grimacing map of rutted roads. The ship leveled and swung sharp to port. Lenore gripped the hand bar bolted to the wall to keep from losing her feet and tumbling against the engine. Jupiter held her arm in a vise grip that numbed her fingers.

"Are you well?" he shouted. She nodded. He pointed in the general direction of the exposed sky. "That's why we're still spinning. There's a horrific just about on top of us."

She nodded, understanding. Stop the engine and propeller, and they'd lose not only speed and power but maneuverability. The *Terebellum's* formidable arsenal didn't work alone. She still needed to get out of the way and to do so she needed all her engines running.

"Why do you need me?" she asked.

Mr. Jupiter raised one hand and wiggled his fingers before shouting again. "The opening to reach the splinter is too small for any of us to get in there and pry it out. We need someone with small hands who knows the engines and don't need a lot of instruction. That's you."

Lenore's stomach lurched as she turned to look at the crankshaft and gearbox, the spinning rotation of a hundred metal teeth that notched and turned tooth over tooth in constant motion. They'd stop the engine so she could dislodge and retrieve the splinter. She tried not imagine the impossible scenario of the engine somehow restarting on its own. Those teeth would chew her hand off, pulp it into a bloody hunk of crushed bone and shredded muscle. Her fingers twitched at the gruesome thought.

For one moment, she wished herself back home, safe in the parlor, drinking tepid tea and listening to her Aunt Adelaide abuse their pianoforte. She'd hated every second of it, craved adventure and freedom from the strictures of stifling society.

Be careful what you wished for.

She nodded to Mr. Jupiter. "Whenever you're ready."

A shout traveled down the shaft. The master mechanic slipped past her to stare up at his junior still hovering at the top of the shaft. He nodded and returned to stand next to her. "The helm's taking the engine down now."

"What about the horrific?"

He grinned. "Seems that bone keeper might have made a kill shot. The monster fell back into the rift."

Lenore closed her eye and tried not to think of Nathaniel. All of her focus needed to stay here, in this tight, damaged, vulnerable gondola.

She and Mr. Jupiter waited several tense minutes. The engine's noise abruptly changed, slowed and finally whirred to a stop on a mechanical exhalation. The slowing rotation hum of the propeller followed until it was just the wind and the endless boom and vibration of gun and canon from the *Terebellum* and the other ships around her.

They waited even longer for the engine to cool to a temperature that wouldn't cook her hand off her wrist. The mechanic tapped his foot impatiently. "We're an easy target while that engine is down."

"I'll be quick, sir," she said, eyeing the spot in the gearbox where the splinter jammed the gears.

She eased her hand inside. The metal was still warm, but not so much that it burned her skin. The blunt teeth scraped her knuckles, pressing shallow depressions into her arm as she reached for the shrapnel piece. Sweat poured down her torso under her clothes and trickled down her neck.

Her fingertips gripped the splinter, earning a slice across her index finger for her efforts. "Got it!" she called to the mechanic. She growled under her breath as the metal, wedged hard against the gear, refused to dislodge. "Bloody hell," she snapped. She didn't have all day for this. Neither did the *Terebellum*.

Blood from her wounded finger made the metal slippery, but with more cursing and careful joggles of the splinter first one way and then the other, she managed to pry it loose. Mr. Jupiter's whoop of triumph when she straightened to show him her prize made her grin. No bigger than a bodkin tip on a practice arrow, the sliver had nearly caused a catastrophe. That something so small could cause such problems!

She turned the sliver over to Mr. Jupiter who pocketed it with an approving nod before returning to the shaft. This time she heard him clearly when he ordered the junior to relay the command to start up the engine again. Both he and Lenore wilted in relief when the powerplant coughed back to life and set the propeller in a proper rotation speed. He grinned and shook her hand. "Good work, lass."

"Thank you, sir." She might have been more elated if it weren't for the knowledge that a man she loved and thought dead was once again playing a game of suicide on the weapons platform. But she didn't have the luxury to worry. She climbed the shaft ladder back to the hull, returned the junior mechanic's cap to him with a word of thanks and raced back to the sick bay.

Voices crackled over the speaking tubes from the control room, following her as she made her way to the keel corridor— Nettie's, strong and sure, her boatswain's equally commanding, a few stray remarks overheard behind the commands, one that made Lenore pause and clench her fists until her nails dug into her palms.

"That bone keeper is a crackin' good shot! Just blew away two of that horrific's eyes!"

"Please," she prayed—to God, to Nathaniel, to Fate, to anyone or anything who'd listen. "Give me a chance. Please give me a chance to say yes."

There were two crewmen in sickbay when she arrived, one with minor wounds, another clutching an arm split down to the bone by the sharp edge of a broken girder. The doctor tended to him as his assistant dealt with the other. Lenore doused her injured hand in carbolic solution, wrapped her finger in a stretch of gauze and took over the assistant's tasks so he could help with the more seriously injured man.

She'd just finished cleaning her patient's last cut when the deafening barrage of artillery fire suddenly halted. The silence hung weightier than a lead bell on a thin rope. Lenore caught herself holding her breath. She glanced at the others in the room. Like her, they didn't breathe.

Nettie's voice, still so calm and so sure, carried a lilt of triumph. "All hands stand down."

Static cheers poured out of the speaking tubes and erupted in the sick bay. Lenore's patient impulsively embraced her and just as quickly apologized, though his grin continued to stretch across his face.

A wave of relief, so strong it nearly knocked her to her knees, crashed into her. Her shoulders slumped, and her eyes filled with tears. "Nathaniel," she whispered. Her leg muscles tensed with the urge to bolt from sickbay and race for the weapons platform.

The sick bay door flew open once more. Nettie's boatswain's mate, Mrs. Markham, filled the entrance. "Brace yourself, Sawbones. We got wounded coming in, six deep."

Reunions would have to wait.

## Chapter Twelve

NATHANIEL EYED NETTIE FIRST and then the Howdah pistol she'd brought aboard the *Terebellum* with her. The sidearm lay on the desk in the captain's quarters. Nettie, fortunately, wasn't within reaching distance. Instead she stood at the small cabinet where the brandy and port were kept. Port sloshed out of the glass as she poured from the decanter with a shaking hand.

Combat fatigue. He recognized the signs; he suffered them himself. His own hands were steady, but bolts of muscle spasms ratcheted up his back periodically, coming and going in a rhythmic echo of the thump-crack from the Dahlgren guns each time he fired at the horrifics. Not only that, but his body refused to shed his armor in favor of the soft vicar cloth. No matter how he willed it, the armor didn't soften and melt back into his skin. He only hoped that as things continued to calm aboard the *Terebellum*, his body would recognize the lack of threat and relinquish its defensive shell.

Nettie gulped down her port and stared at him with hard eyes. "You step foot again on any ship I captain, and I'll have you shot on sight," she vowed in a shrill voice. Her pupils were wide and dark.

Nathaniel didn't take offense. "I'm fine, Nettie. No worse for wear." He held out his arms and pivoted in a slow rotation so she could see all of him. "Not even a scratch."

Such couldn't be said for everyone. With the exception of four, most of the *Terebellum*'s crew had escaped injury. That was a blessing as her sick bay was currently bursting with the wounded and the dying from the three damaged ships. Because her speed topped that of the *Gatria* and the *Bellatrix*, the *Terebellum* was chosen to transport the injured and the dead back to London while the others trailed behind, towing the disabled ships.

Victory celebrations had been brief as the crews on all ships bent to their tasks of transferring people from one ship to another and coordinating plans for the return trip home. And all had paused to commemorate and mourn the loss of the *Castra* and her crew with the sounding of eight bells and a prayer from Nettie.

He'd listened to a last watch commemoration more times than he ever cared to. Britannia had lost a lot of men, women and ships to the Redan over the decades, along with all the other nations with coastlines bordering the Atlantic. No matter how often you heard eight bells, they never sounded any less mournful.

Their sad pealing made Nathaniel itch to hunt down Lenore, yank her into his arms and hold her until her body melted into his. No amount of reassurance from Nettie or even confirmation with his own eyes when he saw her running back and forth between sick bay and captain's quarters calmed his fears. He'd only be satisfied when he actually held her.

"What if Lenore wants a permanent place aboard the *Pollux*? Or even the *Terebellum*?" He'd heard about Lenore's help in the forecastle. The master mechanic had even remarked to any who'd listen "Bricky girl, that Kenward. I'd be happy to train her up as a mechanic."

Nettie downed another round of port. "I'll have her shot too," she snarled.

Nathaniel held back a grin, both amused and delighted by her answer. He braced a hip on the edge of the desk and watched Nettie pace. "Well that would put Jane Kenward into the dither you've always wanted to see."

"That girl is going straight back to her mother as soon as they tie this ship down for repairs in Maldon."

He hoped not. At least not permanently. He wanted her to come straight to him—and stay. He'd caught her wide-eyed stare in the battle's chaotic aftermath, when the crew had breathed a collective gasp of relief that the fighting was temporarily over. She'd mouthed his name—Nathaniel, not Colin. The expression on her face had been an odd combination of anger and yearning. Commands and tasks separated them, and they hadn't crossed paths since. He was desperate to see her, to hold her. To explain.

"You're still the best damn gunner in the fleet, dead or alive," Nettie said, interrupting his thoughts. "But worrying over you will kill me faster than any tussle with a horrific."

A knock at the door made them both turn. Nettie cast him an enigmatic look, put away the port and tucked the Howdah into her belt. "I know that knock," she said. "Looks like you have some explaining to do. I'll leave you to it. Don't drink all the brandy while I'm gone."

Butterflies bashed themselves to death against his ribs when he spotted Lenore standing at the threshold. What would she say now that she knew?

Lenore inclined her head as Nettie eased past her. "Captain."

The older woman grasped her shoulder in a brief display of affection. "Go in, Lenore. He's waiting." The door closed behind her, leaving Nathaniel alone with the person most precious to him. He waited, letting the silence bloom until she was ready to speak.

She clasped her hands in front of her and looked down for a moment before settling her gaze on him once more. "I knew," she said softly. "Somehow I always knew, from the first moment I saw you again." Her lips flattened against her teeth, and her eyes turned glossy. "Were you ever planning to tell me?"

He edged closer to her. Tension made her entire body quivered, and she balanced on the balls of her feet as if she'd bolt if he moved too swiftly. "Not at first," he admitted, hoping she heard the apology in his voice. She flinched. "Look at me,

Lenore." He sketched an invisible line down his torso. "This isn't even my body. It belonged to a comic droll stabbed to death for the three crowns in his pocket. What was left of me wasn't worth saving. Harvel's experiment might be viewed as miraculous if it weren't so heinous."

She crossed her arm, rubbing them briskly as if she stood before him with no coat and the windows open. "You're still Nathaniel."

What faith she had in him, this resolute, loyal girl. "No, I'm not."

Her arms dropped to her sides, back straightening with an indignant snap. "Yes you are. I knew it the moment I saw you again at Highgate, leaning on that cane and scaring the mourners.

He sighed. "Lenore..."

"Don't 'Lenore' me. Even before you were dropping hints a blind man could see, I knew it was you. Everything inside me that broke when they said you'd died suddenly healed." She dragged her braid over her shoulder to worry it between her fingers. "I didn't recognize what it was at first. Maybe if I weren't grieving my father, I might have figured it out sooner."

She'd have to be stubborn to defy her strong-willed mother. He shouldn't be surprised Lenore refused to budge in her assertion he was the same man he'd been five years earlier.

Nathaniel inched a little closer, close enough to hear the sudden hitch in her breathing. "I can hear and speak to the dead, love. I don't need to eat or drink or sleep. I can lust; we've both ascertained that." He grinned when she blushed. "My blood is poisoned with *gehenna*, and the changes it wrought are obvious. I am no longer the man you knew."

His eyebrows lifted at the low growl rumbling from her throat. This time she narrowed the distance between them until they were toe to toe. His armor made a dull *tink-tink* sound when she tapped him on the chest.

"Where it counts most, you are. The soul, the mind, the heart. The body might not be yours and changed beyond comprehension, but the small things you do—the way you tip that invisible topper, how you tilt your head when you're considering a question, even the pitch in your voice when you're impatient. Those things belong solely to Nathaniel Gordon."

His grin coaxed one out of her. "You plant your feet when you believe in something don't you?" It was one of her many charms that made him fall in love with her a lifetime ago.

She considered him for a moment. "I was more than suspicious when you told me your name was Colin, but the surname threw me off, not to mention the improbability that you weren't actually dead. Who is Whitley?"

His dear Nettie. She'd guffawed when he told her the name he'd assumed to hide his identity from Lenore. He hadn't missed the pleased blush that flagged her cheekbones. "That secret isn't mine to tell. Maybe one day the person who possesses it will."

Her hand splayed across his chest, fingers dancing up to his neck and down to his abdomen, undaunted by the hard armor. He felt her touch all the way to his bones. A hot shiver replaced the fading spasms in his back. He choked back a surprised laugh. While his protective shell might not obey his every command when he wished, Lenore's touch had beguiled it the same way she had beguiled him. The armor began to thin and soften in random spots, transforming to fabric.

"Even the way you kissed me was Nathaniel Gordon."

He captured her hand and pressed her palm flat over his heart. "I never thought I'd be fortunate enough to taste you again," he said in a voice gone low and thick. Lenore's eyelids lowered to half-mast. "Especially in a graveyard or on an airship."

"You should have told me," she said. "I suspected but to hear it confirmed over the *Terebellum*'s speaker tubes by Nettie threatening you?" She shook her head.

He pressed her hand even harder to his chest. Her eyes grew wide when the armor collapsed there and transformed to cloth. "I could live with your first rejection, Lenore, because there was hope. I wasn't giving up, despite your mule-headed insistence on me claiming an inheritance I didn't want." He closed his eyes, forcing back the fear that reared a cobra's head inside him. She had kissed him and welcomed his embrace when she thought him nothing more than a Guardian. Surely, now that she knew all, she wouldn't turn him away? "Were you to reject me a second time, it would have been because of who I'd become, not what I was born to. In that, I found no hope."

Lenore lifted her free hand to trace the contours of his face. Cheekbones and jaw, eyebrows and forehead, the blade-thin bridge of his nose and curvature of his nostrils. Did she see a reflection of the old Nathaniel in the black expanse of his irises and scleras? She grasped his chin and tugged him down to her. "I hate Harvel for what he did to you." Her breath caressed his lips. "Yet I'd thank him if he were alive because he gave you back to me."

In this moment, with all his dreams sparking to life at Lenore's words, Nathaniel thought he'd thank Harvel too—then disembowel him later.

Lenore freed her other hand from his gasp and slid both into his hair to cup his head and hold him in place, looming over her. "Nathaniel Gordon," she declared in a fierce voice, "I will love you until I'm one of those spirits who whispers in your ear and bores you with my repetition."

He laughed and gathered her into his arms, no longer armored but garbed in fabric that welcomed the press of Lenore's body against his. He nuzzled his nose against the side of hers. "Love, by then we will be dust together."

Lenore's laughter chorused with his. "That's because when my mother finds out my Nathaniel is back and keeping company with the dead, she'll immolate us both with a single, well-aimed glare."

## Epilogue

ONE YEAR AND A DAY after her father's death, Lenore Kenward became Lenore Gordon by marrying a man who guarded the dearly departed.

Having resigned herself to spinsterhood more than a half decade earlier, she never imagined she'd marry or that the ceremony would take place in a tucked-away grotto in a graveyard and be attended by an odd array of guests, both living and deceased. Then again, Nathaniel was an unusual groom and Lenore a flouter of society's more rigid rules, so it seemed perfectly appropriate that the ceremony itself mirror the uniting couple.

Highgate's rector, John Morris, oversaw the proceedings with his wife acting as witness. They were joined by Nettie, dressed in a far more conservative frock than what she usually preferred. It didn't bare her knees and was a subdued shade of blue. She or someone else had tamed her wild hair into a neat chignon, though a beaded braid had managed to partially escape its prison of pins and bounced with every nod of her head.

Two Guardians attended as well, their presence the cause of wide-eyed astonishment, disapproval and unease from Jane Kenward and the Kenwards' long-time housekeeper Constance. The two men introduced themselves by first names only and the cemeteries they guarded—Gideon of Kensal Green and Zachariah of Nunhead.

Lenore herself found it hard not to stare at them. Like Nathaniel, they had been remade by Dr. Harvel. They possessed the same coloring as Nathaniel—long white hair and Stygian eyes with pupils as bright as stars and wore the severe garb reminiscent of the clergy. They were unique beyond that, in both stature and demeanor.

While the more jovial Zachariah came alone, the taciturn Gideon brought a guest. Almost as tall as Gideon with a dignified grace that put any aristocrat to shame, Rachel Wakefield had taken Lenore's hands prior to the ceremony and given them a squeeze.

"My sincerest congratulations, Miss Kenward." The woman smiled not only with her mouth but her eyes as well, exuding a warmth that made Lenore think of summer and meadows and wildflowers. "You are a fortunate woman to marry such a fine man." Her smile widened. "And I've been informed he is an even more fortunate man to take you to wife."

"Thank you, Mrs. Wakefield. I've loved him for a long time."

The ceremony was short and infinitely sweet. Lenore noted the tremor in Nathaniel's hands when he held hers through the sharing of vows, but his kiss was firm and sure, promising so, so much more once they were alone.

Lenore invited their guests to the newly cleaned and furnished rectory Nathaniel once dubbed as nothing more than a place to occasionally take shelter from the elements. The dust and cobwebs were gone, and the clear windows caught the watery winter light, casting pale sunbeams throughout the parlor, made far more comfortable with a rug, furnishings and a fire in the fireplace.

Nathaniel had encouraged her to make the rectory hers and decorate it in whatever made her happiest. She had at first been hesitant.

"Nathaniel, I have no dowry or funds to bring to this marriage. We will live in Spartan surroundings."

"I'm not without means," he said gently. "I possess a hefty account funded by the Necropolis Company and the Mage Guild.

There's been no reason to touch it until now, and it's grown impressively from lack of pilfering on my part."

Lenore gawked at him. "You're paid to guard Highgate?" She didn't know why that news astonished her so. It was employment after all.

He grinned. "Handsomely. Guardians are social outcasts but valuable nonetheless. The Guild and the Company understand our worth and contribution. Even if they didn't, Gideon would make certain to enlighten them."

Having now met the dour, imposing Gideon, Lenore wondered what exactly his form of enlightenment entailed. She gave a delicate shiver and sipped the warm tea Constance and Rachel served to everyone.

Once the guests departed with good wishes and congratulations—even from Jane—the house settled into an intimate silence. Nathaniel reclined in a chair near the fire and tugged Lenore into his lap. Lenore wound her arms around his neck and stole a kiss from him.

"Are you glad it's over?" she asked.

He nuzzled the warm spot near her temple, just above her ear. "I'm glad it's just begun," he said.

She melted in his arms. "You always did have a honeyed tongue, Nathaniel Gordon."

He trailed a line of soft nibbles across her cheek to the corner of her mouth. "Care to taste?"

"Oh yes."

He did taste of honey and the pomegranate wine he'd chosen over the tea served earlier, and Lenore savored the feel of his mouth on hers, his tongue gliding across her teeth to tangle with her tongue in a match neither won and both excelled.

She gasped into his mouth when he suddenly rose in one smooth motion, still clasping her tightly against him. "Bedroom," he muttered when they took a second to breathe. She nodded and laid her head on his chest, listening to his strong, steady heartbeat as he carried her effortlessly up the stairs.

Their bedchamber, once an empty room shrouded in dust, held a bed, wardrobe, vanity and mirror. A chest footed the end of the bed. Lenore had proclaimed the room complete when she filled the chest and the wardrobe with personal items and clothes, including the precious ambrotype of a Nathaniel gone but not forgotten.

Her new husband set her down so that they stood pressed together by the side of the bed. His mouth curved up on one side. "I will give you anything you desire if you let me play lady's maid."

Her fingers walked across his shoulders. "You are a man of many talents, it seems."

"No, only a few, but I excel at those."

How very, very fortunate she was to finally call this man hers. The joy welling up inside her threatened to burst free in an embarrassing barrage of tears guaranteed to alarm her Nathaniel and turn her face into a splotchy, hideous visage. Instead, she clutched the safety of lighthearted innuendo and teasing. "Prove it," she said.

His eyebrows shot up, and the wicked grin spreading across his face made her laugh. "I could never resist a challenge."

True to his boast, he made short work of her wedding dress and corset with its miles of lacing. They made a growing pile on the floor, along with her petticoats and crinoline, shift and small clothes. He paused when she stood before him wearing only a pair of filmy stockings that did nothing to warm her legs and a pair of garters. His spectral gaze blazed, burning hotter as it touched on her shoulders and bare breasts, the curve of her waist and flat expanse of her belly, the slope of her hips and length of her legs.

He had seen her naked before, years earlier. Then, it had been a furtive, forbidden union, no less pleasurable for its risk but infinitely less stirring than this moment when they stood together in the room they shared as man and wife. Lenore fought down a blush and raised one leg, her stockinged toes caressing his shin. "Don't you want to finish?"

Nathaniel's voice was guttural. "I suspect I'll be finished before we've truly started." He gestured to her stockings. "Leave those on and loosen your hair for me."

She did as he requested, sauntering to the dressing table to seat herself naked before the mirror. Nathaniel didn't follow, but he turned to watch her, his eyes bright in the room's dim light. Lenore took her time removing the pins, setting each one carefully on the vanity. With each pin out, a curl unfurled to fall down her shoulders and back until her hair cascaded over the chair and pooled in her lap.

Her husband's breathing panted harsh and loud in the room. She met his eyes in the mirror's reflection, noting the flare of his nostrils, the silvery shadows that smudged his cheekbones and the way his chest rose and fell as if he'd run across London Bridge a dozen times without stopping.

"My God," he said in a choked voice. "You're even more beautiful than I remembered."

She smiled, warmed to her toes by his fervent compliment. Desire unspooled in her belly, sending liquid heat through every part of her before settling into a throb between her thighs. "Your turn," she said softly.

Her startled bleat nearly ruined the sensual atmosphere when Nathaniel closed his eyes and went from being garbed in black from neck to feet to bare, pale nudity in an instant. His expression had sobered, a touch tentative as he watched her leave her seat at the vanity to stand before him.

She once likened him to a marble statue. How unknowingly accurate she'd been in that comparison, and he was garbed then with only his hands and face hinting at his overall paleness. The Nathaniel she'd first fallen in love with had been a man of average height with broad shoulders, muscular arms and a powerful, easy stride. The Nathaniel who claimed a droll's body as his was muscular in his own right, taller and leaner with the long, wiry body of an acrobat.

Looking at him was like looking at the living representation of a Greek myth gone awry, in which a mad Pygmalion begged an even more perverse Aphrodite to bring a male Galatea to life.

The doctor had done it with torture and lightning. The sculptor scientist perished, but his creations lived on. One of them married Lenore.

"You are truly lovely," she said, breathless at the sight of him. The silvery color shadowing his cheekbones spread down his throat and across his chest. Lenore's gaze dropped, and her lips parted. "Oh my." He might share the same milky skin tones and muscular physique of any of the Greek and Roman statues but God, or the mercurial Aphrodite, had been far more generous than the sculptors when endowing the living man.

Nathaniel followed Lenore's wide-eyed gaze to his erection, swollen and stiff. His hands fluttered at his side as if to cover himself and went still at Lenore's abrupt "Don't."

Lenore wet her lips with her tongue, smiling faintly at Nathaniel's sudden focus on her face. "It must have been a...challenging task, flipping and tumbling about with such a..." She frowned, searching for the right word.

"Weapon?" Nathaniel offered. They shared a chuckle.

"Just so," she said.

He glanced down a second time. "Believe me, I was just as surprised as you when I first saw it."

"Impressed too, I'll wager." Her short time aboard the *Terebellum* had been an education in many ways, not the least an observance that men in general possessed an obsessive interest in the size and potency of their own genitalia, along with an insatiable need to brag about it to each other.

Nathaniel confirmed that belief when he shrugged and said "Hard not to be."

Lenore grinned and shook her head. She padded to him, the floor cold under her feet, her nipples drawn tight in the room's cool air, despite the heat from the hearth lit in one corner of the room. "Make me warm, husband. I'm freezing here."

He leapt to do her bidding, lifting her in his arms to carry her to the bed. They burrowed under the covers, wrapped around each other in a tangle of limbs.

Lenore learned every angle and sweep of Nathaniel's body, its taste and scent, the way his narrow hips angled so that he seated himself firmly between her thighs. She carded his soft, white hair and mapped the length of his back with her lips. She followed the path of silvery veins just under his skin with her fingers, tickling and teasing in a way that made him laugh and moan by turns.

Unlike her, he knew her body, remembered how to make her back arch as he sucked the tips of her breasts and played his tongue over her nipples. He recalled just how to make her mew his name when he slid down, propped her legs over his shoulders and tipped the velvet until her hips bucked hard enough to make the bed bounce and her heels dug into his back. She was sheened with sweat and gasping when he slithered up her body and pounced, his tongue sliding into her mouth even as he spread her thighs with his and thrust deep.

Nathaniel paused, his chest heaving like hard-worked bellows. He rested his forehead against Lenore's, and she heard the strain in his voice as he fought for control. "I remember this," he whispered. "I remember, and it is paradise."

Lenore, half dizzy with the exquisite feel of Nathaniel buried deep inside her, stole his breath with a slow hungry kiss. "I never forgot," she said when they broke for air. "I dreamed about you all the time."

She didn't know if her words or the involuntary flex of slippery muscles sent him over the edge, but he gasped and shuddered, eyes rolling back as his back arched. He angled his hips so that his pelvis rubbed just the right way in just the right spot. Lenore climaxed a second time, and Nathaniel groaned her name into her neck as he came.

They lay together in a knot of limbs and twisted bedclothes. Lenore no longer felt the chill and played idly with idea of opening the bedroom's single window to cool them. She lay under Nathaniel, whose long body was draped over hers and most of the bed. His head rested between her breasts, a most convenient spot for him to press a kiss to a plump curve or a rosy nipple.

Lenore jumped and tugged a lock of his hair when his tongue flicked out to tease the tip. "Stop that," she ordered and giggled. "I'm ticklish now."

He raised his head to stare at her. She liked his half smiles very much. "I remember that too," he said before returning to his favored spot with the promise to behave himself.

Silent laughter made his shoulders shake. Lenore tucked her chin and stared down at him. "Why are you laughing?"

He rose, bracing himself on his forearms where they rested on either side of Lenore's shoulders. His fingers traced the contours of her ears and played in her hair. "Your mother must be beside herself. Her only child married to a bone keeper."

Lenore harrumphed, not at all liking her mother's intrusion, even in casual conversation, into the bedroom. "I think she'll secretly be glad I finally married. Maybe with enough time, and a few glasses of sherry to help her along, she might even refer to you as the Honorable Mr. Gordon, protector of the dignified deceased instead of 'that creature'."

Nathaniel's expression brightened. "You truly think so?"

"No."

He grinned. "Ah well, it's a rare man who gains the affections of his mother-in-law."

Lenore grimaced. "In this case, please consider it a blessing if Mama withholds hers."

The grimace melted, and she sighed her pleasure when he feathered kisses down her nose, to her sensitive philtrum and finally to her lips, still swollen from his earlier attentions. "It's of no importance to me, as long as I keep the affections of her daughter."

Lenore cupped the sides of his head and lifted his face so she could look deep into his strange, ethereal gaze. "You will bring me great happiness," she said in tones that demanded he believe her. "You already do."

His lids dropped for a moment, hiding the expression in his eyes. She gasped when he opened them again, revealing the fires of devotion and hope. "You will bring spring and white roses to the graveyard," he said, and his voice echoed back and back as if all eternity rose inside him to spill from his lips in a declaration of his faith in her.

Humbled and stunned, Lenore blinked back tears. She stroked his hair, his elegant face. "I will be content to bring you joy," she said, her words thick in her mouth.

Nathaniel kissed her deeply before pressing his lips to her ear. "You do that simply by breathing. My Lenore."

## —END—

ELIZABETH HUNTER and GRACE DRAVEN are both writers of paranormal and fantasy romance with over twenty works of fiction between them. Both love writing complicated characters who fall in love. They really like each other's work and thought it would fun to do some creepy, creepy Gothic romance stories together.

They also both like hummus and large dogs, red wine and traveling. They spend too much time talking about books and probably not enough time doing the laundry. Their readers are grateful they live very far apart, because if they lived closer, they probably wouldn't get as much work done.

You can find out more about Grace Draven's work at: GraceDraven.com

You can find out more about Elizabeth Hunter's work at ElizabethHunterWrites.com

They are also both on Facebook and Twitter more than they should be.

## Also by Grace Draven

Master of Crows
The Light Within
The Lightening God's Wife
A Brush of Black Wings

Radiance
Eidolon (2016)

Entreat Me
All the Stars Look Down

Drago Illuminare
Draconus
Wyvern
Arena
Courting Bathsheba

## Also By Elizabeth Hunter

The Irin Chronicles

*The Scribe*
*The Singer*
*The Secret*

The Elemental Mysteries Series

*A Hidden Fire*
*This Same Earth*
*The Force of Wind*
*A Fall of Water*
*Lost Letters & Christmas Lights*

The Elemental World Series

*Building From Ashes*
*Waterlocked*
*Blood and Sand*
*The Bronze Blade*
*The Scarlet Deep*

The Elemental Legacy Series

*Shadows and Gold*

The Cambio Springs Series

*Shifting Dreams*
*Desert Bound*
*Waking Hearts*

Contemporary Romance

*The Genius and the Muse*

Made in the USA
San Bernardino, CA
05 December 2016